"Look, Saku.
You're hot,
and girls
love you,
so you're
bound to
have haters."

Yua Uchida

Haru Aomi

"Man, I hate a tight tie, especially after getting all sweaty during club practice."

Yuzuki Nanase

"I go the extra mile for the guys I like."

Asuka Nishino

"Ah, it's you. I had a feeling I'd see you today."

"Is something on your mind, Saku?"

"Yeah. I'm thinking about how best to execute a sudden tactical brake so I can get some boob-to-back action."

"..."

# Chitose Is in the Ramune Bottle

## contents

**Saku Chitose**

# Chitose Is in the Ramune Bottle

1

## Hiromu

### Illustration by
### raemz

YEN ON
NEW YORK

# Chitose Is in the Ramune Bottle 1

**Hiromu**

Translation by Evie Lund
Cover art by raemz

CHITOSE-KUN WA RAMUNEBIN NO NAKA Vol. 1
by Hiromu
© 2019 Hiromu
Illustration by raemz
All rights reserved.
Original Japanese edition published by SHOGAKUKAN.
English translation rights in the United States of America, Canada, the United Kingdom, Ireland, Australia and New Zealand arranged with SHOGAKUKAN through Tuttle-Mori Agency, Inc.

English translation © 2022 by Yen Press, LLC

Yen On
150 West 30th Street, 19th Floor
New York, NY 10001

Visit us at yenpress.com
facebook.com/yenpress
twitter.com/yenpress
yenpress.tumblr.com
instagram.com/yenpress

First Yen On Edition: February 2022

Yen On is an imprint of Yen Press, LLC.
The Yen On name and logo are trademarks of Yen Press, LLC.

Library of Congress Cataloging-in-Publication Data
Names: Hiromu, author. | raemz, illustrator. | Lund, Evie, translator.
Title: Chitose is in the ramune bottle / Hiromu ; illustration by raemz ; translation by Evie Lund.
Other titles: Chitose-kun wa ramune bin no naka. English
Description: First Yen On edition. | New York, NY : Yen On, 2022
Identifiers: LCCN 2021057712 | ISBN 9781975339050 (v. 1 ; trade paperback) |
    ISBN 9781975339067 (v. 2 ; trade paperback) | ISBN 9781975339074
    (v. 3; trade paperback) | ISBN 9781975339081 (v. 4 ; trade paperback)
Subjects: CYAC: High schools—Fiction. | Schools—Fiction. | Friendship—Fiction. |
    LCGFT: Light novels.
Classification: LCC PZ7.1.H574 Ch 2022 | DDC [Fic]—dc23
LC record available at https://lccn.loc.gov/2021057712

ISBN: 978-1-9753-3905-0

10 9 8 7 6 5 4 3 2 1

LSC-C

Printed in the United States of America

**Saku Chitose**
One of the most popular guys
in the school.
Ex-baseball club.

**Yuuko Hiiragi**
A popular class princess.
Tennis club.

**Yua Uchida**
A self-made popular girl who tries
her best at everything. Music club.

**Haru Aomi**
A small and perky girl.
Basketball club.

**Yuzuki Nanase**
Every guy's favorite, along
with Yuuko.
Basketball club.

**Asuka Nishino**
A strange upperclassman,
socially unaware.
Likes books.

**Kaito Asano**
Popular jock.
Star player of the boys'
basketball club.

**Kazuki Mizushino**
A logical-minded, handsome guy.
A leading player in the soccer club.

**Kenta Yamazaki**
A shut-in, otaku nerd.

**Atomu Uemura**
Insecure popular kid, seeking
dominance over his nemesis, Saku.

**Kuranosuke Iwanami (Kura)**
Homeroom teacher of Saku and his
group. Fairly hands-off and laid-back.

# Chitose Is in the Ramune Bottle

Hiromu

Illustration by
**raemz**

## Hiromu

I always wanted to write a story about my home prefecture of Fukui, and my dream has finally come true. One of my favorite Fukui words is "skrishing." For example, "I turned on the TV in the middle of the night, and it was really skrishin' up a storm." (The answer will be in the story sooner or later.)

## raemz

Born in California, USA.
Works mainly on social-network games and game illustrations, with this as their first light novel project. Please have a look!

I was walking in the direction of the school gates with a cute girl I'd just met only an hour before.

We were close enough to almost bump shoulders every now and then, and we were both aware of it. I guessed that we looked like a would-be couple who were just too scared to take that first step—or maybe a couple who had only started dating recently enough for it to still be awkward.

The girl had a hint of stranger-like formality in her tone as she said, "Um... Thanks for earlier. You were a real lifesaver. You're really good at studying, aren't you, Chitose?"

A warm, pre–spring break kind of breeze wafted past just then, bringing with it the sweet, clean, soapy scent of the girl by my side.

"Don't worry about it. It's a personal policy of mine to never turn my back on a girl who needs a favor."

After school, I had been in the library studying for a test when the girl sitting next to me had started sneaking peeks at me. Then she turned to me and said, "Um, do you mind if I ask you a question?"

She told me there were some math problems she didn't understand. The school crest on her blazer was the same color as mine, indicating that we were in the same year in school, so I was familiar with the problems and able to explain the answers.

"But you were in the middle of your own studying, weren't you? Why did you spend so much time helping me out? After all, we'd never even spoken before today."

She stole a quick glance up at me as we walked along, side by side.

"Well, you said you'd treat me to a coffee. It was a fair trade."

Apparently, that wasn't enough for her. "Hmm... So if another student offered you coffee, you'd help them out in the exact same way? I don't get it. Well, you're always surrounded by pretty girls, so I guess someone ordinary like me doesn't even register on your radar..."

"Nope. If you were a guy, coffee wouldn't cut it. He'd have to cover the bill for ramen if he wanted my help."

That's what I told her, but I knew it wasn't the kind of answer she was after.

I thought I'd handled that pretty well, but as I glanced back down at the girl and took in her disappointed expression, I decided to add more of an explanation.

"...Besides, anyone would look at you and see you're pretty yourself. And your light-pink scrunchie is perfect for you."

An obvious blush spread across the girl's cheeks.

"Really?! Hey, Chitose, are you dating anyone right now?"

"Sadly not. What about you?"

"Uh, it's kinda complicated..."

The girl hesitated.

"Hey!!!"

Someone grabbed my shoulder from behind and yanked me backward violently, as if deliberately trying to prevent me from hearing the rest.

"..."

I stumbled but managed to stay upright, my arms flailing wildly as I turned around.

There was a guy standing there. I didn't know his name.

He was much taller than my five foot seven, and he had an unconventional hairstyle held in place with wax. His eyebrows were shaved thin, and his unorthodox take on our uniform's dress code was instantly attention-grabbing. His face was nothing special, but he had a "cool-guy" aura girls would probably like. If you asked me to categorize him as a popular kid or a nerd, he would definitely fall in the first category.

"The heck do you think you're doin'?!"

The guy was pissed about something. I checked out his school crest and realized he was in the grade above ours.

"Uh, I'm going on an after-school date with this cutie from my grade. What does it look like I'm doing?" I shrugged flippantly.

Before the guy could react, the girl yelped. "What's your problem?!"

The guy took a step toward her, frowning and clearly irritated. "Excuse me? What's *your* problem? You've got a boyfriend! What do you think you're doing going off to hang out with some other guy? That's Saku Chitose, a first year, you know. I hear he's got his fingers in all the girls' pies, if you know what I'm saying!"

This guy seemed to know about me, but I was pretty sure I'd never met him before. For now, I'm calling him Jock Blocker.

As I was chuckling to myself over that, the girl took a step toward Jock.

"Chitose helped me out with studying, so I was just about to buy him a coffee in return. What, can I not study with people now?!"

"Not with guys like him! I heard him calling you pretty just now. He says that to all the girls!"

"You were sneaking up behind us listening? Gross!"

I decided to interject. "Aww, c'mon! Don't fight over little old me!"

"…You think you're funny?"

Welp, that backfired. Now Jock Blocker's ire was focused on me.

"Keep your hands off other people's girlfriends, got it?"

*Ah, so we're doing this now.*

I sighed internally.

It was obvious they were dating. I don't know if their relationship was on the rocks already, or if I was just too darn handsome and charming, but it seemed like the girl was interested in me. And Jock Blocker did not like that.

Clearly, he was lower on the school hierarchy than I was, and he barely even passed for good-looking. In my position as one of the most popular guys in the school, girls asked me out basically every day.

Meaning he had to vent his anger at me for ensnaring his girlfriend.

"Sorry, man, my bad. I didn't realize she was already dating you. And you're right, I do have a bad habit of calling girls cute. I just call it like I see it."

The entire time I was speaking, Jock Blocker's face was darkening with rage. The girl looked embarrassed and kept sneaking glances at me.

"She may be just another girl to you, but to me, she means a lot! She's my girlfriend! I won't let you treat her like a toy and break her heart!"

*Wow, look at this guy riding in on his white horse.*

Yeah, he probably wasn't such a bad guy. Even the girl looked a little bit impressed by his manly speech. She was gazing at her boyfriend with something like wonder in her eyes.

Now the kids who were coming out of the school on their way home were all staring at us.

Here was a boyfriend, publicly proclaiming embarrassing, personal feelings in the name of protecting his girlfriend from a nefarious trickster. Deeply moved by said boyfriend's gesture, the girl awakens as if from a bad dream to face reality. What a splendid scene. How fresh, how youthful, how…springlike.

So I decided I'd better play my part, too.

"Sure, I'd like to duke it out with you down at the riverbed, but I'm a lover, not a fighter. Still, you should be more careful. If she matters that much to you, you should take better care of her, so bad guys like me don't come swarming."

Jock Blocker scowled and put his arm possessively around his girlfriend as if to say he didn't need any advice from the likes of me. The girl was gazing at me. "Chitose...," she said sadly. So I decided to throw her a bone.

"As for you, when you get bored of this guy, I'll be there to bring some excitement back into your life. Rain check on the after-school coffee date until then, yeah?"

I gave her a twinkling grin and a wink, and Jock Blocker flung his schoolbag in my direction.

"Screw you, dude!"

"Ooh, scary."

I deflected the schoolbag easily, then dashed off toward the school gates with a jaunty wave.

I wished them all the best for their future together. I guess.

All I did was help a girl out with her studying when she asked me. It wasn't my fault she caught feelings for me. And then her boyfriend ended up making me the bad guy.

Oh well. This kind of thing happened all the time.

I was feeling pretty good, though. I picked up speed, kicking up dirt behind me as I ran past all the other students who were making their way home.

The sky above me was bright blue. The sun was blazing away, heralding the ending of winter and the coming of spring. The cool breeze felt good, even though it was full of dust coming from the sports field.

Someone catching feelings for me. And someone else, out to get me.

Yep, everything in my world was just as it should be...

# CHAPTER ONE
## Popular Bad Boys Do Well in High School

A parade of students in blazers made their way down the high path that ran along the river embankment. A flurry of playful cherry blossom petals whirled and swirled in the air, coming to rest on their hair and shoulders. Beneath their blazers, they wore crisp white shirts with unfashionably long plaid skirts, or still-baggy pants meant for growing into. Stiff loafers, not yet broken in to the wearers' feet, clattered with every footstep.

*Clunk, clunk, clunk.*

*Scuff, scuff, scuff.*

The rhythm of my feet in ripped, stained, and generally worn Stan Smith sneakers was a mismatch to the heavy clunking of brand-new school shoes.

All of a sudden, I noticed that my shoelace had come undone, so I crouched down. My Gregory-brand backpack, which had seen better days, slid sideways and made my square schoolbag swing off my shoulder.

I gazed out across the scene, feeling a stirring in my heart as I drank it all in. The gentle springtime sun. The burbling of the stream below. The new students walking beside me, heading earnestly to school in the midst of their still-unknown peers. What unbreakable friendships would form? Who would end up dating? It was all still ahead of them.

*       *       *

Saku Chitose from Class Five is a total man-slut shithead.

High schoolers are the center of the whole world. You see it all over media, too. Think about it. Every novel, manga, TV series, and film made these days features a high school kid as the protagonist. It's never an elementary schooler, right? And only occasionally do you see a college student or working adult. I mean, the word *youth* itself is synonymous with high school. It's like when you grow up and become an adult, you want to look back on your time in high school and get all misty-eyed about it. You want to reminisce about those slightly embarrassing yet completely precious three years.

…But that's all just superficial.

The truth is something everyone knows. If you're lucky, you spend your days goofing around with your buddies, getting into silly fights, then laughing it off and throwing your arms around each other's shoulders. You confess your feelings to that girl you've had your eye on. You wait for her club practice to get out, and then the two of you stop by a park bench on the way home and chat. You go to the summer festival together wearing *yukata*s and watch the fireworks. You stroll hand in hand to a secluded corner of the shrine, and then when no one's watching you have your first…y'know. Stuff like that. But only a few people get to experience those kinds of sickly sweet, heartburn-inducing moments. Only the ones who manage to claw their way to the top of the school hierarchy and become the elite, the few, the *popular* kids.

You have your popular kids and your unpopular kids.

I've always hated those definitions, ubiquitous though they are. Ever since those terms came about, high schoolers have cared about only one thing: *Please, let me be popular. Or at the very least, not at the bottom of the heap. Please.*

The entrance ceremony the little first-years were heading to was only the first round of the battle. By the time they came back along this pathway later today, they'd have a pretty good idea already of what was up. They'd know which of their peers was likely to be the life and soul of every class and which ones were destined to spend three years trying to blend into the walls. If they weren't nervous right now, well, then they'd have to be crazy.

Saku Chitose from Class Five is a total man-slut shithead.

*Don't believe what society tells you, little first-years. Forget about who's hot and who's not. Forget about who's "sociable" and who's "anti-social." Tell them all to go screw themselves—and just be a little stone that rolls where it wants. After a year of bumping and colliding against each other, you'll be a nice, smooth rounded-off little pebble anyway.*

In my position as a second-year student, who had already been stuck with the "popular" label by everyone, I felt more than qualified to give these little newbies some advice.

*Clunk, clunk, clunk.*

*Scuff, scuff, scuff.*

The breeze felt pleasantly warm on my cheeks as it blew away the last vestiges of the cold, depressing Hokuriku region's winter.

Spring is the season of new beginnings. The pastel blue of the sky, the fluttering black hair and the flapping skirts of the girls, the cherry-blossom pink blush of their cheeks—it all spoke to new encounters, new romantic possibilities. As I walked toward school, I had a light spring in my step, like some sprightly old dude heading excitedly to his favorite public bathhouse owned by an old childhood friend.

*     *     *

Saku Chitose from Class Five is a total man-slut shithead.

You know, I keep reading and rereading this post, but I have to say it sounds like someone might have it in for me. They used my full name and everything.

I grinned wryly down at my cell phone screen. For the past few minutes, I'd been taking it out of my pocket to look at it before putting it away, and then doing it all over again.

On my phone, I had the underground school gossip site open.

It's kind of like an anonymous forum, and each school has its own section where anyone can post anything they want. There's *a lot* of posts. It was super popular for about ten years, but then it became this big "social issue" because of online bullying, so it started to die off and fall out of use.

Well, these days we have Twitter and LINE to vent our stress on. But those kinds of social media platforms come with risk. Make one wrong move, and your true identity can be uncovered just like that. So we elite students from Fukui Prefecture's top-level Fuji High have all taken our bitching, dissing, and trash-talking back to the underground forums, and they've seen something of a revival recently.

"He's a limp-dick blowhard; that's what he is. Looool!"
"Yeah, I heard he couldn't keep it up when he was banging that senior girl lmao"

Hey! I'm not about to let that one slide!

I felt my spirits sinking as I scanned all the comments that agreed with the OP. Being called a man-slut, okay, I could own up to that one. But having rumors fly around about my sexual performance… That kind of thing could really affect the self-worth of a hot stud like me.

And one more thing… The other kids getting dumped on at least got to have code names or were referred to by their initials. Why was I the only one getting outed with my real name while these fools raked me over the coals…? By the way, my real name first popped up on this site shortly after last year's entrance ceremony, and it's never dropped out of the yearly top keyword ranking, not even once.

Almost all the posts about me were slanderous takedowns.

Why can't people write something nice sometimes? Like, "Chitose's so hot! I wanna be in his arms rn!" or something?

"Good morning, Saku. Why are you just standing there like that?"

Someone tapped me on the shoulder, and I turned to see Yua Uchida, who had been in my class last year. She was smiling, her expression reminding me of a bright, blooming sunflower.

Her long hair was pulled forward over one shoulder, fluttering slightly in the breeze. When she smiled, which was often, the corners of her eyes crinkled in this totally adorable way that could probably end all wars and bring peace to all mankind. She wasn't exactly the undisputed beauty of the school or anything, but she was the type of girl whose name would come up on school trips when talk turned to who's hot and who's not.

Actually, she didn't stand out at all at first, but as the year went by, she started to blossom out of her junior-high phase. During second semester last year, she naturally started to gravitate toward us popular kids.

"Mornin', Yua. Check this out."

I waved my phone in the air, and Yua came to stand shoulder to shoulder with me so she could see the screen. As she leaned in, I got a whiff of her shampoo. Smelled organic.

"Ah, that. Well, don't worry."

Yua grinned at me, her eyes crinkling a little as she patted me reassuringly on the back.

"…Excuse me? Is that any way to react? It's like you're saying, 'Well, there's no way to deny it, so get over it.'"

"That *is* what I'm saying. Look, Saku. You're hot, and girls love you, so you're bound to have haters. It's all jealousy."

Honestly, I agreed with Yua. It was pointless even trying to figure out who could be writing all the online burns about me. It could be Jock Blocker, the meathead I tangled with just before spring break started. Or it could be some rando with a grudge against me, someone who wasn't even on my radar at all.

Just think about any famous creative…an actor, a musician, a writer, what have you. The more popularity they get, the more haters they accumulate at the same time. There are plenty of jerks out there who want to drag down successful people and expose whatever weak points they might have.

In fact, when your proportion of fans to haters is about fifty-fifty, that's when you know you're doing all right. The thing that really scares me is not being gossiped about at all.

"But it's crazy! I mean, here's a super-hot, stylish guy, gifted at sports, with top-notch grades, excellent at getting along with everyone, is super nice and is also an excellent leader—with, I might add, a real penchant for wit and dirty jokes. I'm great. Why do they hate me?"

"If you really can't guess, I'd be happy to fill you in. But I have a feeling you already know."

\*

As we passed through the now-familiar school gates, we picked up our copies of the class lists being handed out. Starting in second year, the classes would be separated into sciences and humanities, and the class list would show the breakdown. Personally, I prefer the system where they post it up on the bulletin board—it's more exciting somehow—but this way it's easier to see what class everyone else is in, so I guess it makes more logical sense.

As she scanned the class list, Yua's face lit up.

"Yes! We're in the same class again. Here's to another year together!"

"It's not just us. The class list is basically the exact same as last year."

"Yeah, but…you could at least act a little more excited to be in the same class with me again!"

I chuckled, shrugging off Yua's sulking. Then I took a closer look at the list. Along with me and Yua, the main players from the popular group of last year's Class Five were all reunited, having opted for the humanities course.

Our school has a policy of trying to keep kids together as much as possible, even when they need to separate us for the course selection.

This helps mitigate the stress that comes with an abrupt change of peers, and it helps us focus on our studies instead of trying to make new friend groups all the time. You get to stick with your buddies, and the social hierarchies remain in place. It's a common policy with high-level, college-admission-oriented schools like ours. So it really didn't come as too much of a surprise to me.

That said, outside of our original group, there were plenty of unknowns from other classes mixed in, too. I heard from an upperclassman once that the social sciences and humanities groups both always end up with a mishmash of students like this.

Even though they try to avoid switching us around as much as possible, because each class of students chooses their own courses, there's a limit to what they can do on the faculty side. So some kids end up without many of their old friends where they're placed, or no friends at all. They try to fix that to an extent by lumping them all together—with, of course, the troublemakers and the nuisance kids. Then they try to plug up the gaps by shoving in small groups of amenable popular kids who are good at getting along with everyone.

I mean, the faculty doesn't actually *admit* to this, of course. But everyone talks about how the second- and third-years definitely have both "popular classes" and "loner classes."

"And we're still Class Five, too. Aw, I was just thinking about how those '*Saku Chitose from Class Five*' online takedowns would soon be outdated. But for at least another year, they'll stay current."

"Yeah. I'm sure those anons will be thrilled they don't have to go back and edit all their messages to say '*Saku Chitose from Class Two*' or whatever."

"Hey, whose side are you on anyway?"

*

"'Sup? Mornin'."

I lifted a casual hand in greeting as I opened the door to Year Two, Class Five's classroom, my voice bouncy and perky. I had no idea who I might find already in the classroom, but I had carefully tailored my greeting to fit all eventualities. It was very much a greeting meant for a brand-new class of unknown variables.

"Hey, Saku! Morning! Aaah, hey, Ucchi!"

A greeting came floating my way, cutting through the excited classroom chatter and hustle and bustle, as clear and sharp as a bird singing in the morning light. The owner of the voice was Yuuko Hiiragi, and while her greeting was rambunctious and unrefined, she had the looks of an elegant young lady, the very definition of the class princess.

Her hairstyle must have taken three times as long to arrange as Yua's had. Her curves were in all the right places; she had that "ideal" figure that has all the guys doing a double take. You could put her in one of those all-girl pop ensembles with, like, twenty members, and she'd still stand out as one of the best. Everyone fawned and fussed over Yuuko, and she took it all in stride. She almost expected it. Kinda like how a newborn baby never thinks to question whether it's adorable or not. And she was so natural about it that everyone gave her a free pass.

Sometimes, perfect girls do exist—and not just as the main female character in novels and manga. She transcended petty concepts like being stuck-up or arrogant and was accepted by everyone.

Incidentally, the kids at school had all pretty much decided among themselves that Yuuko and I were endgame. Or at least, that she was "first-wife" material for me.

"We've got Yuuko, Kazuki, Kaito... Wow, the key players are all here."

"Hey, Yuuko. Hey, you two."

Yua and I both returned Yuuko's greeting and walked over to where Yuuko and the others were standing in a circle, while they naturally moved aside to make space for us.

"Yay! We're all together again!"

Yuuko raised both hands to solicit a double high five from me. I slapped her hands with mine, then interlaced my fingers with hers.

"Are you glad, too, Saku?"

"Of course. If you and I had been separated, Yuuko, I'd have to drag myself to school every day in despair."

Yuuko always treated me like the funny guy friend. She thought nothing of getting touchy-feely with me like this. In fact, she had probably greeted Kazuki and Kaito the exact same way only moments before.

Yuuko never even thought about things like being disliked or thought of as annoying by other people. She was very affectionate with everyone. And she didn't just act that way with us popular guys. She acted like that with everyone, even the nerdy ones. And of course, they would get the wrong idea, actually think they had a chance with her, and then try to ask her out.

She'd end up with this total *???* look on her face. It had happened way too many times to even count.

Her character being what it was, she was always walking a fine line between being loved or being despised by everyone. But she never crossed that line. Yuuko was naturally sweet and kind, and she treated everyone the same, be they popular or dorky, boy or girl. People loved that about her. That's why she was at the top of the hierarchy, one of the most popular girls in school.

I was just contemplating the popularity of Yuuko when Yua turned a scornful eye on me.

"This guy here was really enjoying himself on the walk to school, scoping out all the new first-year girls."

Yuuko turned to look at me, too, quickly linking arms with Yua and furrowing her brow.

"Ew, Saku, what a creeper! When you have such pretty girls like us in your grade already!"

"…You're just jealous you didn't have a hot guy like me from the year above you waiting to appraise your looks when it was you making that first innocent, heart-pounding walk to high school. Am I right, Yua?"

The adorable twosome giggled and rolled their eyes at me. We were having a good time—until all of a sudden, someone karate chopped me in the midsection. Ouch.

"Sorry, dude. I thought you were due a punch or two."

The one responsible was Kaito Asano, who was grinning teasingly at me. He was already the star player of the basketball team and had barely even started second year yet. He was your typical jovial jock type with a great physique and superior sports skills.

And he was taller than me. I could only hope that male-pattern baldness was in his future.

"You gotta give it to him for the timing, though. He had to cut you off; that flirty playboy shtick was wearing thin on your charming concubines."

Kazuki Mizushino grinned like a shark. How was he the star player of the soccer team already, when he was barely in second year? He always acted so suave, but the kid knew what he was doing.

And he was arguably better-looking than me. I could only hope an explosive diarrhea attack during class lurked in his future.

"Saku, you seem somewhat annoyed."

…Hmph. *And* he was always pointing out the elephant in the room.

"It's cool. I was just thinking about how you two are a couple of annoying bugs trying to get between me and my harem. Three's company, but five's a crowd, you know. And I'd cut out that 'concubine' business real quick unless you want to read your name on the school gossip website sometime soon."

Everyone snorted as I snarked at Kazuki, keeping one eye on Yua.

Grinning, Kaito threw his arm around my shoulder.

"Aw, Saku. The message boards getcha again?"

"Screw you. Why do you look so happy about it?"

"Why wouldn't I? A rogue like you who leaves girls weeping all over school… You need to suffer the consequences, or the cosmos will fall out of alignment!"

"If I'm up there with my real name, this jerk ought to be, too. That's where the universe is off-balance."

But Kazuki merely smirked. "Hate to break it to you, but I never leave girls crying. I simply love 'em and leave 'em wanting more."

"Oh, spare us."

Now that I was done verbally sparring with Kaito and Kazuki, I cleared my throat to indicate a change of subject.

"Anyway, it looks like Team Chitose is back in business."

"I prefer Yuuko Hiiragi's Angels."

"Nah, Kaito's Dynamite Bombers."

"Kazu's Creative Agency."

"Yua 5."

"Welp, time to disband! Too many creative differences!"

We all shared a fist bump to seal the deal.

*

"Morning!"

"Mornin'!"

The classroom door kept sliding open as we stood talking and goofing off together, and kids kept coming in all bright-eyed and bushy-tailed. Everyone seemed nervous, walking into a new classroom and an unfamiliar social environment.

"Hey, it's Chitose. You grow your hair out over spring break? I can cut it for you."

"No, thanks. Knowing you, you'll cut a major artery by mistake."

Haru Aomi was the girl who had offered me the haircut. She was in Class Three last year.

She had long limbs and was the shooting guard on the girls' basketball team. She wasn't really all that tall, but she had a model-like physique—not exactly skinny, just sort of lean and small-boned.

She didn't fuss over her hair like Yua and Yuuko did; instead, she kept it in a short ponytail so it didn't get in the way. She didn't have the assets of the other two girls, but there was something about her bobbing ponytail and exposed neck that tended to catch your eye.

Kaito inserted himself into our conversation then.

"Hey! You should greet me first. We're both on basketball teams."

"Oh, I've seen enough of your face. There's nothing exciting about it. Right, Nanase?"

"I'm sick of Kaito, too. But I'm glad Chitose and Mizushino

are here. A little eye candy for once!" Yuzuki Nanase popped her head over Haru's shoulder. She had glossy shoulder-length hair that made me think of a shampoo commercial.

She was in Class Three last year, too, the point guard on the girls' basketball team. She and Haru were BFFs, probably known throughout the whole prefecture. But mostly for their plays on the basketball court.

If you did a poll of who was the most popular girl in our year, Nanase's name would definitely pop up alongside Yuuko's. If Yuuko was a pop-idol type who combined cuteness with status, then Nanase was more like an actress. She could go from playing a cute role to an absolute beauty, from friendly to aloof, from ballsy to a shrinking violet you ended up wanting to protect.

Personally, though, I had the feeling she was more calculated than Yuuko. Yuuko was oblivious to her own charms, but Nanase radiated an aura of perfection that seemed perfectly constructed. I had the feeling she was always thinking about how she was perceived at school. I could tell, because so was I.

Both girls had great figures, but where Yuuko was marshmallow-soft in all the right places, Nanase was nice and firm.

…I wasn't talking about their chests. Get your mind out of the gutter.

Nanase was grinning now, walking up to me. "Well, now that we've got the hot guys all here…I guess it's time to feast our eyes! Show us those pecs, boys!"

Kazuki and I immediately leaped into theatrics, covering our chests with our schoolbags and squealing.

"Nooo! Don't objectify my body!"

"Women are only after one thing!"

Then Haru got in on the action. "Aw, come on, don't be prudes, boys. Just lie back and count the stains on the ceiling tiles. It'll be over before you know it."

"Er, what year were you girls born in, again? Why are you acting

like creepy, mustache-stroking advertising executives from the fifties?"

While the two of us were squealing and hopping about, Yua joined in the fun and provided the heckling for the two girls' little comedy skit. She hadn't been a member of the popular kids for that long, but you wouldn't know it by looking at her.

"Ucchi!" Haru squealed. "Perfect, we were missing a heckler in Class Three last year! Nanase always gives up when I'm on a comedy roll. You should be my new comedy partner!"

"Ucchi, when she goes off the rails, you gotta roast her mercilessly. And me," added Nanase.

"...Er, okay. But shall we start over? We've never really talked before, so we should introduce ourselves first, right, you guys?"

Yua blinked a little as she gazed at Haru and Nanase. Ah, she was really getting overwhelmed. But these were two of the most popular girls in the school; not a single kid didn't know their name. That's how it goes.

But the natural-born princess, Yuuko, was as cool as a cucumber.

"Yuzuki, Haru, it's so great to be in class with you this year! I've always wanted to be friends with you both. But don't forget that Saku and I are endgame! And Ucchi is his...uh, sidepiece, okay? But apart from that...sisters!!!"

Like Yua, Yuuko had never really interacted with Nanase and Haru before. In her own laid-back, bumbling way, she was trying to mark her territory. It was sort of cute. Except it was clear she had no idea what a sidepiece was.

"All that aside, it's great to welcome two new members to Team Chitose," I said.

Haru and Nanase didn't miss a beat.

"I prefer Aomi's Dangerous Challengers."

"No, no, Yuzuki's Moon Crusaders."

"Ah, I had a feeling it would be this way."

Yeah, our group was definitely going to end up consisting of the most popular members in our new class.

I looked around at the other students. Some of them I remembered seeing before. Several looked nervous. Others were talking with loud voices, and some were even glancing enviously at our group, maybe wishing they could join us. Others stared unseeing and silent at their desks or the blackboard. And there was another group who obviously hated our guts.

It was an understandable reaction to have toward us. Here we were, laughing and talking with raised voices, all buddy-buddy so soon into a change of class. I could understand a few dirty looks.

Sorry, but that's just how we are.

I know I was a little self-aware, and I think Kazuki and Nanase were, too. But it wasn't like we were trying to show off or flaunt the new additions to our group. *Hey, everyone, look at us! We're so popular!*

No, we were just happy we were in the same class again with friends. Just old buddies, goofing off.

I swear, that's all we were doing.

But considering how many people don't get to enjoy high school the way we do, it was perhaps no surprise that they were always painting me as an obnoxious popular kid with zero self-awareness and dissing me online by my real name.

The unpopular kids, the losers, and the otaku, they stereotype us just as much as anyone else. *Popular kids are all like this; they should be more like that; they're all style and no substance; they're a bunch of assholes who think they're better than us.*

I guess that's why it's obvious that the teachers try to keep the popular kids together. Like together with like, you know? Let the kids be with other kids who they're most likely to be friends with. And fill the gaps with the ones who won't get along with anyone. Maybe they could even learn a thing or two from us popular kids. Maybe our coolness will round off some of their idiosyncratic edges. And everyone can relax and focus on studying, without any discord in the pecking order.

Anyway, the status quo suits Saku Chitose just fine.

*Death is better than an unbeautiful life.* That's my philosophy. And by *beautiful*, I mean a life where I'm cool and attractive and have tons of girls fussing over me.

\*

"All right, take your seats, everyone."

Suddenly, there came a languid, slightly irritated voice from the front of the class. Not really the kind of fresh attitude you expect on the first day of school, now, is it?

Once everyone realized that our homeroom teacher had entered the room, they scampered to their desks. He didn't even really need to tell us—maybe the guy was just saving his energy. Anyway, we're one of the top schools in the prefecture, so it's not like we take all that long to settle down and listen, unlike some schools.

"I'm Kuranosuke Iwanami, homeroom teacher for Year Two, Class Five. Let's get straight down to it and make it through another year, all right?"

He had residual bedhead, which he clearly hadn't bothered to comb and gel down, and stubble. He was also wearing a shabby suit and an old pair of straw-soled thong sandals.

This fellow, who looked like some madcap artist who had retreated into his craft and turned his back on the human world, was also our homeroom teacher last year. His particular subject of expertise was the Japanese language.

He was kind of a slob, but he was pretty well-liked as a teacher. Every class he taught for Japanese language got the best grades. At a school like ours, which has plenty of top-notch teachers, his laid-back, "meh" sort of attitude toward class endeared him to his students. We even called him Kura.

"Aw yisss! We got Kura for homeroom! I was just saying I hoped we would!"

Since we were all seated alphabetically by surname, Haru was at the desk next to mine. Now she was grinning at me. I could smell something sweet, probably scented body spray she'd put on after morning club practice. It made me feel restless for some reason.

"Yeah, you guys had Miss Misaki last year for homeroom, right? Man, she sucks. Every time she sees me in the halls, she tells me to tighten my tie up. She's hot, but she's got a mean stare."

"A lot of guys like her and her stare. Not you, Chitose?"

"Hmm… Nah, I don't like that type. Too many pheromones. Too much of a hard-ass. I much prefer laid-back women like you, Haru. You're easy to talk to."

"…What? I sure hope you're not trying to hit on me this soon into the semester. Please don't; it's very tacky."

"Yikes. Sorry. I got confused and thought I was talking to a girl just then."

"Yeah, big mistake. Come see me after school, behind the old building."

"I give you points for the classy choice of venue, Milady. The standard option for an impromptu brawl is usually the men's toilets."

I got to know Haru last year through Kaito. She had this kind of refreshing, sporty girl vibe. And she was easy to hang with. You could treat her like one of the guys. She was a real bro.

"You know, I think Miss Misaki is a pretty good teacher, though. A lot of students like her. But I guess you're right about her being kind of a hard-ass. Kura, though, he seems totally laid-back."

"Yes, he's as loosely wound as his tie."

"I see it, I see it. Man, I hate a tight tie, especially after getting all sweaty during club practice."

Haru fiddled with the neck of her shirt, flapping it to get some air inside.

What a naughty girl. But she did it so innocently. I said she was a bro, one of the guys, but that doesn't mean she didn't have feminine appeal. In fact, it was often kind of distracting.

"You could wear a neck ribbon instead of a tie. That's less constricting."

"Dearest, can you really see me with a ribbon?"

"Hmm…"

"I know my image, but I'm not a fan of hearing people point it out; you know what I'm saying?"

"…Okay, I prefer you in the tie, Haru. We cool?"

"Ah, Chitose, the light is glinting off your hair like a halo. Like a basketball hoop, so tempting…"

"Don't dunk me!"

Miss Misaki aside, the Fuji High faculty were actually pretty chill for an elite school. We were allowed to straighten or perm our hair, experiment with different hairstyles, and personalize our uniforms to a limited extent. We could even check our phones in class as long as we were subtle about it. A lot of the teachers, Kura included, also allowed us to take pics of the blackboard for later reference.

You have to be pretty smart to get into this school in the first place. The teachers don't want us all having mental breakdowns and going neurotic over college entrance exams, so that's probably why they give us a lot of breathing room.

"All right, we need to decide on the class president and vice president, and determine the seating order. Well, Mr. Chitose, can you take over? And try not to suck-u, Saku."

I was so distracted thinking about the contrast between Haru's sporty style and femininity that I barely even noticed Kura calling my name. Of course I was the one he called on to do the grunt work. As usual.

Haru poked my elbow. "Chitose, you've been nominated. Even got a lame Dad joke, too."

"All right, all right."

I had learned in the past year that there was no point trying to worm out of Kura's requests.

Besides, ol' Kura never gave anyone more homework than they could handle or more class duties than they could cope with. But he vacillated in a range between "They could do this easily" and "This would be a real stretch." On this occasion, the first category applied to me. Any complaining would be met with a languid "Just get on with it" from Kura.

Still, it wasn't like Kura to be *this* lax on the first day of a new school year, in front of students he hadn't even met yet. Eh, I wasn't going to dwell too heavily on it.

I headed on up to stand behind the teacher's lectern.

Then I cleared my throat.

"Uh… So… I guess everyone in second year knows my name already, but just in case…"

I started off arrogant, plucking at the lapels of my blazer in a cool way. Then I gave the kids a sharp nod.

"I'm Mr. Iwanami's personal maid, apparently. The name's Saku Chitose. You may know me from certain websites as a man-slut and/or a shithead. ♪"

They all grinned, first the girls and then the guys. Their reaction told me they had all read the BS on the underground website.

"Tch."

"…Lame."

As I looked more closely, I could see that several of the smiles were sarcastic. Probably the same students who were giving me the evil eye just before.

Still, it was the first day, so I decided to try to appease them a little. I flicked my gaze over to Kazuki.

"All right then, everyone close your eyes. Now, will the person or persons who have been writing such libelous things about me online raise their hand?"

…

"All right, all right, I see. You can open your eyes. Kazuki, we're going to have to settle this like men later."

"I'm sorry. It was only a prank. I was trying to cheer up my sick mother."

"The heck? Show her a funny rom-com, then! Incidentally, I saw your mom riding her bicycle the other day—she's smokin' hot, by the way—and she didn't look sick at all!"

"Listen, Saku… I mean, Saku Man-Slooten…"

"What's with the weird Dutch-sounding nickname?!"

"Tsk, tsk, what would my mother think?"

"Yeah, because of you!"

The tense atmosphere in the class dissipated, and now everyone was grinning.

It was calculated, yes, but I wasn't trying to one-up my fellow students. I just wanted to get along with everyone and have myself a nice time in high school. To that end, I needed to make it difficult for people to ruin the fun with name-calling and negativity.

Even the dissenters had settled down now, although their lips were still pressed together in tight lines.

"Anyway, jokes aside, let's all get along and make some new friends this year, yeah? Okay, so for the class president and vice president, does anyone have any nominations?"

Kaito piped up right away. "After that introduction, nobody's gonna wanna take over! You do it, Saku. You were class president last year, after all."

Nanase and Haru backed him up.

"Eh, sure. He can't be any worse than anyone else."

"It's just a title, after all."

And…decided in ten seconds.

Eh, but I was kinda expecting this after setting the mood for the class just then. Still, it wasn't an unfavorable outcome for me.

My bad to any idealistic students who were planning to shake things up this year by becoming new class prez and changing everything, though. If any such person did speak up, then sure, I'd concede. But I'd have to warn them... Change doesn't go down too well in the second year of high school. Being class prez isn't a whole lot of work, but you do have to watch out for the haters, like that group earlier. And you have to be aware of the needs of not just the popular kids, but the losers and the loners, too. Yeah, you've got to be able to make shrewd decisions and then carry them out, for the good of everyone.

"Any other nominations? No? Okay. Then I'll do it. From today forth, I hereby claim you all as my subjects."

I put one hand on my hip and struck a humorously arrogant pose.

"Big talk for Teacher's Personal Maid," Haru quipped.

"Oh dear, I do apologize! I look forward to serving you all to the best of my ability!"

Several of the girls cracked up at this. "Too funny!" one gasped.

"Okay, now to choose the vice president. Any nominations?"

This would be another five-seconder; I just knew it.

"Me, me, me! If Saku's gonna be president, I just gotta be vice president!!!"

As expected, before I even finished talking, Yuuko had her hand in the air. No surprises there.

"Er, as I recall, the vice president last year goofed off a lot and pushed all the work onto the president. If I'm not crazy, I have a feeling she looked an awful lot like...you."

"It's cool; it's cool! I took great care of the class bunny and class turtle in elementary school! I got this!"

"...Excuse me; I am not a class pet."

Nobody voiced any opposition to Yuuko as vice prez.

"Thanks, everyone! I'll be your new class vice president, Yuuko Hiiragi!"

Waving, she trotted up to join me at the lectern without even bothering to look at the class to see if they were cool with this.

That's just how she was. It blew me away how she could act so chill without needing to scheme about stuff. Unlike me.

"All right, now let's decide the class order. Any ideas?"

Beside me, Yuuko shot her hand up into the air again.

"We should all be able to sit with the guy or girl we have a crush on!"

"No, thanks! I'll never be able to study if I'm surrounded by a harem of hotties."

*Er, Yuuko? This is a class of mostly popular kids, remember? (And a few loners.) Better not force everyone to sound each other out just yet.*

"We should arm wrestle. Winners get to choose where they sit."

"Kaito, please. The grown-ups are talking."

"We should be seated based on last year's grades."

"Kazuki, please. I really think your contribution to this discussion should be silence. Although… Let's talk about *your* grades last year…"

"I want to sit at the back so I can snooze during class!"

"I appreciate the candor, Haru. But I really think your seat should be right under the teacher's nose."

"I like that logic. Put me in the back, too."

"If we're going by number of personality flaws, I think you and Kazuki ought to be seated first, Nanase!"

"We should just draw paper slips and make it fair."

"Now, now, Yua… Don't spoil the fun with logic."

"Wait, why am I getting chewed out?"

I heaved a huge, put-upon sigh before casting my gaze over the class. Then I suggested the immediately obvious choice.

"Okay, kiddos. Since we can't agree, I'm going to exercise my presidential authority. Now as I look at you all sitting here so bright-eyed and bushy-tailed, I think to myself, *Ah yes, how fresh, how befitting the new school year this setup is!* So I propose we stay seated alphabetically. What say you?"

I waited for a few seconds, but since there was no opposition, I continued.

"Anyone with any issues, come talk to me. Issues may include but are not limited to 'I can't see the blackboard because my eyes are bad,' 'Kaito's big head is blocking my view,' 'Kazuki keeps staring at me, and it's making me uncomfortable,' and so on and so forth. We'll take it on a case-by-case basis. Okay?"

I was well aware of the fact that only the popular kids had been contributing to the discussion so far. The others probably felt too afraid to.

Those who ended up seated at the front by alphabetical order may have had their grievances, but it was also easier to see the board from up there. It wasn't worth coming to the class president and complaining. And since I'd chosen alphabetical order, no one could accuse me of prioritizing the popular kids. My plan was calculated to avoid as much class discord as possible.

"All right, so everyone seems to be on board. Then let's stay seated like this for second year. I look forward to serving you all as class president."

"Wow, what a lame ending. What happened to the humor?"

"…Ah, I'll also agree to seating changes if the sight of Kura puts you off your schoolwork, ha-ha-ha!"

\*

Since it was the first day of school, and we had the opening ceremony and all, we didn't have any classes beyond homeroom. Half the kids headed off to club activities, and the other half headed home. Kaito, Haru, and Yuuko had tennis club; Yua had band practice—all my buddies had clubs to go to. I was the only one with a wide-open afternoon stretching out in front of me.

I bought a can of coffee from the vending machine and made my way up to the school roof, slippers slapping on the steps. I could hear the band's trumpets somewhere far-off. I could hear the shouts of the soccer club, warming up by running laps. The rubbery bounce of the basketball club's balls and the squeaking of their sneakers. And the dull thwacks of the baseball team's mitts coming into contact with the hard baseballs. As I listened idly to all these typical after-school sounds, I was overcome with a sense of melancholy.

I opened the roof door and was met with the sight of the railings towering over me, fencing in a square of blue overhead. The sky was so blue it felt almost oppressive, so vast it made me feel suffocated. And there were tiny puffs of gray, lighter than clouds, floating just above the railings. I headed over there to see a familiar face I'd rather not have encountered.

"Ah, hello, hello."

Kura was leaning up against the housing unit of the water tank, enjoying himself a cigarette.

"I thought this school was nonsmoking anywhere on the premises?"

I made my way up the little ladder and sat myself down beside Kura.

"Just another silly rule invented by the education board to keep up appearances. As long as I don't blow smoke on the kids, who cares?"

"And who am I, then, if not one of said kids?"

"You're the one who's smart enough to figure out which is the better option between tattling on me to the other teachers or having free use of the spare key to the rooftop. That's who."

"Well, thanks for the compliment."

Like most high schools in Japan, our school frowns upon kids coming and going on the rooftop as they please. Essentially, it's forbidden. Still, you can sometimes get permission from Kura, the Keeper of the Key, to eat bento lunches here with your buddies. But you have to ask in advance, and it's kind of a hassle, so most people don't bother.

Me, though? Well, Kura appointed me Roof-Cleaning Officer, a totally made-up role, so I get to come up here whenever I want, without having to ask anybody. It's pretty sweet.

"Aren't you ashamed to be a smoker in this day and age, though? Society is trying to stamp out your kind, you know."

"Eh, people are just looking for an easy scapegoat."

"You're telling me."

I popped the tab on my can of coffee, thinking bitterly about the school gossip website.

"Well, it's true that secondhand smoke affects the health of others. And if someone tells me they don't like the smell, well, I can't really argue against that. It's the self-righteous jerks I can't stand. They just want to sling mud at others. It's the same anywhere in society, from school to the workplace. It's like a modern-day witch trial. They'll burn you at the stake no matter what you say."

Kura was spitting some feisty words here, but all the while, he continued to placidly blow smoke rings.

"Yeah, it's the ones who sling mud without even stopping to consider if they're right or wrong that I can't stand. You kids grow up to be adults like that, and I'll have failed in my duty as a shaper of young minds."

"I so agree. Spot me one?"

I held out my hand for a cigarette—not seriously, of course. Kura smacked it away lightly.

"Don't push it, kiddo. If I end up jobless on the street, it'll be on your head."

"You're an excellent example to us all why adults shouldn't be trusted, Kura."

"Oh, go stick your head down the blouses of Hiiragi or Nanase like a good horny high schooler, would ya?"

"Now, now, that's no way for an educator to talk, even in jest."

I took a delicate sip of my coffee.

"…So whaddaya want, Teach?"

As homeroom ended, Kura had told me to meet him at "the usual place."

"So you're class prez, right?"

Kura pulled a crumpled packet of Lucky Strike out of his breast pocket and lit up his second cigarette in a row.

"Oh, whoops, I just realized I'm late for practice..."

Sensing danger afoot, I tried to get to my feet so I could beat it. But Kura grabbed me by the shoulder and yanked me back down. He was skinny as a stick but plenty powerful enough. I sat myself down obediently.

"Listen, Chitose... Don't you think it's better for the class to be all together? No one left behind, and all that?"

"Ah yes, depending on the charms of the homeroom teacher, I think that's the best way to be..."

I had noticed there was an empty desk in the back of the classroom. I figured the kid was maybe out sick, but I guess not.

"We were missing a student today, the first day of Year Two, Class Five, right? His name's Kenta Yamazaki. Last year he was in Year One, Class One. He wasn't a star student or anything, but he got decent grades and had a couple friends. But beginning in third semester, he started having absences, and soon he stopped coming altogether."

I'd never heard that name before. No-shows were kind of a rarity in our school. Attendance was pretty solid, generally speaking.

I don't know how it is in other schools, but most students at Fuji High plan to go to college. That's why they take the exam for Fuji in the first place, since it's a college prep school. Our student body consists of mostly smart kids. And yeah, there are some jerks who write shit about people on underground school gossip websites, and sometimes they try to outdo each other when it comes to test scores (the stress buildup can get ugly), but basically bullying isn't an issue here. Sometimes students who only scraped by on the entrance exam end up dropping out because they just can't keep up, but this didn't sound like that sort of situation.

I shrugged. "So why'd he stop coming?"

"His previous homeroom teacher visited his family home several times but wasn't able to speak to Yamazaki directly. Asking his friends didn't turn up much, either; they weren't that close with him. They only hung out because of shared interests."

"I see. So now you get to show off your skills as an educator."

"Anyway, that's all the information I have right now. The shared interests in question, incidentally, are anime and light novels. That whole genre, you know."

"Er, that's nice and all, but I get the sense we're talking past each other. Conversation is a game of catch, you know."

Kura pretended not to hear me. I heaved an exaggerated sigh. Then I continued, a little more seriously than before.

"All right, I'll bite… Why are you talking to me about this?"

"You're class president, Chitose. Class president is a position of responsibility, with a duty of care to their fellow classmates…"

"Yikes. It's just symbolic, though, isn't it?"

"I thought you were my maid, Chitose."

"Aw, screw you."

Kura had me trapped. I figured he'd deliberately had me take over as class president so he could stick me with this conundrum right after. There was no limit to the stuff he could make me do, using the "class president" angle as leverage.

"Only kids know what other kids go through at school. Like adults are the only ones who know what other adults have to deal with. Do you have any idea why a catch like me is still single past the age of thirty, hmm? Do you have any idea why I have to spend the majority of my meager teacher's salary down at the local titty parlor, Don't Make Me Take Off My Blazer? Well, do you?"

"Okay, well, now I know you're a total failure as a man, not just as a teacher! …Tch. So you want me to go and convince this

Kenta Yamazaki kid to come back to school, right? Why didn't you just ask Yuuko?"

"Hiiragi doesn't have the subtlety needed for something like this. She'd charge in without knowing all the details and end up driving the kid even farther into his shell. You're better at analyzing a situation and acting accordingly."

"In other words, you know I don't even have the option of saying no, huh?"

"So here's an issue that a kid of your skills could easily solve, but you're just going to turn your back? I thought you were more capable than that, Chitose. Everyone's superhero."

Kura gave me a grin loaded with meaning.

Tch. This unshaven old dude was such a pain to deal with.

What's that saying? *Don't chase what eludes you; don't reject what comes to you.* I didn't usually go out of my way to help others, but in a situation like this where I've been asked specifically, I found myself wanting to do a good job. To swoop in there and tie this problem up in a nice, neat bow and get credit for a job well done.

After all, I have appearances to keep up. If I want to keep my life running smoothly, I have to be the Saku Chitose everyone wants to believe I really am.

"You'll let me handle this my way, right? And I want proper compensation for my troubles."

"Oh yeah? You want me to bring you along to the titty bar, too?"

"No need. I know plenty of cute girls who are more than willing to 'take off their blazer' for free."

"…You know anyone into older guys?"

"You are so gross…"

\*

I found myself back once again on the river embankment path from this morning. But this time, I was walking in the opposite direction.

There're a lot of paths and roads to take to school, but I like this embankment path. The riverbed's around twenty meters in width, flanked on both sides by an assortment of old and new houses. And I enjoy the symmetry of the electricity pylons standing at neat intervals with cables strung tight between them. And then there's the view of the mountains in the background. No cars, either, so it's a good place for a casual stroll. Lots of feral cats, too, basking in the sun and yawning without a care in the world.

As the sight of homeward-bound students became sparser and sparser, I spotted someone sitting beside the sluice gate. Walking with careful, quiet steps, I headed down the little slope meant for accessing the gate. I didn't want to disturb her peace. She was radiating such an aura of stillness.

I spoke up, hoping my voice would be no more jarring than the soft trickling sounds of the river's water.

"Hey, Asuka."

She lifted her face from the paperback book she was reading and fixed her eyes on me. Then, the upperclassman Asuka Nishino responded, in a voice as dismissive as a cool spring breeze:

"Ah, it's you. I had a feeling I'd see you today."

The late afternoon sun made the downy hair on her cheek seem to almost glisten, and her eyes crinkled into a smile, making the small mole underneath her left eye rise. That expression drew me in as she raised a hand in greeting. She was both curvaceous and delicately built, and she wore her tie tight around her collar. Her skirt was in that modest gray zone between short and long. Her understated, muted beauty struck me all of a sudden in that moment.

"What are you reading?" I asked.

"It's *Phantom Lady* by Cornell Woolrich."

"'*The night was young, and so was he. But the night was sweet, and he was sour.*' That's the new edition, isn't it? I like that opening passage better than anything in any other novel I've read."

"...Of course you've read it. Man, you're annoying."

*

I had first met Asuka in September of last year. I quit baseball club over summer break, and I was heading home along the embankment, not sure what to do with myself.

"Hey! He's getting away!"

"Let's chase him!"

*Scuff, scuff, scuff. Clomp, clomp, clomp.*

A little ways ahead, I could see a bunch of kids playing together and having themselves a good old time. They seemed to be playing a game of samurai. The three of them were running at top speed, carrying "swords," aka loose branches they'd picked up somewhere. And they were chasing a fourth kid. The fleeing kid also had a branch-sword, but he didn't seem willing to use it. He must have been the weak link in that little group.

I watched them for a while, and then the kid who was being chased ended up slipping and falling into the river. The flow was pretty light there, so there was no real danger of the kid drowning or anything. But the embankment was steep, and a kid his size would have a lot of trouble climbing out by himself.

"Loser!"

"Ew! You're covered in mud and river goo! You stay far away from us on the walk home, got it?"

The kid's three "friends" were jeering at him as they peered down the embankment. None of them seemed willing to lend him a hand.

There were other students about, heading home from school, but they seemed to be ignoring the scene on purpose. Some of them even visibly picked up speed in an effort to hurry past.

Probably it was just friends roughhousing and not genuine bullying. But I figured the least I could do was scoop the tearful-looking kid out of the river, lend him a towel, give his friends a gentle scolding, and admonish them to go easier next time.

Now that I'd noticed it, I couldn't just look the other way and walk past. It would be lame.

Just as I was about to step in…

"Hey, guys, let me play, too!"

With a splash, a teenage girl appeared, plunging down the hill into the river.

I blinked, trying to process the new development in the situation. I was just standing there open-mouthed, staring at her.

Ignoring the gawking boys, the girl began splashing the fallen boy with river water in a playful manner. I clocked her school uniform immediately. She was one of ours.

"Hey, come on! Splash back!"

The students who had been ignoring the scene just before had now stopped and were gawking down at the girl with their noses wrinkled. Some of them were whispering to each other and smirking. I couldn't hear what they were saying, but it was obvious they were talking about how the girl must have a few screws loose.

I'd be lying if I told you I wasn't thinking the same thing. It was definitely a very odd, illogical scene. The river wasn't dirty and stinky or anything, but it still wasn't exactly the kind of place you'd want to splash around in, either. You had to expect to end up covered in mud if you started playing down there.

But the girl didn't seem to pay any attention to the state of her uniform or the stares of the onlookers. She just kept splashing the kid.

Her smile was so bright and beaming that the kid soon seemed to shrug off the weirdness of the situation and began splashing her back.

"Come on and join us, you guys!"

The girl called out to the other three kids who were still standing on the embankment. At first, they seemed weirded out, but the girl's exuberance seemed to take hold of them, too. They exchanged shrugs and flung themselves down the slope into the river.

"Hey, lady, you are seriously bonkers."

"Splash battle! Splash battle!"

"Hee-hee! You'll never win against me! I've got years of splash battle experience on you! Hey! Little squirt! Why are you sneaking up behind me? That's a dirty move! And just after I helped you!"

"You didn't help me. You just started splashing me."

Now the bullied kid was ganging up with his so-called friends against the girl.

"Don't let her get away!"

"Get her!"

*Tromp, tromp, tromp. Sploosh, sploosh, sploosh.*

They began a game of tag, right there in the river. It was the same kind of game as before, but this time, instead of yelling, they were all laughing together.

…What the heck was going on?

After they had all played in the river for a good amount of time, they made their way back up the bank.

That's when I finally stepped in and offered my sports towel. The four kids shared it, wiping off their faces one by one. Then they called "You're a weird lady, ya know that?" and all ran off together, shoulder to shoulder, soaked T-shirts clinging to their backs.

The girl watched them go, then slowly turned to look at me. Her school blazer, hair, face, everything, was dripping wet. Her blouse had gone see-through, and I could make out the camisole she wore underneath. But I couldn't really appreciate the sensuality of it under the current circumstances. I checked out her blazer crest and saw she was in second year.

"Enchanted by the lady of the lake? Well, river."

"Uh, no. I was just thinking you look like the ghost of someone who drowned at sea."

"Seriously?"

But the girl laughed loudly with amusement.

"Aw, man, I need to get this uniform dry-cleaned. Hey, you—you got any extra gym clothes in your bag or anything? I didn't have gym class today."

The girl blinked at me as she tried in vain to rub her hair dry with my towel, which was already completely saturated after the four boys had used it.

"I do, but they're pretty sweaty. They don't smell so fresh."

I handed her my gym bag, and she stuck her face right in there and began sniffing.

"Aw, man, that reeks! It's like someone used a dishcloth to mop up spilled milk at an elementary school."

"Hey now, it's not *that* bad. You want me to shove you back into the river?"

"I was only messing with you. It smells nice actually, like fabric softener. Can I borrow this? I swear I'll wash it and give it back to you. I'll just head back to school, change, and then walk home. If I walk around at dusk dripping and muddy like this, people will start calling the local priest."

But the girl herself didn't seem all that concerned about the fact that she was wet and muddy.

"Sure, but can I ask you one question?"

"Ye-es?"

"Why did you do that? A normal person would have scooped the kid out of the river and given his friends a lecture. I mean, I was just about to do that myself until you showed up."

The girl rubbed her chin. "Hmm," she said pensively. It seemed she'd acted on instinct and hadn't really thought it through beforehand.

"Well, I was kinda thinking about how it would suck for that kid to be the only one having to walk home wet and muddy. If everyone got in and splashed around, then they would all be in the same boat, and they could head home as friends. That would be much better in my opinion."

"Yeah, but you ended up wet and muddy, too. You weren't even part of the situation until you inserted yourself in it. And all the kids walking home were laughing at you."

The girl smiled, looking me in the eyes. For some strange reason, I had the feeling she was seeing right into my mind.

"I'm not sure why something like that is supposed to bother me, but okay…"

Her gentle smile became a challenging grin.

"If I cared what people thought, I wouldn't fling myself into a river like that in the first place, right? Anyway, I just thought it seemed like fun… So what you're saying to me now is, like, irrelevant."

I had no idea how to respond.

Most normal human beings factor in other people's perceptions before doing, well, anything.

I mean, I was planning to help the kid out, but in a way that would make me look like a hero. Then people would be like, "Wow, what a good guy." Otherwise, I guess I wouldn't have done it.

But this crazy girl was standing here saying she did it because it "seemed like fun."

It was almost like she accepted herself or something. Like she was exactly where she was meant to be in the world, and she only had to answer to herself.

And in the act of being herself, she'd solved the situation for the kid in a way that was going to benefit him much more than what I'd planned to do.

"Can I ask one more?"

"Sure."

The girl was wringing out the towel, seeming totally unbothered by anything I may have had to say.

"What's your name?"

"Asuka Nishino. You write Asuka with the characters for *tomorrow* and *breeze*."

Silhouetted against the deep-red setting sun, the girl gave me a soft smile.

In that moment, she seemed so beautiful. The wet hair stuck to her cheek? Beautiful. The brown smudge of mud on her nose? Beautiful. She had taken off her shoes and socks, and I could see her bare toes. They were beautiful, too.

A soft, late summer breeze swept across us both.

After this, I would be looking out for her at school—and on the path home.

*Tomorrow. Breeze.*

The name suited her. This girl who lived free, by her own rules. It suited her perfectly.

✶

"So I'm class president again, and Kura wasted no time in forcing me to do something for him."

I had plopped down next to Asuka, and now I was telling her all about Kenta Yamazaki.

"You're imperfectly perfect, as always. Like a spotless park you're not allowed to set off fireworks in."

"That's a weird comparison. Anyway, everyone prefers a nice tidy park, don't they?"

"But the park prohibits ball games and dog walking, too. No play equipment, either, in case kids get hurt. So no kids around. Just stone-faced adults, reading books like a bunch of statues."

"…Yeah, it sounds super boring."

"Then change the rules if you think that. Then the pretty park will become a fun place to play."

"It's difficult to change the rules once they've been established."

"Is it? All you have to do is pull down the signposts telling people not to do stuff. Boom, done."

"We live in a litigious society. If anything happens, you'll have a lawsuit on your hands."

Asuka closed her book and stashed it in her schoolbag. Then she got to her feet with a "Hup!" before gazing at the river for a few moments. After that, she turned to look back at me.

"Here's a question. If the girl you're closest to in your class and I were both drowning—like in the ocean or a big lake—which one of us would you save? You get a kayak in this scenario. A bright-red one. But the kayak only seats two."

"The second person could just cling onto the back of the kayak."

"No, no, the water is infested with piranhas and crocodiles." Asuka wagged her finger in my face like she was telling off a small child.

"I dunno if I'd be able to even row in such dangerous waters."

Asuka continued, as if I hadn't even said anything.

"I'd save you. No contest. Even if it was between my favorite guy in my class and you. I like you more, you see."

"So what happens to the Favorite Guy in Your Class, then?"

I turned the question back around on her, my heart pounding all of a sudden. Still, I knew she wasn't using the word *like* in the romantic sense.

"I'll pray for his soul. I'll pray that the piranhas and crocodiles eat him up quickly. It must hurt a lot to be nibbled to death by piranhas, don't you think?"

Asuka clasped her hands together in prayer, her eyes unfocused as if seeing the scenario play out in her mind.

"But if it was between you and a cat, I'd save the kitty, of course!"

"I'll hold the cat. I swear. Let me on the kayak!"

"…I bet you wouldn't bother saving anyone. You'd just paddle off by yourself." Asuka crouched down in front of me, hugging her knees and gazing at me.

"No, I'd give up the kayak to you two. I'd swim and take my chances. That's the most beautiful choice. That's what I'd want to believe."

"Yeah, right. You'd be squealing, 'Don't let the piranhas get me!'"

"No, I'd accept my fate. While the fishies were nibbling on my toes and earlobes."

"Geez, they're going right for the places that hurt, huh?"

Her comment had wounded me a little, so I'd just been trying to laugh it off. I often had the feeling that she made no attempt to filter herself around me and just said whatever she wanted.

"...Yep, that's Saku Chitose."

See what I mean?

Asuka scooped her bag up from its spot beside me and shouldered it. I wanted to keep talking, but it looked like she was done for now.

"So why'd you bring up the kayak scenario anyhow?"

"There's no real reason. It just came to me. If you insist on being the hero, then fine. Go sleep with the fishies. But if you make it back...we'll have a duel."

"You'd fight a man with piranhas dangling from his body? Maybe I'm just extra-tasty bait."

∗

That evening, I was lying on my bed scrolling on my phone.

I'd been in various LINE app friend groups since Year One, but today I had a bunch of messages from girls I'd met in my new class and swapped LINE IDs with.

I went down the list, sick of the same old boring group chats. Sending basic responses. I put a little more effort into responding to the girls I wanted to get to know better. It was like going through veggies at the grocery store, picking out the tastier-looking ones, and tossing the rest back.

Relationships with other kids can be complicated when you're popular. You have to know where to draw the line. Other kids approach you freely, either because they like you or because they hate you, and you have to decide how and when to cut them off. Sometimes you get caught up in a trap. It's like walking across a minefield. You can never let your guard down.

And once you put on the "good guy" mask, you have to keep it on right up until graduation.

About thirty minutes later, I finished dealing with my personal correspondence. Then I could finally open the messages from my actual friends.

First was Kaito's.

Breast-Master Saku, I have a question. What cup size sayest thou, on the subject of our basketball queen, Yuzuki Nanase?

"Hmm. I'd say it's approaching solid C-cup territory."

Wait, how big are Yuuko's again?

"I estimate a pillowy D cup."

Thank you, Master!!!

Kaito was such a dork. And fast to text back. Entirely too fast.

Kazuki's message was simple.

What's up for lunch tomorrow?

"Cafeteria food, I guess. Shall we invite Nanase and Haru?"

Yuuko's message was littered with emoji.

Darling! (a ton of pink hearts) Let's both do our best as class prez and vice prez! (a ton of faces with star eyes) (a ton of thumbs-ups) (tons of red hearts)

Nanase's message was interesting, very interesting, indeed.

I was hoping to get to know you more, Chitose. looking forward to talking to you.

"I was hoping to get to know you, too, Nanase. Let's chat it up anytime."

For some reason, Haru's message was just a super-close-up photo of a hot dog on a stick.

HOT DIGGITY DOG! I'm sizzling with excitement for the new school year with you!

"Can't you send me a cute selfie like a normal girl?"

*All right, that's enough of that.*

Putting my phone down on the bedside table, I headed out

onto my balcony. The moon was a perfect circle in the sky, like it had been drawn using a compass.

The air outside was still pretty warm despite the late hour, and it smelled of spring. I felt restless. For some reason, ever since I was young, I've always felt like a full moon heralds the coming of something new.

It was a late country night. All the people you'd see walking along would be tucked in bed by now. No cars running, either. It was ten o'clock, after all. Half the people in town were probably already asleep. The others were probably getting ready for bed. As I stood there in this air pocket of empty time, weird thoughts started coming to me.

Did I really exist in this town? What if I was a character in some fictional place, just playing out the role that was written for me? What if I burst and disappeared tomorrow, like a bubble? Would I leave any lasting marks on anyone? What would remain of my pain, my sadness, my loneliness? Would it even matter?

This pathetic little town, this pathetic little high school…and all the pathetic little popular kids in it. What if we were all just running around in circles inside a glass terrarium, with no way out?

I reached one hand up to the moon, almost trying to gauge how far away from it I really was.

And I thought about Kenta Yamazaki.

*What's on your mind right now, man?*

*If you're looking at the moon right now, is it the same one I'm looking at or one that's completely different?*

I went back inside my room, picked up my phone, and selected a name from my contact list. Then I placed a call.

# CHAPTER TWO
## Kenta Is in His Room

The day after Kura stuck me with his request, I was heading to the cafeteria at lunch break with Yuuko, Yua, Kazuki, Kaito, Haru, and Nanase. All the popular kids in Year Two, Class Five, in other words.

When I looked around, I could see that several new second-years I didn't know had taken up noisy positions at the tables. Since our school's cafeteria is kind of small, there's an unwritten rule that first-years aren't allowed to sit down to eat, unless they're super popular. There was no punishment for breaking this rule, of course, but all the first-years tended to stick to it out of an awareness of the school hierarchy. Most of them took their school lunch out to the courtyard or the classroom to eat. As long as they returned their plates and eating utensils, none of the staff cared.

So the privilege of being able to eat in the school cafeteria was something new and exciting to a lot of kids who had been first-years only as recently as two weeks ago.

As for my group, we had obviously been eating in the cafeteria the whole time, and we were a little taken aback as we were reminded of how it was a year ago. The cafeteria was at its fullest in April, but the numbers tended to taper off around second semester. By the time third semester rolled around, there were a lot of empty seats. We had come straight from class, and yet most of the tables were already filled. The only empty one was located in the farthest corner, which everyone knew was basically permanently reserved for a group of the most popular kids in third year. But that was last year. They were gone now.

"Boy, it's crowded. I guess a lot of first-years felt like cafeteria lunch today."

Yuuko had been mindlessly seating herself in the cafeteria all through first year and hadn't noticed how unusual that was. Typical Yuuko.

Kazuki rolled his eyes. "Uh, no, it's mostly second-years like us. I'm not asking you to remember names, but you could at least learn to identify faces. You're gonna make all the boys cry. They've been staring at you since you came in. You talk to complete strangers like they're your best friends; you could at least try to remember who some of them are."

"What? But you're nice to all the girls, too, Kazuki."

"No, it's Saku who sweet-talks everyone. I pick and choose."

"Wow, that's...kinda awful."

"You might see it that way. But sometimes in this world, you have to be cruel to be kind."

"You know, Kazuki, sometimes I have no idea what you're talking about."

*That table's free, so let's sit there.*

Kazuki and Yuuko sat themselves down at the far table, operating on basic logic. The others all joined them and flopped down casually at the table, too.

As we settled ourselves down at the sacred table, whose location identified its users as the chosen few, there was a hushed murmur across the cafeteria. As if everyone was thinking, *Ah yeah, that checks out.* Our group sat down without much ado, but I knew that starting tomorrow this table would always remain empty and waiting for us. And that we would always make sure to choose this table to sit at. It suited me fine. There was no need to scope out a different spot. Thus, the perks of one petty unspoken high school rule had just been inherited by our group.

"What's everyone eating? I'm having the katsudon, jumbo size, obviously!"

The dish Haru had just mentioned was popular among the guys in the sports teams. It was pretty calorific. A mountain of white rice soaked in special sauce, then covered with two big pieces of breaded, deep-fried pork drenched in the same sauce. Unless you ordered the jumbo, in which case you got three pieces.

By the way, if you order katsudon in Fukui, you get the sauce-soaked version every time. I guess in other prefectures it's normal to get it served with egg, but in Fukui, if you want egg you gotta ask for "katsudon with egg," or you'll be disappointed. But we Fukui-ites rarely order that.

I love the stuff. I would totally order it as my last meal. When I was a kid, we took a family trip to Tokyo, and I ordered it at a highway rest area. I got a nasty shock when it arrived dripping with egg.

Yua blinked rapidly in response to Haru's remark as she set down the tray of waters she'd gotten for everyone.

"Haru, you sure can eat a lot for someone so skinny. I ordered that last year in the regular size, and I had to give up halfway through. Asano had to finish it for me."

"Whoo! Thanks for the water, Ucchi! But yeah, I can really pack it away. I have breakfast in the morning, then after early club practice, I always eat a rice ball. Then once after-school practice is done, I always pick up a steamed pork bun or a hot dog on a stick at the convenience store. Oh, and then there's dinner when I get home. I mean, that's just high school sports club life, though, isn't it?"

Nanase made a face.

"Er, no, it's just you. Normal girls learn to fear the repercussions of that. I'll order the Fuji Lunch, I guess. With only a small serving of rice and extra salad."

Yua handed Nanase her glass of water. "I think I'll have the same," she mumbled.

Today's lunch special was Hamburg steak with grated daikon radish and ponzu sauce. Following strong pressure from the female student body, our school serves extra salad for those who order a smaller portion of rice. Sadly, they rejected the requests of male students who pushed for a "less salad, extra rice" option.

Yuuko, meanwhile, always had a decent appetite.

"Oh, won't you be hungry later? I'll have katsudon as well. Just the normal portion, though."

Nanase raised an eyebrow at this.

"Er, what?! I figured you'd be the super-calorie-conscious type, Yuuko. Is tennis club really that much of a hard-core workout?"

"Oh, not at all. Sure, we have our medal-hungry maniacs, but a lot of people just play for fun! I'm one of those. Anyway, I don't really factor my activity levels into what I eat. I just eat whatever I want, whenever I want. I don't like to over-complicate things!"

"Oh my gosh. Ucchi, can we punch her?"

For some reason, Nanase nudged Yua, who had just finished distributing the waters.

"Oh, I totally get how you feel, Yuzuki-chan! But we can't allow ourselves to get mad, mon! We gotta rise above, mon!"

Who are you, Kumamon?

I watched as Nanase and Yua threw their arms around each other in solidarity against some perceived injustice. Female friendships. They're a beautiful thing.

*

We bought lunch tickets, picked up our orders at the counter, and then returned to the table. Kazuki and I both ordered a dish that was right up there with katsudon on the popularity scale: chilled ramen. Jumbo size, of course. To be honest, it's just soy-sauce-flavored ramen served cold, and it's not actually all that good. And yet I found myself addicted to it. The addiction took over a lot of the guy students, but for some reason, girls never ordered it. Just another Fuji High mystery, I guess.

"Cheers to our new class!"

Yuuko led us all in a toast, and we all cheered as we clinked glasses together. Water glasses, of course.

Then, between bites of his pork and rice, Kaito started talking with his mouth full.

"So, Yuzuki, Haru, how'd you like your new class? It's all the same old stuff for us, but you're transplants from Class Three, right?"

Haru was packing it away, too.

"It's only the second day, dude. Anyway, I can adjust to just about anything, so yeah, I'm having fun! Besides, I already knew Chitose and Mizushino from before. And Ucchi and Yuuko are easy to get along with. And I bet we'll be the group to beat in the inter-class sports tournaments!"

Meanwhile, Nanase finished delicately swallowing a bite of her Hamburg steak and put her chopsticks down before speaking.

"I feel the same way. But it's also daunting. There are so many new people I've never spoken to before."

"Oh yeah. There are so many people who I've never even seen before, either!" Yuuko commented lazily.

Kazuki rolled his eyes.

"Er, that's not the same thing. You just have selective amnesia when it comes to people's faces. As we already discussed."

"Oh, shut up, Kazuki. This afternoon we've got math, biology, *and* English, right? Ugh, I've got a headache already. Is it time to go home yet?"

I joined in, seamlessly picking up the rhythm of the conversation. "Well, that's what you get in an elite school." I paused for a second before continuing. "By the way... Has anyone here ever felt like just not coming to school?"

""Why? All the sports are here,"" Haru and Kaito answered in unison.

"All the cute girls are here," Kazuki added.

"Are you okay, Saku?" Yuuko asked. "Are you having a post-puberty crisis?"

"All right, all right, I guess I phrased that wrong."

I wanted to face-palm, just a little. I was figuring I could get their opinions on Kenta Yamazaki's situation in a subtle, sneaky way, but what was the point of asking popular kids about something like that? They were far too popular to relate.

Ah, but perhaps I just overestimated their intelligence. Maybe if I simplified the question, they'd handle it a little better.

"Okay, so say there was someone who didn't want to come to school, now, why might that be?"

Kaito and Haru answered first.

"You mean an absentee student? I don't really know, but I guess bullying?"

"Maybe things aren't going well in their school club. You know, some of the upperclassmen can be too harsh sometimes. You wouldn't really call it bullying, but sometimes kids don't see eye to eye with their teammates."

Both of them had provided uncharacteristically sound arguments. And from the sounds of it, common ones, too.

Kazuki offered his own idea, eyes narrowed.

"Well, this is an elite school, so maybe they can't keep up with classes? Maybe the stress of the entrance-exam cramming broke them? This school's full of kids who were at the top of their class in junior high, then got here and discovered they were actually completely average in comparison. What do you think, Yuuko?"

Based on Kura's intel, I didn't think that was it. But maybe Yamazaki himself wasn't happy with his average grades. It was possible.

"I think it has to be romance-related! You know, it's super sad when the person you like doesn't like you back. Or even worse, flat out rejects you! Or even worse than *that*—starts dating someone else! I know I wouldn't want to come to school."

That was a very Yuuko response. Not that I really expected her to be able to fathom why someone might be refusing to attend school, of course. But usually it would be because of friendship issues, problems with schoolwork, or an after-school club, right? The three big things that plague every high school kid to some degree, at some point or other.

"Even if they're skipping school, it doesn't necessarily mean that school is the source of the trouble."

This hypothesis came from Nanase.

"I mean, if something bad happens in your home life, for example, you might not have the willpower left to go to school. You might be too scared to interact with anyone, whether at school or outside it."

I found this concept interesting. We popular kids tended to think of school as the center of the universe, but I guess there were some kids who had other stuff going on.

But Yuuko took the opposing stance.

"That's weird, though. If I had something bad going on at home, I'd want to come to school even more so I could see my friends."

"That's because school is a safe space for you. But some people don't care much for school to begin with, so they focus on their home life. And then if things go wrong with those relationships at home, it might have a knock-on effect that stops them from wanting to interact with people at school, too."

"I see," said Yuuko. "So it's like when your favorite mascara is sold out at the drugstore. You can't just buy another brand as easy as that. And if people say your makeup sucks, you'll start over-thinking your whole routine, and it'll become this huge complex!"

"...I guess that analogy tracks, technically," Nanase replied. "I'm gonna give you that one."

Their contributions to the conversation had distracted everyone to the point where no one thought to question why I'd brought up this topic to begin with. Good.

Still, all this posturing and conjecture wasn't getting me anywhere. I was going to have to hear it straight from the horse's mouth. In the meantime, I applied myself to my chilled ramen.

Yep. It tasted the same as ever. It was just soy-sauce-flavored ramen. Only cold.

*

"Chitose!"

After lunch, we were heading back to the classroom when Nanase called my name.

We came to a stop in the hallway. Since we were bringing up the rear anyway, none of the others noticed and just kept on walking.

"What's up?" I asked. "Did you want to separate me from Yuuko and Yua so you could ask me on a date?"

"Oh yeah? A surprise attack like that might be good, I guess."

Nanase giggled, covering her mouth with her hand. She didn't seem flustered or indignant at all. Her hair fell forward in front of her ears in an elfin sort of way, like a fairytale sprite from a children's story. Man, she was cute.

"But right now I have something else I want to talk to you about. That thing you brought up over lunch… Are you having some kind of issue, Chitose?"

So she noticed.

I mean, it's weird, isn't it? Why would a popular kid like me even bring up kids not coming to school? Still, while this mission of Kura's wasn't exactly something I wanted to make widespread public knowledge, I didn't need to go to desperate lengths to hide it from my friends, either. Also, Kura hadn't told me to keep my mouth shut. That had to mean it was cool for me to talk about it, right?

"Kura asked me to do something for him. You noticed we're

missing a student today—and yesterday, too? His name's Kenta Yamazaki. Apparently, he stopped coming to school around the end of last semester."

"So he wants you to go convince this kid to come back to school? Boy, it's hard being Mr. Popular, isn't it?"

"Tell me about it. Anyway, I won't be able to help him if I don't find out what his damage is, so I'm going to go see him after school. Still, I don't see how a class prez he hasn't even met is supposed to convince him."

"Hmm…"

Nanase frowned thoughtfully, tapping her chin with one finger. It was sort of a theatrical gesture, but somehow it suited her and made her look even more beautiful. Weird.

"I could go with you if you like? I can get my club buddies to cover for me. It might go down better if you bring someone with you, after all."

I knew Nanase and I were birds of a feather.

I hadn't even told her much at all, but she still came to the same conclusion I did.

"Thanks, Nanase. But I think you and I are too similar. Things are still in the early stages, and I wanna gather some more info. So I've already asked someone else."

"I see. I guess I should butt out. If you're sure, then okay. But just know you can call on me anytime."

Nanase gave me a cheeky grin. "I go the extra mile for the guys I like."

"…Can I interpret that to mean whatever I'd like it to mean?"

"Nope!"

"Damn, you're good!"

She made an X with her fingers, and then with a smirk she left, taking her C cups with her.

★

After seventh period, I was waiting by the bike racks when Yua came running out around five minutes late. She didn't seem to notice me, since she paused for a second, pulled out a compact mirror, and fixed her hair. I smiled a little.

"Sorry, did you wait long?"

"...Oh no, I just got here. Actually, I lied. I was here half an hour ago, just *dying* to see you. Tee-hee!"

"Wow, now I'm not sorry at all." Yua gave me a mock scowl, fanning her face with her hand.

"All cool with music club?"

"Yup. It was a free practice day anyway. I just said I had stuff to take care of."

Last night, when I made that phone call, it was to Yua's phone. I told her about the situation and asked her to come with me to Yamazaki's house. I mean, I could have gone alone, but for reasons both good and bad, I tend to stand out. And there are a lot of kids who sneer at the mere mention of the name Saku Chitose. Mostly other guys.

...Sob.

Anyway, if Yamazaki was one of *those* guys, there was a high probability I'd be met at the door with a "Whaddaya want, you man-slut shithead?" I think Nanase offered to come with me to prevent something like that from happening.

However, Nanase was also school royalty. If Yamazaki was one of those "Die, normies!" kinda types, bringing her with me would be counterproductive. Worst case, he'd be like, "I get it; you two normie scumbags are trying to convince everyone what good people you are, is that your game? Go to hell!"

...Wait a minute, who said I have to help this guy again?

Anyway, that aside, I couldn't bring Yuuko with me for similar reasons. And also because she had no filter.

So that brings us to Yua. She's the least standout member of our group, and she doesn't give off too much of that popular, normie vibe. She gets along well with the mousier girls, too, and she knew how not to get too close too fast without seeming cold. Even people she hadn't met before tended to like her from the start. And I had another crafty reason for bringing a girl with me, too.

I mean, think about it. No guy wants to show his bad side in front of a pretty girl, right?

"Saku?"

"…It's a compliment, really, when you think about it, Yua. Being a girl who's a bit plain, I mean."

"Er, I have no idea what you were just thinking about, but I know it's something rude. Anyway, Yamazaki's house is kind of far. How are we gonna get there?"

"I've gotcha covered. I borrowed Kaito's bike. He said it's cool as long as we return it before club practice ends."

Yua and I walked to and from school since we liked the riverbank path, but most kids at our school—most kids in Fukui Prefecture, really—travel to high school by bicycle. The only ones who don't are the ones who live pretty close to school or those who live so far away they've gotta take the train.

And I have to add, Kaito's choice of the classic granny bike didn't mean he was uncool. For some reason, every kid in Fukui has a granny bike as his or her ride of choice, rather than a mountain bike or hybrid. As a fun fact, every guy in Fukui, regardless of height, lowers his bike seat down to its lowest setting.

"But I don't have a bicycle."

"We'll ride double. It's a granny bike, so there'll be plenty of room."

I unlocked Kaito's bike and was fiddling with the seat as I spoke.

"But what if a police officer sees us? They'll tell us to get off."

"Listen, Yua. Riding double with a girl on a bicycle is a rite of passage for every high school boy. I know, I know, it's dangerous, it's frowned upon, it's technically illegal, and people get all heated about it on online forums. But don't you think it sucks to bash people where they can't defend themselves? Kura said something super philosophical about that the other day."

"Yeah, and we all know that Mr. Iwanami's personal life is a colossal disaster…"

Huh, she had a point. Still, that was no reason to be deterred.

"Well, I for one think it's sad we might graduate never having participated in the classic high school custom of riding double on a bike. Anyway, if anyone gets mad at us, all we have to do is apologize."

"Well, that's not really the issue that's holding me up…"

"Actually, when you think about it, the combined weight of two passengers on a bike has to slow you down, so it's totally safer. And the brakes have been recently serviced. As long as we go at a nice steady pace, we'll be way safer than we would be on a racing bicycle. And we can get off and push whenever there's a lot of pedestrians around."

"It won't be *that* heavy. I didn't have a big lunch today, after all."

Yua pouted and sat down on the bike's rear luggage rack, legs to one side.

"Kaito's bike has one of those footrests that stick out of the back wheel where the chain is, see? You'll be more comfortable if you put your feet there, on either side of the bike. It'll be easier to sit on the luggage rack that way, too."

Adding one of those footrests to a bicycle was an easy customization and made it much more comfortable for a passenger to sit behind the rider on the bike. Popular kids in Fukui have been adding footrests to their bicycles since way back, and recently the trend had seen something of a revival.

"I am not doing that in this skirt."

"Well, it's your call. But you'd better hold on tight to my shoulders or waist, or it'll be dangerous."

"Huh?"

Yua looked intimidated for a few moments, then she reluctantly reached out and grasped my shoulders with her fingertips.

"You don't have to touch me like I'm a dirty dishrag."

All this prevaricating was getting us nowhere. I grabbed Yua's hands and repositioned them to hold my shoulders more firmly. Her fingers felt slimmer than I had imagined and were cool to the touch. Her grip on my shoulders was surprisingly strong now, too. It kinda hurt.

Slowly, easily, I started pedaling. We headed off down the narrow side street that ran in the opposite direction to the river path. There weren't any students out and about here. It wasn't even close to getting dark yet, but for some reason, there was no one around.

We rode for around ten minutes before we came out onto a wider road, and the town disappeared on us. To the left and right, there were only rice fields. You've never seen such a quintessential Fukui countryside scene. The fields were still brown and a bit sad, but come next month, they'd be filled with shallow water, rippling pleasantly in the warm May winds.

"Your back…"

Yua finally loosened up on her death grip and said something.

"Your back, Saku… It's much wider and more muscular than I thought… Very masculine."

"Well, I used to be the best baseball player in the prefecture, you know. You may not believe me, but I've always ranked first during the school athletic tests, ever since elementary school. I even beat out Kaito and Kazuki."

"I know. I saw one of your games out on the athletic field last summer, from the classroom window. I was having band practice."

"Before we became the great buddies we are now? Have you always been a secret fan of mine, Yua?"

"…Hmm, maybe I have."

Then, hesitantly, as if fumbling about in the dark, Yua switched her grip from my shoulders to my waist. It tickled a little, but I faced front and kept pedaling at the same pace and cadence so it didn't show.

"Is something on your mind, Saku?"

"Yeah. I'm thinking about how best to execute a sudden tactical brake so I can get some boob-to-back action."

"…"

"I apologize, I apologize. Can you please stop squeezing my jugular?"

"You are *such* a jerk."

Huffing, Yua put her arms around my waist again.

"I know, I know, but never mind me. We're here to help Kenta Yamazaki. Did you have any ideas while we were all discussing things at lunch?"

"Hmm, I thought about it, but without any hints to go on, it's impossible to guess what could be wrong. I guess we just have to press ahead and ask him ourself."

"I think you mean ourselves."

★

We arrived at Yamazaki's house with some help from my phone's GPS. It was just a boring, ordinary house with a tiled roof. It wasn't particularly new, but it wasn't particularly old, either. It was probably built in the eighties. You can't walk fifty meters in any direction in Fukui without seeing at least one house like this. (In the suburban areas, at least.) It had a faded wooden nameplate on the gate that said YAMAZAKI.

I let Yua off in front of the house, then parked the bike at the end of the bike rack. Yua shot me a "What now?" sort of look. Without hesitation, I went up to the door and rang the doorbell.

*Ding-dong.*

I could hear the doorbell ringing inside the house. I quickly fastened the top button of my shirt and straightened my tie. Then I grabbed Yua's hand and made her stand beside me. We stood there for around ten seconds before we heard a voice from inside.

"…Hello?" the person asked suspiciously.

"Hello! I'm Saku Chitose, a friend of Kenta's. We're in the same class in second year. I'm going to be class president this year, so I brought some class handouts for him!"

I was polite, but not so polite as to sound phony. I faced the security camera and gave it my best "Trust me" smile.

At the same time, I gently whacked Yua on the back, where the camera couldn't see, cueing her to speak, too.

"Hello, I'm Yua Uchida. Kenta hasn't been coming to school lately, so we were a bit worried and wanted to see if he was feeling okay!"

Classic Yua.

She was a little more reserved and polite than I was, but with a friendly, caring air. *Yes, yes, that's why I brought you, Yua!*

"Oh my, to go to such trouble…! Hold on just a second!"

We could hear a commotion inside, with plenty of rustling and clanking. Then we heard footsteps running to the door. It sounded like Yamazaki's mom was doing a rush-job cleanup.

"Thank you for waiting! I'm Kenta's mother."

The face that appeared at the door belonged to a woman in her late forties. She was slim, in a bony sort of way. The skin on her cheeks and the backs of her hands looked worn-out, and her hair was peppered with gray streaks and seemed to have been hastily smoothed down. She looked us both up and down as if appraising us quickly, then refocused her gaze on our faces.

"We're sorry for the sudden intrusion. Is this a bad time?"

I bowed politely to Mrs. Yamazaki, giving her the old winning smile. Beside me, Yua lowered her head as well.

"Oh my, of course not! I apologize for the mess, but please do come in."

Mrs. Yamazaki's voice had gone up two octaves as she ushered us in and gave us both a pair of slippers. I figured one octave was because she was stunned to discover that her son really did seem to have friends who gave a damn, and the other was because it was obvious to anyone that Yua and I were probably two of the best-looking kids in our school.

It's handy being attractive at times like this. You can bypass the whole process of earning people's trust after you meet them. They just give it to you. And while parents tend to recoil when teachers pay home visits, their kid's friends don't have that same intimidating effect. So it was no surprise that Mrs. Yamazaki was being so welcoming. I guess that's another reason why Kura put me up to this.

She showed us into the living room, and we sat down on the sofa. Mrs. Yamazaki then served us black tea, from teabags and not leaves. Yua asked for milk in hers, but I had mine straight.

"Ah, before I forget. Here are the handouts we got today."

I pulled out a bunch of handouts I'd gotten from Kura. Mrs. Yamazaki took them, sighing as she scanned them quickly.

"I'm really sorry for all the trouble my son is causing…"

I ignored her, folding my hands solemnly in my lap and clearing my throat hesitantly.

"How *is* Kenta, though? We've all been worried. We weren't sure how to reach out, and then time just kept marching on… I really wish we could have come sooner."

"You're so sweet to be concerned. But I don't even know what to say to him myself, to be honest with you."

Mrs. Yamazaki lifted her head and looked at me.

"But the important thing is that Kenta has friends like you, who care. As his mother, I'm so happy to know that. I always worry that he's all alone at school."

I'd heard he had "friends with mutual interests" at school, so it wasn't like him being alone and friendless was the problem. I bet his so-called friends didn't turn heads when they walked down the hallways like we did, though.

"So Kenta won't even talk to you, his mother? About, uh, the reason why he won't come to school?" Yua spoke hesitantly.

"It's embarrassing to admit, but he never tells me anything. He just suddenly announced in January of this year that he didn't want to go anymore, and then he locked himself up in his room. I put trays of food outside his door at meal times, and he does eat them, so at least there's that. And I can tell he's been roaming around the house while I'm out shopping—or late at night when everyone's asleep."

"It's a relief to know he's eating properly."

The atmosphere was getting more and more depressing, but Yua was trying to keep it light.

"I'm really sorry... Oh, for a cute young girl like you to have to concern herself with this..."

Yua looked guilty all of a sudden, so I quickly jumped in.

"But you know, for kids our age, there's nothing more embarrassing than telling your troubles to your parents. So it makes sense he hasn't confided in you. I'd be more worried about him if he spent every day putting everything on you."

I kept my tone light and easy-breezy.

"You...you may be right. He's my own son, but I don't understand him at all..."

"Well, that's no surprise. We don't know ourselves at this age, you know? But would you allow us to try to talk to Kenta? If possible, just us two. If you're nearby, he might not want to talk."

"Oh, I was just about to ask if you'd talk to him. But I have to warn you, he may be very rude to you as well. When his teacher came by the other day, he said, *'I'm not interested! Get rid of him!'*..."

"My apologies for saying so, but a teacher is just like a parent. There are some things high schoolers can only admit to other high schoolers, you know? He might be rude to us, too, but we won't give up. We'll keep coming back. I want to graduate with Kenta, all of us together. So would you be okay letting us handle this situation and not saying anything more about it yourself?"

Mrs. Yamazaki gasped and nodded, eyes filling with tears.

*...Hook, line, and sinker.*

\*

"...You could be a scam artist."

As we headed up the stairs to Yamazaki's room on the second floor, Yua hissed at me.

"Wow, that's mean. I didn't tell a single lie."

"You said we're his friends."

"That was just common sense to win her over."

"You said we've been worried about him."

"I have. Ever since yesterday at lunch. I actually wish we'd come earlier. The situation seems very dire."

"You said we'd keep coming back! You said you want to graduate with him!"

"I do. 'Cause otherwise, Kura is never gonna let me off the hook."

"Saku, did your mother never teach you about how you shouldn't *talk back*?"

We reached the second floor and stopped outside the door at the end of the short hallway. Yua gave me another "What now?" look, but I just knocked on the door.

*Knock, knock, knock.*

Three slow knocks. I had gotten his mother to tell me the kind of knock she usually used. A pair of unfamiliar voices calling out all of a sudden might give the guy a heart attack.

*Knock, knock, knock.*

*Knock, knock, knock.*

I waited a few seconds before repeating the knock.

*Knock, knock, knock.*

"Shut up! I can hear you! What do you want?!"

An answer finally came after the fourth knock.

"Hey, man. It's Saku Chitose from Year Two, Class Five. We're in the same class, right, Yamazaki? 'Sup, homeroom homie? Our new teacher, Mr. Iwanami, asked me to bring you some handouts. But since I'm here, you feel like talking?"

I started off light and casual. After a few moments, the voice from the room barked a very confused "What?!"

"Saku...*Chitose*?"

He sounded like he was still trying to process what was going on. He and I had never even spoken before, so this must have been very out of the blue for him.

"What? Why? Why are you here, you man-slut shithead?"

Welp. Time to murder him.

I lifted my foot to kick the door in, but Yua grabbed me.

"Chill out."

She whispered in my ear, giving me some of that boob-to-back action I'd been joking about on the bike. I put my foot down quickly.

"Yamazaki, hi," she said. "I'm Yua Uchida, I'm in Class Five with you this year, too. Sorry to show up so suddenly like this. When we heard you hadn't been to school in a while, we were both worried..."

"Uchida...? Aren't you one of Chitose's harem skanks?"

*...Hey, Yua? That saxophone of yours is a fine instrument, meant for bringing joy to music lovers with its sophisticated sound. It is not a weapon meant for bludgeoning a certain potty-mouthed shut-in to death. Okay?*

"Chill out," I whispered in her ear, restraining her.

"I don't agree with your descriptions of us, but yeah, we're the

Chitose and Uchida you're thinking of. Anyway, instead of shouting through the door, why don't you open it? It's okay; we're not here to lecture you about coming back to school or anything."

"What? I've got nothin' to say to a pair of dirty normies like you. Are you kidding me right now? Chitose, you dragged a girl here to win points with her by pretending to care about poor, underprivileged me? I bet the teacher forced you to come here, and you're hating every second of it!"

Hate to say it, but he was right on the money.

Ah, but things were also going exactly as I expected. Disappointing, really.

"I'd be lying if I said the teacher wasn't involved in this at all, but that's not the main reason we're here. We just wanna talk, Yamazaki. You know a lot about anime and light novels, right? Recently, I've started getting into that stuff, too."

"Oh, here we go. A normie dips his toes into the world of otaku culture and thinks he's *sooo* cultured and original! I bet you've never seen any anime that wasn't some mainstream movie! Okay, if you're really so interested, tell me which of these titles you've read!"

Then Kenta began reeling off a long list of titles like he was chanting some kind of curse. I caught a few of them: *In the School Social Order, I'm Right at the Bottom!* and *I'm an Otaku Geek with a Hot Girlfriend!* Honestly, I hadn't heard of any of them, but I wasn't sure if they were even real titles or if he was being sarcastic.

"…Sorry, no dice. I guess to you I would be a bandwagon jumper. You know them, Uchida?"

I looked at Yua, but she shook her head.

"Sorry, Yamazaki. I don't really know much about light novels. I haven't read any of those. But they do sound interesting; could you maybe lend me some?"

"Uh… I don't think a popular, normie girl like you would enjoy them."

Yamazaki had been a complete jerk through this whole conversation, but now he seemed to have remembered that he was talking to a girl—and a cute one at that. And Yua was being super polite, so perhaps that had disarmed him somewhat.

"Oh really? Well, I've read a few of the more popular boys' manga. I'd like to see your bookshelves, Yamazaki!"

"Uh, no… My room's a mess…"

"Then let's chat through the door like this. If that makes it easier for you, I don't mind at all!"

"Uh, but I don't know what the bubbly kids like to talk about."

I was glad he'd simmered down some, but we were still just going around in circles here.

"Actually, I'm more low-key compared to Chitose. I wish I was better at making conversation, too, but I tend to go blank, heh. Sorry I'm not a better conversationalist, Yamazaki."

"Uh, no… From what I've seen of you at school, you're a total girly-girl normie."

"You think so? Maybe I'm just surrounded by people who stand out that way? But it sounds like you're the type who prefers time to yourself over rowdy groups, right?"

"Uh…yeah."

"I envy you. You have the peace and quiet to really get absorbed in your interests."

Up until now, I'd been leaving the talking up to Yua, but I had to interject.

"Yamazaki, I'm glad you and Yua seem to have hit it off. How about if just the two of you chat for a while? No need to hold back. Yua and I hang out so often we have nothing to talk about these days anyway."

"…Are you kidding me? Could you be any more of a supercilious dick? 'Here's my woman, you can borrow her for a while'…? I don't want one of the used sluts from your harem anyway!"

"Ah, my bad, man. I didn't mean it like that. Oh well, never mind."

Actually, I totally did mean it like that. I was baiting him on purpose.

Another sucker. Like mother, like son.

Anyway, listening to their conversation gave me some ideas as to what might be the root cause behind Yamazaki's abnormality.

Meanwhile, Yua was about ready to hit me with her sax for that little offer I just made, so it was about time to call it.

"All right, well, we're leaving now. We'll come back again next week."

"Don't ever come to my house again, you shithead man-slut."

*Oh, I'll be back, all right! And next time, I'll bring my baseball bat!* ♪

*

We told Yamazaki's mom he wouldn't open up to us after all, either, and left after receiving her profound thanks anyway. We also let her know we'd be back next week.

Outside, I looked up at Yamazaki's window, figuring he would probably be watching us. But the curtains remained drawn.

Then we headed back to school to return Kaito's bike.

"So what do you think, Yua? Did you glean anything interesting from your conversation with him?"

"Honestly, it cracked me up to hear him call you a shithead man-slut. But how dare he call me a harem slut!"

"Yeah, it would have maybe made more sense the other way around, right? …Ack! Stop! I told you—don't squeeze my jugular!"

Yua let go and refastened her arms around my waist.

"Honestly, though, I didn't really get a very positive impression of him. I don't like to label people this way, but it was so obvious from our conversation that I can't help it. He's like the most stereotypical otaku you've ever seen, isn't he? I mean, obviously he's going through something, but that's no excuse to be so nasty and rude to someone he's never even met before."

"Yeah, I agree."

Personally, I was used to it. But Yua had not yet experienced an unprovoked attack from someone she barely knows. It's par for the course when you're a member of the in crowd, but it doesn't feel great. Still, she held up well under the circumstances.

"Did you notice anything, Saku?"

"Hmm, yes, something very important. He hates my guts."

"Yeah, I kinda picked up on that."

"Waahhhhh…"

I pretended to bawl like a baby. Yua unhooked one arm from around my waist and thumped me on the back soothingly.

"There, there. You've still got your looks, Saku."

"Nice save. Very classic."

I couldn't see Yua's face, but it sounded like she was stifling a laugh.

The squeaking of the old bike's wheels sounded like laughter, too.

The setting sun was dying the clouds all kinds of colors—from apricot pink, to deep orange, to burnt sienna, and then finally indigo blue. It went through a whole spectrum. Beautiful, like something out of a movie.

The shadows of the boy and girl riding double on the bicycle grew longer, too. They stretched into eternity—or at least into the rice fields. The textbook young-love scene.

That was like something out of a movie, too.

It felt like Yua and I could keep riding forever, never stopping, going wherever the road took us.

*

One Tuesday around a week after my first visit to Kenta Yamazaki's house, I was chilling by the bike rack after school, waiting. My upper eyelids were playfully kissing my lower ones, like tentative lovers. Then they started smooching.

What I'm trying to say is that I was tired.

"Saku!"

Ah, here came Yuuko, D cups a-jiggling, one arm waving, her high voice snapping me awake. If any other guys caught a glimpse of this scene…Yuuko running joyfully to meet me… they would want to kill me. In fact, they'd immediately start plotting my demise. Death by fire? Water? An anvil to the head? What would be best?

"Thanks for agreeing to come with."

"Not at all! Anything for you, Saku! So all we're going to do is convince this Ken-something Yama-what'sit to come back to school, right?"

"It's Kenta Yamazaki. Don't act like such an airhead."

I'd been mulling it over and asked Yuuko to come along this time. After explaining the gist of it to her, of course. Yua was nice and all that, but that was exactly why I couldn't keep using her as my partner in this little endeavor. Last time had made that clear.

Before, my objective was to gather information. So bringing Yua along had been the right decision. But now I needed a cunning strategy going forward.

If I was going toe-to-toe with that twisted, complicated, broody guy, I needed a clear display of power. To borrow Kura's words, I'm great at analyzing a situation and acting accordingly.

"It's too far to walk, so I borrowed Kaito's bike."

"Oh, you did? Cool, cool!"

Without a moment's hesitation, Yuuko hopped onto the bike in a standing position, feet on the hub steps, hands gripping my shoulders.

"Tallyho!"

"Hey, have some dignity. You can't stand up in a skirt that short. Everyone will see your panties."

"Oh, but this is how riding double works! Anyway, what do I care if some randos see my underwear?"

"If you're that cool with showing them off, perhaps I could have a glance?"

"No, you don't get to look, Saku. You're special."

"Usually the special ones get to see."

"Only when the timing is special, too."

Ah, Yuuko, sneaky, sneaky.

I kicked away the bike stand, and we set off with Yuuko yelling "Wahoo!" and "Put the pedal to the metal!" Then she suddenly leaned forward, wrapping her arms around my shoulders.

I could smell her sweet body spray and feel her impossibly silky hair against my cheek. She was giving me serious boob-to-back action, too. Please stop that, Miss. Or I'll never be able to get off this bike.

"You don't smell as sweaty compared to last year." Yuuko's voice was right in my ear.

"Yeah, 'cause I quit baseball club."

"Aw, boo! I used to like your post-sports stink. And I wanted to have more chances to cheer you on at games."

Yuuko sat down on the luggage rack, probably tired from standing. This time, she put her arms around my waist. Because of my blazer, I didn't get to feel the softness of her cheek pressing against my back.

"So, Yuuko, after hearing about Kenta Yamazaki, do you have any ideas?"

"Uh, I'm not good at stuff like that. I don't even know. But you'll figure it out somehow, Saku! You're my hero, after all!"

"Hmm. Well, all I want you to do is just say whatever comes into that pretty head of yours. I'll follow your cues."

"Sure thing."

What does it take to be considered a hero? And is that something you have to keep living up to your whole life through?

I mulled it over as Kenta Yamazaki's house appeared in the distance, growing closer and closer.

*

*Knock, knock, knock, knock.*

No point emulating Yamazaki's mom's knock this time. I just rapped on Yamazaki's bedroom door the way I normally would.

Speaking of his mom, apparently Yamazaki told her, "*Those freaks are* not *my friends. Don't let them in next time.*" But clearly, Mrs. Yamazaki trusted in the power of school friendship over the words of her own son. We told her she could leave it all to us.

Oh yeah, she wanted to be off the hook.

She'd balked a little at first when I showed up with Yuuko, a girl twice as beautiful and showy as Yua. But with her natural charms, Yuuko soon won her over, and before long, it was like watching a loving aunt coo over her very own niece.

"Yamazaki, it's Chitose again. I told you I'd be back this week, remember?"

There was no response from beyond the door. Actually, to be more precise, there was a sudden silence from beyond the door.

"Uh, maybe the silent treatment would work if we didn't know if you were in there, but we know you never leave this room, so what's the point? But fine, if you're not going to talk to me, I'll just entertain you instead by rapping the Heart Sutra! I've gotten kind of into it lately. Ready? Yo, yo!"

Shut-in or not, the kid was still a student of the elite Fuji High. He would know what the Heart Sutra was. Then I heard him speak, sounding crabbier than ever before.

"...Shut up. I told her not to let you in. You seriously came back?"

"Ouch. We're your friends. We're worried about you. Or at least, that's what your mom thinks."

"So you used your pretty-boy face to charm my mom, huh? Of course she'd believe whatever crap you told her over her own son. Is…is Uchida out there?"

Ah, so she's graduated from "Chitose's Harem Slut" to "Uchida," has she? Yua, you really tugged on the guy's heartstrings. I bet he's been mentally replaying that precious five minutes of chitchat with you all week long.

Still, too bad. Have to get on with things.

"No, Yua had music club and couldn't come."

"…See? You popular normie jerks are all like that. She only came to win points with you. Then she got bored and dropped it. I freaking knew that would happen."

Yamazaki was sulking.

Ah, he was so easy to read. Made my job a lot simpler.

"Yua's not like that. She really was worried about you. If she didn't have club, she would have come for sure. But today I brought a different girl with me."

Yuuko took a step closer to the door. "Hello! I'm Yuuko Hiiragi; we're in the same class. I heard you're skipping school? That's not good. You okay?"

Her voice was perky and lighthearted, a total sucker punch.

"…"

There was a long pause of about ten to fifteen seconds.

"…H-Hiiragi?! *That* Hiiragi?! Queen Skank of the Chitose Harem? What's your game, bringing a floozy like that here? You trying to show off to your groupies?!"

He was underestimating me and how popular I was with girls. I knew I was hot stuff, and I sure didn't need to assert dominance over a little shut-in like him to prove it. Also, I was embarrassed for him. No one uses terminology like *floozy*, *harem*, or *groupies* in real life. Unless they're trying to be ironic.

"...Saku, what's a harem skank? What's a floozy?"

"When he says harem skank, he means close, personal female friend. And a floozy is, uh, a loose woman, I guess."

Yuuko and I were whispering together.

"Hey! I'll admit to being a harem skank, but I draw the line at floozy! I'm only loose for Saku, got it?"

Well, that's good to hear!

Kenta Yamazaki did not like this.

"Yeah, you've gotta say that in front of Chitose. But everyone talks about you. You've done it with that Mizushino kid *and* that Asano kid from your group, too!"

"I have not! Kazuki and Kaito are my good friends! Saku's the only one I might date. Anyway, who is 'everyone'? Tell me. Explain yourself!"

"Everyone is...everyone. The whole school was talking about it."

"I need names. If there are too many, then just tell me the name of the person you heard it from directly. So. Who told you?"

"...I don't remember. But there's no smoke without fire. No slut rumors without slutting."

"Let's talk about you, then. You're a sweaty, shut-in high school no-show, obsessed with anime and light novels! I bet you're a pedo! See, I can make up nasty rumors, too! Now, why don't you open that door and show your face? We came all the way here; it's the least you can do!"

Yamazaki fell silent. Yuuko was giving it to him straight and undiluted, and what's worse, she had a point. He didn't really have a leg to stand on.

If only he could own up to his flaws, there might be hope for him yet.

"Don't push your normie values on me. I didn't ask you to come talk to me. I'm not bothering anyone anyway, so just leave me alone!"

"Uh, no. You are bothering a *lot* of people. You're bothering your poor mom and dad, your old homeroom teacher, your current homeroom teacher, Kura, Ucchi last week, and now me! Everyone's worried about you; everyone's trying to help you and taking time out of their busy lives to come and see you!"

Yuuko paused for breath before continuing.

"And the person you're bothering most of all with your sulking and skulking in your room is our new class president, Saku! If you really don't want to bother others or have anyone else worrying about you, then get your ass back to school, get your ass back to class, and freakin' graduate!"

*Finish him, Yuuko!*

This was excellent entertainment. I wish I'd brought up some of Mrs. Yamazaki's tea for refreshment. She'd upgraded to tea leaves since my last visit.

But Yamazaki himself still wasn't backing down.

"Say what you like, but everything you're doing is really for your precious Chitose, isn't it? You and Uchida might be here to win points with him, but you don't give a damn about me, do you? This is why people hate you!"

"Uh, excuse me, what's wrong with caring for a friend? I came here because my *friend* Saku asked me to. That's what you do when you have *friends*; you want to help them out! So yeah, I do want to 'win points,' if that's how you wanna put it. If Saku wasn't the one who asked, you really think I'd be here trying to convince some nobody I've never met to come back to school? What do I care?!"

"See? See? You normie scum rely on trampling us geeks to claw your way to the top of the hierarchy. Then you only pretend to care to make yourselves look virtuous! Once you've won points with whoever you're trying to impress, you drop us!"

"Ugh, you're impossible to have a conversation with! Like I literally *just* said! What the heck is wrong with that? Everyone wants to put on their best self when they're around someone they like! And I'm not gonna lead other guys on when I've got a boyfriend!"

Yuuko had her face pressed up against the door, scowling with fury, probably picturing the guy she was arguing with.

"What I'm saying is: Don't pretend like you're interested in them in the first place! Being nice to guys will give them the wrong idea! Then you laugh with all your buddies, like, whoops, I was only being nice, and then he fell in love with me! Just leave us the hell alone! And you're being played, yourself! You think Chitose likes you? Hah! He's like that with all the girls! Including Uchida!"

"What's that? So you're admitting that a girl was nice to you once, and then in all your pimply, inexperienced glory you asked her out, and she turned you down? That's it? If you think it's only okay to be nice to people you're romantically interested in, you're never gonna make any friends, you know!"

"I didn't…say that…"

Ah, it was all making sense now. The reason why none of his friends at school knew what was wrong with him. He had fallen for a girl outside of school. A girl who was actually popular, and he lost her to a guy who was equally popular.

Yuuko shot me a glance, then faced the door again.

"Also, I know that Saku is nice to all the girls, and that a lot of them like him! But it's not just girls—he's nice to everyone! I admire that about him! That's why all I want is to be his number one someday! If he ended up dating another girl, yeah, I'd be crushed. Maybe I'd even take some time off school. But it would just show that I didn't end up being the type of girl he likes! That wouldn't be his fault for being nice to me, though! I'd never blame him, not even for one second!"

"…"

Kenta Yamazaki had fallen silent.

Ah, I really did make the best decision bringing Yuuko here.

Last week when I left this house, I had two options open to me.

The first was to continue to wear the mask of niceness with Yua at my side and keep coming by week after week until he finally opened his heart to us. Once he let us in, Yua would soothe him and cajole him back to school. Based on what I'd just seen, I'd give it about a 20 percent chance of success.

The other option was to find the root of the problem and deal with it directly. Classic and clear-cut, if also extremely annoying.

The first way would be effective, yes. And low effort. But it would have only been a makeshift solution. He probably would have gotten fixated on Yua, confessed his love to her, and then been shot down in a sweaty mess of pubescent disillusionment. And using Yua as bait that way…just wasn't a very beautiful solution to me.

I had chosen the second option.

But that required getting our shut-in friend to spill his guts. Yua and I, working in tandem, could have pulled it off (maybe), but it would be time-consuming. I needed Yuuko to cut through the bullshit.

It was obvious Yamazaki had a chip on his shoulder about "normies" and popular kids. My bringing Yua seemed to get him really steamed, especially when I was being ultra-nice to him in front of her. He hated that. I figured that if I brought the school princess herself, Miss Popularity Yuuko, with me, she would enrage old Yamazaki until he blew up and spilled his guts in a blaze of self-pitying vitriol.

But to be honest, I never expected it to go quite *this* well.

"Yuuko, calm down. I understand how you feel, but you should take a step back, go downstairs, and pull yourself together. I'll talk to Kenta."

I gave Yuuko a "That'll do" kind of smile and dropped her a wink for good measure. She gave me a billion-dollar smile back, plus a saucy wink of her own.

I watched as Yuuko clattered down the stairs, and then I called out to Yamazaki.

"All right, I see what the situation is now. But I think I can help you."

"...Oh, is this the part where the generous, popular normie helps out the geeky, lovelorn otaku? Spare me! How dare you look down on me like that!"

Goodness, what a pill he was being.

When you start feeling like people are looking down on you, perhaps you should start by asking yourself if it's not just because you're looking *up* at them. Hmm?

"Anyway, can you open the door? This whole shouting-back-and-forth thing is getting old. Come down and have tea with your mom and Yuuko. Your mom will supply the teacups, and Yuuko will supply the D cups, if you get what I'm sayin'."

"Go die! I'm never opening this door."

"Never? No matter what?"

"I just told you: I ain't openin' it! Get lost, you slutty man-whore shithead!"

...I think I've earned the right to get a little angry by now, wouldn't you say?

I went next door into what looked like the parents' bedroom. Then I stepped out onto the balcony, which connected to Yamazaki's. The curtains were closed tight in his room. I tried the window, but it was clearly locked.

*Guess I made the right choice bringing you with me after all, eh?*

I removed my metal baseball bat from the carry bag I had slung over my shoulder. The weight of it in my hands felt nice and familiar, and the grip was just right.

The balcony itself wasn't very wide, so I didn't have enough room for a full swing, but...

Batter up. Player number nine, Chitose.

*Sorry to have to use you for something like this, old friend.*

I stretched my arms out in front, then readied the bat. I focused on my target. It was the same routine I'd done so many times when I stepped into the batter's box. I counted to three, loosened up, then swung the bat with all my might.

*Crash!!! Tinkle, tinkle, tinkle...*

The crash was much more muted than I'd been expecting. And the sound of the breaking glass was almost musical. And thus ended the life of Yamazaki's faithful window glass.

It didn't come close to knocking a ball into the outfield, but still, that felt *good*.

I did feel a little bad for the glass. *I hope you get reincarnated as one of those glass marbles you find in old-fashioned soda bottles, to someday meet the lips of a young, fresh, high school beauty like Yuuko*, I thought to myself.

"What. The. *Hell*?!"

A half-hysterical yell came from inside the room. Understandable. I'd be taken aback, too, if someone busted their way in through my bedroom window. The drama was warranted.

Careful not to cut my arm on the jagged pieces remaining in the frame, I reached through and unlocked the sliding door. Then I pushed it open, parted the curtains, and stepped carefully into the room, bat slung over my shoulder.

"You're completely crazy! This is a criminal act! You're a criminal!"

I shrugged, unfazed by his dramatic reaction.

"Oh, don't you know the song? 'Laugh Maker'? By the band Bump of Chicken? '*You can't be serious! I hear the window on the other side break as you take an iron pipe with a tearful face. I've come here to bring you a smile.*' It's a sweet song. Kind of an oldie now, though. I'll play it for you sometime."

"What the hell are you talking about?! Are you for real right now? What is wrong with you?!"

"Oh, now, there's no need to be so salty. I just told you, *'I've come here to bring you a smile,'* dude."

Man, am I the coolest guy in the universe or what?

*

Let's go back half an hour, shall we?

*"Mrs. Yamazaki, to return to my proposition, which would be easier to repair, the door or the window?"*

Mrs. Yamazaki looked like she had no idea what to say. I plowed on anyway.

*"Kenta's not coming out, not unless we do something drastic. I'm sure he only meant to skip a few days of school in the beginning, but things have gone too far now. He's missed his window of opportunity to emerge on his own. He knows he needs to do something before it's too late, but after all the fuss he's made, he's too proud to come down and announce that he's done renouncing school. So we need to create some convenient pretext for him, so he can act like he's being forced to return. That way, he can save face."*

Mrs. Yamazaki still didn't seem to be following me.

*"So my proposition is that I break into his room by force, either by bashing the door down or breaking the window. That's why I brought this baseball bat with me. Then Kenta can tell everyone: 'Crazy Chitose busted into my room, so I had no choice but to give in.' You see?"*

Finally, the light seemed to dawn in Mrs. Yamazaki's eyes. Her blank expression was replaced with anxiety.

*"...I understand, Chitose, but won't that make things worse? I don't want Kenta getting upset. I would hate for there to be any violence..."*

*"I don't think we need to worry about that. If Kenta really didn't want our help, he would have put on headphones or something and just ignored us when we knocked or tried to talk to him. But he's been quite chatty with us, actually. I think he's looking for a way out."*

I wasn't just saying that, either. Kenta Yamazaki wasn't committed to his shut-in, school-dodging plan for the long haul. He was probably kicking himself for getting stuck in this position in the first place. That was why I needed to go hard now. I needed to go totally OTT on his ass.

*"You won't hurt him, will you?"*

*"It'd take a while for me to bash down the door. I'm sure Kenta will back away to a safe distance when he hears the commotion. And the curtains are drawn, so if I smash my way in through the window, he'll be safe from any flying glass. But I recommend the second option. Repairing the window will be less expensive than replacing a door. And Kenta won't be able to put up any resistance if I go in fast. Of course, I'll pay to replace the window."*

I predicted that Mrs. Yamazaki would refuse to allow me to foot the bill if it came to that. But I was prepared to pay if necessary. I'd just have to hit ol' Kura with an invoice and get reimbursed later.

*"I couldn't possibly take money from such good students who are doing so much for my wayward son! All right, I understand your plan, and I agree to it. May I ask you to opt for the window, though?"*

Ah, all according to plan.

If this was a syrupy teen novel, you could expect me to sweet-talk Yamazaki through the door until he finally opened it of his own free will in an emotional, heartwarming scene. But I didn't have the patience for that. And the end result would be the same, so who cares? I just prefer to cut to the chase. When I'm on the case, all roads lead to Saku-cess, after all. Heh.

*"Thank you for agreeing to my plan; I know it's a bit on the wild side. But I'm certain we can get Kenta back in class if I do this. Yuuko, when I give you the sign, can you head back downstairs where it's safer? I think it will be better if I talk to him man-to-man, as well."*

I smiled at Yuuko, keeping my ulterior motives to myself.

"*Okey dokey. We can have that tea together while we wait, Yumiko!*"

His mom's name was Yumiko? Must have missed that.

✳

...So you see, everything was aboveboard. No criminal act here.

While I was trying to explain this, Yamazaki kept pacing the room. Sitting on the bed. Sitting on his desk chair with his legs tucked under him. Every now and then he made as if to interject, then shut his mouth again. He kept looking at the door furtively. Clearly wondering if he should make a break for it. It was quite funny, really.

"Just take a deep breath and calm down, Kenta."

"Don't say my name like you know me."

He was much less feisty now that I was on the other side of the door. His voice had lowered a notch or three and taken on a tremulous quality.

"Remember what Yuuko said? Looking the other person in the eye when you speak to them is rule one of basic human communication. We've finally reached the starting line. We've finally both stepped into the ring."

I was sweeping glass pieces into a corner of the room with the end of my bat as I spoke.

"Now, let's try to understand each other here. I can tell you have a ton of things you want to say to me, right?"

Now that I was able to finally get a glance at Yamazaki—well, Kenta now—my suspicions were totally confirmed. He was the most stereotypical sad-sack otaku I'd ever seen.

He was extremely disheveled, the effects probably worsened by a long spell of being a shut-in. Dressed in slobby sweatpants and a matching sweatshirt, he had unkempt hair and scrubby stubble growing all over his face. But I tried to overlook that.

He wasn't fat, exactly, but he was a bit round for his frame. Behind his unfashionable, cheap-looking glasses, his eyebrows were bushy and had clearly never felt the loving touch of a pair of tweezers. And he had a twitchy, restless air about him. If you looked up *sweaty otaku*, he'd be the first image result.

"Come on. No sense in clamming up now. If you've got something to say to me, you'd better get it all out."

"…That swagger of yours, it's all because you honestly believe you're better than everyone else at the end of the day, don't you? All you jocks are the same. Doesn't matter what I say or how good my argument is. Guys like you just resort to using force. Pulling pro-wrestler tricks. Getting violent. You prey on guys like me. Anything to make yourselves feel superior."

"You couldn't be more wrong. Though, I guess me saying that kinda rings hollow after I just busted open your window. But I'm actually a totally peaceful kinda guy. I abhor violence. I'd never do anything to escalate a situation. Anyway, I'm confident I could best anyone in an argument using just my words. Didn't I tell you? We're both standing in the ring here. It's going to be a totally fair fight from now on."

I rested my bat against the desk and sat myself down on the chair.

Kenta was still watching me with suspicion and a touch of fear in his eyes.

"You're pretty different when Uchida and Hiiragi aren't around, huh? You decided to quit the whole 'Look what a good person I am' shtick?"

Hmm, he wasn't totally wrong. I certainly wouldn't want the girls to hear some of the truths I was about to lay on old Kenta. Especially not Yuuko. It would really spoil her shining image of me as the hero.

"I just changed up my angle now that we're talking face-to-face and not through the bedroom door, that's all."

"W-well, let me warn you, if you get physical in any way, I'm calling the police."

"Fine by me."

I shrugged. Kenta hesitated for a second more, then sat himself down on the bed as if resigned to his fate.

"Fine, then. I'll tell you what I think. Why not? All you popular kids shit on us unpopular ones like it's your freakin' birthright. Just 'cause you got to the top of the school hierarchy using your athleticism, your study smarts, your good looks...all stuff the universe just handed to you! Well, it's not right! You should at least try to get to know who we are as people before you discriminate against us based on what we look like and who we hang out with!"

Oh boy, he's mad.

But I could point out at least ten reasons why he was wrong.

"Don't just assume that good looks, athleticism, and good grades are 'gifts' from the universe. Yeah, maybe until the end of elementary school, you can coast. But from junior high on, there's good reasons why the popular kids are popular."

I thought of my buddies as I spoke.

"You think Yuuko doesn't spend hours every day working on her hair and makeup skills and doing her skincare? You think my buddies in the soccer and basketball clubs aren't spending precious hours of their irreplaceable youth every day doing hardcore training? You think Yua didn't spend two to three hours every night studying just to pass the exams to get into our school?"

"That's just polishing up the skills and stuff they were born with..."

"Fine, let me put it this way. Would you quit an RPG just because your character has to start at Level 1? Would you call it a shit game unless your character started off at Level 99? We all have different initial stats, you know? Everyone's got different parents and home environments. It's not realistic to expect every-one to begin on equal footing."

"That's...a reductionist example."

Kenta was mumbling to himself.

"Yeah, maybe. But it's true. We all choose our own paths. That's called having free will. We get to make our own destinies."

"Easy for you to say, and for everybody else who's got it made. It's impossible to beat someone with natural ability, no matter how much effort you put in. Trying your best is just a waste of time."

"That's the kind of comment I'd only allow from someone who's put their absolute heart and soul into something, worked their fingers to the bone and wrung out every last drop of blood, sweat, and tears, and only then failed to someone with natural talent who expended no effort. Even Ichiro, the best batter in all the world, puts an incredible amount of effort into his game, so much so that his major league teammates give him grief for it. And he's been working that hard ever since he was in elementary school."

"...So he was born with natural talent and then cultivated it a bit."

He still wasn't getting it.

Or perhaps it would be more accurate to say he was deliber-ately not getting it.

"Okay, have you ever even tried to work hard at anything? You talk about how some people are just blessed. About how you can't win. But who are you trying to win against? Yeah, if it's a competition to see who is the best in the world at something, then natural ability is definitely going to be a big part of that. But at our school, anyone should be able to get great grades if they just put a little work into it."

"Oh, here we go. The whole, 'Just pull yourself up by the boot-straps' speech."

"Am I wrong? Sure, some of us are more cut out for certain things. But it's knowing that difference and going for the thing you've got more aptitude toward, and working hard on it, that defines real success. If you put in the time and effort toward something you're good at, then results will follow. Like they say, once a child prodigy grows up, they just become average. Even if you succeed at something by coasting along on natural talent, that doesn't mean you'll be able to keep it up forever. You'll be overtaken by people who work harder."

I gave Kenta a meaningful smile.

"I mean, if you took all the time you've spent not going to school and applied it to, I dunno, solving the Rubik's Cube or something…then by now I bet you'd be the fastest in the whole school at solving it."

"…Oh, whatever."

I caught Kenta smiling for a second. But he quickly blushed and looked away.

"Well, all I'm saying is that if you made it into our school, then you're already ahead in terms of society. You know how many people failed the entrance exam? You *do* have abilities, Kenta. In the future, you'll be able to walk into any job in Fukui Prefecture with Fuji High on your résumé. In fact, our school's name holds more clout around these parts than some of the best universities in the country."

Of course, Fukui's a small, rural prefecture. So it's not that big of an achievement in the grand scale of things. But what I wanted to get across was that Kenta wasn't the loser underdog he thought he was.

"Huh. Maybe you're right… Okay, so hard work does factor into it a little. But I can't do anything about my shitty communication skills or my personality…"

"Yeah, when you prefer being alone, it's hard to go out and try to become a party person. But I don't think you need to go that far. And communication skills are easy to pick up. To put it simply, you can start with asking why, offering information about yourself, and finding points in common. Get it?"

"What?"

I coughed pointedly and put a little extra energy into my voice.

"Ah, man. I am hella sleepy today."

I raised an eyebrow and gestured at Kenta in a "Go on, then" motion.

"…Uh… Uh, how come?"

"'Cause I have not slept in, like, a week. I've been up all night reading this really sweet light novel…"

I gestured to Kenta again.

"I… I like light novels, too…"

"You do?! No way! What genres are you into?"

"I… I like romantic-comedy-type ones…"

"There, see? We're having a totally normal, functional conversation. It's easy!"

I clapped my hands in an exaggerated manner.

"…The hell? You making fun of me?"

"Nah, man, I'm dead serious. This is *communication*. It's all about trying to get to know the other person, about trying to get them to get to know you. It's like a game of catch, see? You pass the conversational ball back and forth. Think back to your chats with Yua and Yuuko. You kept dropping the ball. '*Why?*' '*What?*' '*I dunno*'—you weren't giving them anything to vibe off, see?"

"Huh, I guess you're right…"

"And then you kept saying dumb stuff like '*I dunno what the bubbly kids like to talk about.*' If you don't know, then just ask. You wanna know what makes people tick? *Ask them.* And then tell them about the stuff you like."

Kenta stared at me, uncomprehendingly.

"Yeah, but, Chitose… I thought you didn't read light novels?"

"Oh yeah? Check it: *I Was the Biggest Dork in School, but Then*

*I Got Reincarnated as the Leader of My Own Harem in Another World!*, *I'm Handsome, but Only in a Parallel Universe?!*, *I'm a Huge Otaku, but the Slutty Girls Are All Up on Me?!*, *Is It Okay for an Otaku to Fall in Love?*, *I Joined the Popular-Kids Group and All of a Sudden I'm in High Demand!*, *The Most Popular Kid in School Is None Other than My Younger Brother!*, *My Hot Senpai Is Obsessed with Me, an Otaku?!*, *I Don't Need to Be Popular, but at Least Let Me Be King of the Nerds!*, *I Can't Get the Hot Girl's Attention if All I Do Is Hang Around with Otaku Scum!*, *In This World, Geeks and Normies Have Switched Positions!...*"

I finally paused for breath.

"...Why do they have such long titles? Thought I was gonna die listing those off."

"Those are all the ones I mentioned last time."

"I'm actually a big reader. But let me know next time how long each series runs. Each one of those had at least five volumes out to date. It took me the whole freakin' week to get through 'em."

"...What? You read them *all* in one week? Yeah, right. Well, prove it, then. Answer these questions."

Then Kenta started shooting questions at me. He wanted me to provide the character lists for each series, plus describe random chapters. But I was up for the challenge. As I said, I spent all week reading them. There wasn't a question he had that I didn't have the answer to.

"...I seriously don't get you. The heck is your game? Why are you so desperate to be friends with me?"

"Whoa, whoa, whoa, hold up. Being friends with you would provide me with zero social benefits. I just want to get your ass back to class. I have no other motivations whatsoever."

"Then why...all this?"

"You know, I hate people who make zero effort to get to know the first thing about someone or something, then jump on what they've heard secondhand from people talking shit and use that to try to drag that person or thing down. Actually, the books were pretty interesting. I couldn't put them down. I can see why you like them now. Like I said, communication is all about actually wanting to get to know the other person. That's where it starts."

Kenta fell silent. I guessed he was in shock.

"And there's something I want to ask you. You just said something pretty interesting. What was it? *'You should at least try to get to know who we are as people before you discriminate against us based on what we look like and who we hang out with,'* right? Fine. Then out of me, Yua, Yuuko, and you, who was discriminating against whom based on looks and friend groups? Hmm?"

"Yeah, but…"

Kenta's lips flapped for a few seconds, but then he fell silent again.

I picked up a book on world history from his bookshelf and idly flipped through it.

"You know, in elementary school, I was hooked on that book series…The World's Greatest Figures from History. Did you ever read them?"

I wasn't thinking too hard about it when I threw out that question.

Kenta shook his head, confused by the sudden change of subject.

I continued, half messing around.

"One of the great men I admired, he had an interesting childhood. This young man was blessed with all kinds of natural gifts. He was so beautiful he was mistaken for a girl sometimes, got the best grades, and beat all the other boys at sports. But he never let it go to his head. He was nice to everyone, boys and girls alike."

Kenta interjected then.

"What are you talking about now? I don't follow…"

"Just listen. This will help us understand one another more. So what do you think of the boy so far, Kenta?"

"What…? I guess…from what I've already heard, he sounds like a jerk. He's got to have some kind of flaw, though. At least one, right?"

Ah, he was so honest.

"Yeah, a lot of people would probably feel that way. And actually, they did. The kids in the boy's peer group started picking on him, looking for a weak spot. He was just too perfect, you know? If he got a ninety-nine on a test instead of one hundred, they would tease him about it. If he had a stray thread hanging loose on his school uniform, they would mock him. They even made fun of his laugh."

"Sounds like he deserved it. Anyway, kids are jerks. And getting one question wrong on a test doesn't change the fact that he's smart in school."

"Like I told you, they were nitpicking whatever they could find. *The nail that sticks up gets hammered down.* They hated this kid. They were like crabs in a bucket. They couldn't ascend to his level, so they dragged him back down with them."

I took a pause for effect then, looking at Kenta.

"So what do you imagine the boy did next?"

Kenta pondered it for a second. "I guess he started fighting back and giving as good as he got. After all, he was naturally gifted, right? All he had to do was assert dominance. Yeah, I bet he was pissed."

"Nope. The boy decided to lower himself down to the level of his inferior classmates. He made deliberate mistakes on tests and screwed up on purpose during gym class. He made himself just like the others. He figured that if he stopped standing out, he'd stop being singled out."

"…Well, that's not really fair. It wasn't the boy's fault his classmates were jerks. He still should have been able to be himself."

"It's always the unremarkable ones who try to drag down the remarkable ones."

I returned the history textbook to the shelf. Then I wandered over to my bat and began to idly stroke the handle.

"So then the boy stopped being picked on?"

"No, sadly not. The situation only got worse. Now that he was making even more basic errors, the mocking got worse. His tormentors were more determined than ever to hammer him down into complete submission."

"Yeah, that's just bullying, then. But the boy triumphed in the end, right? I mean, he was that remarkable, wasn't he?"

I fell silent, rubbing my chin before continuing.

"In the end, a certain schoolteacher noticed the boy's plight. She saw how the other kids were excluding him, and she took the boy aside to speak to him. She said: '*A boy like you, blessed with all these gifts, ought to be standing in front of the class and serving as an example to the others. You may wonder why you're the only one who has to put in this much effort, but the other kids—well, they're wondering why you're the only one who has all these gifts.*'"

I paused to exhale a little. I was getting a little fired up here. I had to make sure to keep my voice cool and steady.

"'*…So you have to fly even higher. You have to run even faster. Until you become a real hero, the kind who inspires the others to follow along behind you…*'"

"…Sounds like a good teacher."

"So the boy stopped trying to hide his talents and focused on being the best he could be. Until he became someone so awesome that he was admired by everyone. And he lived happily ever after. The end."

Yeah, the boy realized that by trying to fly under the radar, he was only putting himself in range of the losers around him, who kept trying to grab him and drag him down by his feet.

He had to fly higher…faster…until he was so far out of reach that the simpletons would look foolish trying to catch him. He had to shine—bright and beautiful.

Like the moon in the night sky.

Like a round glass marble trapped inside an old-fashioned bottle of Ramune soda pop with a lid you can't take off. I read something like that in a book once.

He had to go so high and so far that when he finally looked behind him, he wouldn't even be able to remember why he had gone so high in the first place...

"I see. So which great figure did the boy grow up to become?"

"He grew up to be the great, the exalted, the legendary...Saku Chitose."

"You?!!!"

"By the way, I mostly made up that story on the spot. It's, like, ninety percent fiction. Good, eh?"

"Why'd you make it sound like it was some sort of morality tale?! And which part of it was true, then?!"

"The part about me being great."

"Quit wasting my time, asshole!!!"

✶

"Well, now, I think we've learned the important thing about trying to better ourselves and not just drifting through life, haven't we?"

I folded my arms, sounding purposely pompous.

"I feel like an idiot now. I can't believe I actually fell for your dumb story. But... Well... It wasn't completely fictional, was it? I guess you went through some stuff, too, Chitose. So... Sorry. All right. You're right. I had preconceived ideas about you all. I made you out to be the bad guys without knowing you."

This is the kind of guy who reads too much into an anime series that has a vague, lackluster ending and calls it a masterpiece based on all the things it blatantly isn't.

"Well, I'm glad you've seen the light. So you feel like talking now?"

"…I guess. At least, I'm open to hearing what you've got to say."

I smiled in my mind.

"Great, thanks. I wanted to ask you a few things, to clear up some misunderstandings. First, about those light novels you love that all feature awkward losers. Yeah, as fiction they're enjoyable, but don't get them confused with reality. Okay, they do mention a few skills you'll probably need to become popular, but they over-idolize popularity. And they also demonize it. It's not realistic. They need to skip over stuff and simplify for the sake of the story, you know?"

"I know it's fictionalized, but popular kids are like that, aren't they? They're the winners in life."

"I see. So that really is how you view it…"

I thought about things for a moment.

Probably all the unpopular, gloomy kids felt like that, not just Kenta.

To clear up this misunderstanding for him, I was going to have to show a little of my inner self. I didn't really want to, but I'd predicted this. Another reason why I brought Yuuko with me.

Still, Kenta was far from the point where he'd be able to read any deeper meaning into what I'd been saying. But this was a small price to pay for helping someone change their life. In taking on this endeavor, I was also taking on some small amount of personal risk.

I started talking again.

"So even if you think that popular kids are playing life on easy mode, it's actually hard mode, way harder than it is for unpopular kids. Standing out kinda sucks. I mean, you know about the abuse I have to put up with on that underground website, right? Yeah… I mean, don't get me wrong, being handsome opens doors, but it also makes people think they can say mean stuff about you, like that you're a dick, that you're a man-whore, and so on. I get that kind of stuff on the daily. As I recall, you even did the same…"

"I… I'm sorry about that."

"It's cool, I'm not trying to guilt-trip you about that or any-thing. I just want you to understand that there's two sides to every story. I mean, here I am trying to help you out. And I got named class president."

"Oh yeah, you mentioned that."

"Yeah, but it's like everyone takes it for granted that I'll do whatever they need me to do just 'cause of that position. And that I'll do it right, whatever it is. It's a lot of pressure, and it comes from everyone, and there's no way around it. I mean, would *you* like to have to go to the house of some gloomy shut-in you've never met to try to convince him to come back to school?"

"Uh, no. I really don't like getting involved in other people's business…"

Kenta screwed up his face as if imagining being in my shoes.

"Right? I tell you, you get that 'class hero' label slapped on you. And you end up having to be freakin' perfect from then until the end of time. 'Cause if you slip up just once, they'll be coming for you to drag you down into hell."

"Like in the story you just told me."

Kenta was following right along the trail of bread crumbs I was setting. Yes, he was following along real nice.

I continued.

"Compared to that, these otaku protagonists have it easy. If they screw up… So what? No one's surprised. No one's going to shame them for it. All they have to do is pull themselves together and have a normal conversation with a three-dimensional per-son, and they get praised and clapped on the back. They screw up, no problem. They succeed a little, and everybody loses their minds. Like I said, it's life on easy mode. But for us? When we succeed, nobody cares, because everyone just expects it. We never get to earn any additional points. But if we ever do any-thing wrong, we lose all our points. It's a rigged game. It sucks."

Kenta was deep in silence, thinking about what I had just said. Then he spoke again.

"Okay, I get what you're saying. But that only applies to, like, the most popular of all the popular kids, like you and Hiiragi, right? But the regular popular kids are just jerks, always trying to act so superior to all of us on the bottom of the ladder."

All right, I'll admit I'm exceptional. But he was missing my point.

"But it's just an issue of categorizing people. Those lower-ranked people look at popular kids and think they're all the same. But there're so many levels to it. I don't see kids who constantly try to get one over on the unpopular kids as truly popular. They're just wannabes. I only acknowledge genuinely good people as actually part of the popular set. Jerks don't make it to the top, no matter what kind of special skills or good looks they may have. I mean, take Yua and Yuuko. Were they mean to you? Did it seem like they were trying to put you down?"

"...No. They just talked to me, like we were equals. It was all me... I started off seeing you as the enemy without knowing anything about you, Chitose..."

"And do you know why the girls and I have been so decent to you?"

"Uh...no?"

"To put it in broad terms, it's because we all feel confident in our place in the world. So we don't need to point out the flaws of others and laugh at them when they screw up and act like we're somehow balancing the scales. It's not going to elevate our positions by doing that, and we don't care to try anyway. We don't need to look down on others. We don't even need to look down. See what I mean?"

I lowered my tone a little as I continued.

"Dragging down other people won't lift you any higher. It'll just degrade you until you end up descending to their level."

"…So you're saying I have to work hard to change, until I can have confidence in myself?"

"Yeah, exactly. Forget the others. Focus on becoming someone you'd like if you weren't you. Then you'll automatically become a nicer person. And you won't let other people's opinions bother you anymore."

Kenta was leaning forward, absorbed in our conversation. He was actually a pretty decent kind of guy. Most kids are so convinced they're right about everything that they close their ears to the opinions of others. But not him.

"However… Can I say one more thing? At least for kids like you and Hiiragi…dating actually *is* on easy mode, right?"

"Hmm. Yeah, I can't deny that we usually get to have our pick of romantic partners. But at the same time, it gets awkward when people we have zero interest in get clingy and start crushing on us. We're just trying to get along with our classmates and have fun with our friends, but when someone starts catching feelings, it can end up biting us in the ass. When you turn them down, they start painting you as the bad guy. You try to distance yourself before it gets that far, and they accuse you of freezing them out. You can't win. It's like, sorry for being hot, y'know?"

I threw up my hands and shrugged.

"Yeah, I heard some girls complaining about that in my class last year. At the time, I thought…*Popular sluts, go die!* But when you explain it like that, I kinda get it. Relationships are complicated… I can kinda sympathize… But I mean…not completely."

"Yeah, well, if it's someone you don't care about, you can take the hating on the chin. But if it's someone you actually like and value as a friend who catches feelings and asks you out… Well, it sucks to have to wreck a friendship. It sucks to have to be like, 'Please keep this platonic!' you know? And also…"

I trailed off then for a few moments.

"And also, no matter how handsome you might be, or how

good at sports you are, or how high your grades are, or whatever, it doesn't automatically mean the girl you like is gonna like you back."

"I guess not… But hey, Chitose…can I tell you about, you know, something personal?"

His voice lowered. *Here it comes! One more push and over he goes!*

"Nah, it's okay. I already get what's going on, more or less, and I don't really care to know more."

"What? But… But I was just about to bare my soul to you here…"

"You were in a group for otaku hobbyists. A nonschool group. There was a girl. Kind of a princess, but she was nice to you, so you started crushing on her. But she liked someone else—let's call him Prince, uh, Jiro. Jiro steals your girl. Ever since then, you've felt totally inferior, and you didn't want to be around anyone, popular *or* otaku. So you quit coming to school. Have I left anything out?"

Kenta was staring at me, lips flapping wordlessly, but I knew what he was thinking: *How the hell did you know that?!*

*Dude, how can you seriously not see how glaringly obvious it was?*

Yuuko and Nanase had been right on the money.

"…Wh-when I asked her out…she said…'*Excuse me? Are you delusional? I would* never *date someone like you. Don't you even realize what your own social status is? Loser!*'…"

"Yikes, man. I'm surprised you're still able to even show your face in public after hearing something like that from a girl."

"I'm literally not showing my face in public!!!"

⋆

I sent Yuuko a quick message through LINE and asked her to bring up some iced coffee and iced tea and leave it in front of the door. Kenta and I still had some talking to do.

"So what do you want to do going forward, man?"

I swirled the ice cubes around with my straw before slurping up the iced coffee noisily.

"The girl… Her name's Miki… To be honest, I'm done with her."

"You're traumatized."

"Yeah, I guess so. It was my first time ever liking a girl who wasn't animated. But real-life girls suck worse than I suspected. I'm going back to my waifus."

"What about school, though?"

"About that… I know I can't keep going on like I have been. I'm going to end up screwing myself. With the shock and all, I just couldn't make it to school at first, but once I recovered, I kinda missed my chance to go back. And I know how freaked out I've been making my parents…"

Mm-hmm.

It was just my guess, but it seems like shutting yourself away in your room while at the same time not being fully committed to throwing away your future…that's got to be mentally taxing.

"So if you're really willing to stick with me and teach me how to become popular, Chitose, then I guess I can go back to school."

Kenta lifted his head, gazing into my eyes.

"Er, no way, dude."

I shook my head firmly. Kenta's jaw dropped open in surprise and remained just hanging there.

"What? But…but that's how this is supposed to go…isn't it?"

"Dude, think about it. My mission was to get you to agree to come back to school. That's done now. But to be honest, even if I'd failed, it wouldn't have affected me much. I only came here so I could feel good about swooping in and solving a problem. But who says I have to drag your ass around school with me and make you popular?"

"But…but that's how it's supposed to go…"

"Yeah, no. I'm under zero obligation. Sure, I could probably get you accepted into Team Chitose. But you'd only be depressed. Everyone else is way above your level, after all. The fundamental issue here, though, is that I don't *want* to hang around with you at school."

"Are you serious?! Are you seriously saying this to me? Right now? After all that?!"

"Grow up. You may be the main character in your otaku-to-popular-stud story, but that's not *my* story. My story is a harem comedy starring Chitose himself. You're just a little side character designed to show off my coolness to the readers. Your whole 'Poor me, I can't go to school' plight is just a red herring to kick-start the story and get the readers invested. Go take responsibility for your own story, and write it how you want it to be, Sidey McSide Character."

"Are you trying to be annoying?"

To be fair to him, he probably thought this was going to be a major life-changing event. The day that would change his whole life. But for me, it was Tuesday. I was here to do my thing, like always, and get results, like always. I probably wouldn't even remember this when I was an adult.

This was my way of cutting him loose. It was better for him, to do it this way. He wouldn't get anywhere in life hanging on to my shirttails.

Kenta had this look of abject shock on his face, as if he'd been transported to another world only to find that he'd turned into a hippopotamus.

"But I can see your predicament. You're in a boat with a hole in the bottom, and it's sinking fast. I'd hate to have to watch you drown. So I'll throw you some tips. Enough to help you plug the hole, at least."

"Why bother? You obviously don't care if I sink or swim!"

"Do you want to drown? Huh?"

"…Fine. Help me out, then. It's not like I have any other choice, after backing myself into a corner like this. Besides, I feel like I can, uh…trust you, Chitose."

"Oh gee, thanks. Thanks for the opportunity to serve you, Your Highness."

"All right, all right. Please, Mr. Saku Chitose, most popular and coolest guy in all of Fuji High. Please, please, take pity on this poor, lowly, shut-in otaku loser worm and share with him your wisdom."

Kenta got down on his hands and knees, as if he had already abandoned all sense of self-respect. I could tell he still didn't completely trust me, but after he had already allowed me to smash his window and lecture him at length on not judging a book by its cover…he couldn't very well take a stand against me now.

I smirked secretly to myself.

Good. I was using Kenta to bolster my own image. So Kenta could make use of me, too.

"Very well. You may call me…King."

"King!!!"

Aha, what a fascinating boy this Kenta really was.

"I'll warn you, I don't intend to be your mentor for very long. Maybe three weeks, tops. Let's say, until the Golden Week holiday rolls around. I shall teach you the basics of living as a popular kid. After that, you must use what you have learned to further your growth by yourself."

"Understood, King."

"But you need some sort of goal to aim toward. Are you sure you're over this Miki chick?"

"I'm done with her in the romantic sense. I mean, I'm still sad about it, I guess… And if I got the opportunity, I'd like to show her what she's missing. Just a little bit."

"That's good. Simple is best. Let's make her sorry she missed her chance. And let's smash Prince Jiro as well. Bring him down a peg or two."

"D-do you think we really could? …King?"

"Yeah, we're talking about the prince and princess of some little otaku group. I'm the King of the Popular Kids, y'know? If you can't manage to take them down after receiving my excellent tutelage, then that's on you. If you screw it up, I'll come after you. The only place you'll have left to hide from me is inside your own mind. Got it?"

"You're not a king… You're…you're…a demon!"

"And one more thing." I slurped down the rest of my iced coffee. "You just said that real-life girls suck, right? That doesn't sit well with me, Kenta."

"Yeah, but that's how I feel. It's impossible to tell what real girls are thinking, and you have to worry about your looks and what you say around them. Animated girls are so much better. They just give you unconditional love; you don't need to do anything special."

"Are all you otakus like this? 'Popular kids suck, real girls suck, the voice actress or idol I used to go crazy over got a boyfriend and now *she* sucks.' That's just sour grapes, isn't it? If you can't have something, you make yourself feel better by telling yourself it sucks anyway. Well, I'm about to open the door to popularity for you. Learn some humility."

"Nuh-uh, I'm sticking to my guns on this one. Girls are so much better as abstract concepts. Once they're three-dimensional, they're nothing but a pain in the ass."

"You just want a girl who won't do anything to break your fantasies. You think having to be aware of your appearance and the things you say is a pain in the ass, but you need to master these things if you want to be popular and have an actual life. I know, what you need is an amazing girl to shoot for. It's easier to work on being your best self if you're spending time around a girl you want to impress."

"No… I don't wanna. Seriously. Real girls are scary."

"…Yeah, well, you went all gooey over Yua, didn't you?"

I paused, watching Kenta slyly as he began to sputter. "Wh-what? Yeah, right!"

Then I pressed on.

"Listen, Kenta. When I was reading those light novels you like so much, I really found myself falling for some of the female love interests. And all that stuff about the buildup to a relationship being the best part, and it being downhill from there? That resonated with me, man. And yeah, I know, girls can be a lot of work. But you're missing the big picture."

I got up from the desk chair and picked up my bat. Then I pointed it right at Kenta, the tip mere inches from his nose.

"Listen up, you maggot! Have you ever felt the softness of a real girl's boobs? Do you have any concept of the variety in size, shape, and squishiness that is totally unique to each girl? Have you ever smelled the fresh, clean scent of a girl's hair as you pull her into your arms? Do you know the velvety softness of her belly and hips when you slide your hands up her shirt? Have you ever tasted the salty tang of a girl's neck as you run your tongue along it? Have you ever almost swooned when a girl leans in and licks your bottom lip? Have you ever experienced the anticipation that comes as you peer over a girl's shoulder, fiddling desperately in an attempt to unhook her bra? Have you ever felt the rush of excitement that comes exactly seven seconds later (my personal max time frame) when you get that clasp at last and the bra pops loose and comes off in your hands? Have you ever even dreamed of these things?!!!"

"N-no..."

"Then nothing you say is valid, virgin! Fine, content yourself with animated girls! Rely on your limited imagination to color those fantasies! But never forget! Those 2D girls you so revere... They are flat! They are lifeless! They're nothing more than paper!"

"They're not lifeless! They're alive in my mind!"

"But only in your mind. If you can't bring them truly to life, then the only option for losing your virginity is to pursue real girls! But I have good news for you. You know Yuuko, right? You've seen her face. And her body."

"Uh, yeah… Well, I've seen her around school. She's hard not to notice!"

"Yeah, well, she's kind of my harem slut. If I told her I wanted to do some cuckolding role-playing or whatever, I bet she might go along with it. She might not be thrilled about it, but I bet she'd be your first. Incidentally, here's the specs on Yuuko… Super-plushy D cups. The very size that every woman in Japan considers to be ideal. So what do you say? Don't you want to dive right in there and motorboat the hottest girl in school?"

"K-King…are you being serious right now?"

"The king never lies."

"Yeah but seriously… Are you serious?"

"Seriously serious. So what do you say? Wanna motorboat?"

"Y-yes! I wanna motorboat! I wanna motorboat, King!"

"Do you like three-dimensional boobies?"

"I do! I do! I do like three-dimensional boobies! Forgive me for saying real girls suck!"

"Is your penchant for 2D girls a mere case of sour grapes?"

"It is! It is! Very sour, King!"

"Do you like boobies?!"

"I like boobies!"

"I can't hear you! Louder!"

"I like boobies! I LIKE BOOBIES!"

"Louder!!!"

"BOOBIES, BOOBIES, BOOBIES, BOO-BEEEZ!!!"

"WHAT'S MY NAME?!"

"KING! KING! KING!"

"LOUDER! GIMME ALL YOU GOT! THINK OF YOUR POOR SHRINK-WRAPPED DICK!!!"

"I WANNA MOTORBOAT THREE-DIMENSIONAL BOO-
BIES!!!"

"SELL YOUR SOUL TO ME!!!"

"YES, KING! YES! BOOOBIIIEEESSS!!!"

"TOO BAD!! THOSE ARE MY BOOBIES!! GET YOUR OWN!!"

"Wait... What?"

"I wasn't lying. You said yourself that she's part of my 'harem,'
and I never said she *would* do it, only that I thought she might.
I made no promises of any kind. I just asked what you thought."

"You...you really are a demon."

✳

After that, I brought Kenta downstairs. After all the fuss he'd
caused, I think he was relieved to have an out and was determined not to miss this one chance.

"I hope Mom doesn't start crying. I bet Hiiragi's mad, too..."

He probably went over this repeatedly in his mind, during his
long shut-in period. The moment when he finally emerges.

Not sure how to face people or what to say. Would his mom
cry? Would she get mad? Would she eventually forgive?

I went first and opened the door to the living room.

"Oh, hey, Saku! All done?"

"Oh my! You've finally come out?!"

The two of them were sitting down here sipping tea like old
buddies. His mom had major "We'll be having curry rice for
dinner tonight!" energy.

I was expecting this, though. That's the thing about Yuuko—
she can make friends with anyone.

Kenta had his head hanging low, looking sheepish. He kept lin-
gering in the doorway. In the end, I had to haul him through.
Gave him a smack on the ass for good measure, too.

"M-Mom... Sorry for all the worry I've caused you. Actually,
I—"

"Oh, I heard all about it from Yuuko. You were feeling depressed about your love life, is that it? You might talk big, but you're still just a little boy. I was worried something was really wrong! Now, you'll be going back to school tomorrow, and let's say no more about it."

"Uh… Sure."

Sorry, Sidey McSide Character. You don't get any dramatic reconciliation scenes in *my* novel.

"S-sorry I was a jerk to you, Hiiragi. I don't even know you, but I said some things…"

"Yuuko's fine, you know? Anyway, Kentacchi, it's all fine with me as long as you've already apologized to Saku, too."

Yuuko grinned, waving her half-eaten cookie in the air dismissively. What was with that nickname? Made me think of fried chicken.

"But you should go and take a shower and shave your face, then change your clothes. You reek."

"He does!"

And so ends the touching reunion between mother and son, who have not spoken face-to-face in months now.

Ah, so uplifting!

*

Yuuko being there was probably what spurred Kenta into action. Half an hour later, he reemerged, freshly showered, shaved, and changed into regular clothes. He'd even switched his glasses for contacts.

""Meh…""

Yuuko and I both spoke in unison.

"Hmm, maybe you should have kept the stubble after all," I mused. "I thought your glasses were super dorky, but without them, your face has zero personality. Also, your hair is a disaster. I was going to suggest you get it buzzed off, but maybe a wilder look would be better…"

"Yeah, I could walk past you in the hallways every day and never even remember your face!"

"Wow, that's really harsh."

By the way, Yumiko had stepped out to go shopping for dinner by this point, so it was just us three. And dinner was to be, as I had predicted, curry rice.

Kenta hesitated. "But what about the outfit, though? I actually picked out all my best stuff."

""Yeah, no.""

"Seriously?"

"Give us a break. Who do you think you are, Sid Vicious? Some punk rocker? What's with the long-sleeve T with the English gibberish on it? What does that say? DEAD BOY? Try FAT BOY. And do you really need the skulls, crosses, *and* tribal designs? Are those wings on the back?! And that necklace. Did that come free with the T-shirt? Now the jeans—I thought those were all right at first, but are they boot-cut?! C'mon, *boot-cut*? Even by the most generous interpretation, you are not gonna be the one to bring those back, I can tell you right now! Oh, and did you see the checkered pocket lining? Yikes, honey. What is it with you otaku and check patterns? Do you have some sort of check pattern quota you've got to meet? I'm embarrassed to be associated with you, you walking fashion disaster."

"Y-you don't have to go quite that far, King."

"Well, you've blown my mind, that's why! If you'd come down here wearing the typical otaku uniform of a tucked-in checkered flannel shirt, jeans, and forehead bandanna, maybe I could have dealt with it, but this…? What do you think, Yuuko?"

Yuuko grinned.

"Hmm, well if you showed up for a date with me dressed like that, I'd have to kick you in the crotch and run."

"Dude, is this what you've learned from your light novels with loser protagonists? All right, we'll have to take you shopping at

Lpa next weekend. I'll show you how to pick clothes that look good. You coming, Yuuko?"

"I'll be there if you are, Saku!"

By the way, Lpa is the biggest shopping mall in Fukui City. It has clothing stores and other home goods–type stores, but it also has a movie theater, an arcade, karaoke, and even a Starbucks all in the same complex. It's where basically everyone in Fukui comes to hang out on the weekends and holidays. Lots of junior and high school kids go there on dates, too. College students, too. And lots of families. Everyone knows it. What I'm saying is that it's *the* place to meet up and hang out.

"Thank you. You'd spend your weekend on me? That's so kind. Because I really have no idea what kind of clothes to choose. Can I wear this to the mall, though?"

""No. School uniform.""

Yuuko and I both spoke in unison again. The guy was a mess, I won't lie, but he definitely had potential to improve.

"For now, we can't let you go back to school with that hair. Let Yuuko cut it for you."

"Er, you want me to let Hiiragi cut it? I mean, uh, Yuuko? She doesn't look like the...steady-handed type."

"How rude! I'll have you know, I'm as good as any salon! Anyway, Saku already asked me. I have my haircutting scissors, plus my thinning shears, and even my barber clippers in my bag! While I'm at it, I'll trim those brows for you as an extra bonus, too."

Yuuko rummaged around in her bag, showing off her tools one by one.

"Relax. I can vouch for Yuuko's steady hand. She's cut my hair a bunch of times. What kind of hairstyle did you have before you started skipping school?"

"It was kind of long all over. With bangs that covered my eyes."

"Yuuko, give him a really short cut. With a skin fade."

"Aye, aye, captain."

"Isn't anyone going to ask my opinion?!"

We stepped out into the small yard. It wasn't anything special, but Kenta's mom or dad or both had clearly been caring for it, and it was pretty nice out there.

A cool evening breeze had started up while Kenta and I were talking in his stuffy room together, and now it was quite pleasant out. The twilit sky was tinged with a crimson hue.

Yuuko spread out some old newspapers she'd found in the house, then plonked one of the dining chairs down on it. Then she got out a plastic bag she'd asked Yumiko for earlier, folded it into a semicircle, then cut a small hole in it to create a haircutting cape.

I turned to Kenta, who was hovering about behind us.

"Listen, only hot guys like me can get away with having floppy hair that falls in our eyes. The most important impression guys need to make is neatness. If you've got a face you feel like hiding, the best thing to do is buzz your hair short and own it. But your face isn't a disaster, so I'm going to have Yuuko give you an undercut and leave it a bit longer on top. You've got a natural-curl type of situation going on, so it'll give you some character without looking too wild."

"Oh yeah, I totally agree. Now, Kentacchi, sit down and put this on."

Kenta sat down obediently on the dining chair. Yuuko stood facing him and plonked the bag hole down over his head. It looked like she'd forgotten to cut him any armholes, though.

"You look like a rogue samurai who's seen better days. And in that cape, you look like a *decapitated* rogue samurai who's seen better days."

"Ew, gross! That's so funny!"

" . . . "

But I knew that Kenta's sudden silence wasn't because of rage.

It was because Yuuko's chest was right in his field of vision. And he was trying to surreptitiously inhale her scent. I could see his nose twitching.

Still, I could let him have this.

"Now, let the snip-snapping commence!"

Yuuko's scissors flashed as she immediately began cutting off the long strands around Kenta's jawline. First, she was getting rid of the length roughly, so she could shape it afterward.

"You're cutting off an awful lot… Can't I have a mirror so I can at least see what you're doing?"

"All a mirror's going to show you is a pasty, unhealthy-looking shut-in of a boy. And besides, you have no right to question Yuuko's abilities. So pipe down."

"Aw, it's okay, Kentacchi. First time for you? Just close your eyes and leave it all up to me. I'll even throw in a free head massage!"

*Yuuko, please. I know you're oblivious, but you're going to give the poor virgin a heart attack. And I still have some important things to discuss with him.* Wanting to distract Kenta, I started talking to him again as Yuuko continued her work.

"So you're coming back to school tomorrow, agreed?"

"I guess asking for a little more time is out of the question, King?"

"Hmph. It's out of my way, but for the first few days, I'll pick you up in the morning, and we can go to school together."

"You're not going to back out on me, though, are you?"

"Listen, there's only so much I can do for you in three weeks. Whether this is effective or not really depends on how much effort you put in. First, you need to improve your communication skills. We'll start off by getting you back to school and woven back into the class. Then our goal will be for you to have a normal conversation with a popular kid without freaking them out, okay?"

"That's all? Hah. That doesn't sound so hard."

"Then why haven't you been doing it all along?"

"...My bad, King. Please continue."

Yuuko was focused on haircutting. She could hear what we were saying, but it was clear she was leaving everything else up to me.

"Just so you know, if you're hoping to reach the level of people like Yuuko and me, then you can keep on dreaming. Maybe in a fictional world, you could do it if you had, like, a year. But this is reality, and it's not a matter of how much time you put into it. Being able to enjoy conversations with other students and live a normal high school life is the best it's going to get for you. If you still want more after that, that's on you. But don't think any amount of instruction is going to get you there."

Kenta nodded obediently. *Whoa, don't do that; you're gonna mess up Yuuko's handiwork.*

"One other thing we need to worry about is your appearance. That's why we're giving you a haircut, and why we'll take you to Lpa. I'm going to guide you, but you need to put in the work yourself to fix that bloat you've got going on. You're not chubby enough to make it part of your character, so you'll need to slim down some. Have you been at that weight since before you quit going to school?"

"No, actually, I used to be more on the skinny side."

"That's all right, then. I'll write up a meal plan and a training plan for you. But make sure you put in the work. I'm not going to put you on keto or anything, but you're going to cut out the refined carbs. And we'll go heavy on the cardio, plus some strength training, the kind that will show the fastest results. If we don't fix your hair, clothes, and get you back to your fighting weight, then there's not much I'm going to be able to do."

"Well, my body type and metabolism aren't really under my control..."

"I know, people have different bodies. But it's calories in versus calories out, basic thermodynamics. Don't try to make excuses. And anyway, if you're usually skinny, then a little exercise and a calorie deficit should have fast results. Time to get up and work."

I knew how it was, though. I'm the type who packs on muscle fast with a little exercise, but once I stop, that bulk immediately goes to other places. There're some folks out there who don't get fat even if they eat the house down, but they also can't put on serious muscle no matter how hard they go in the gym. You have to work with your body type, but you can't use it as an excuse.

"Yeah, but…"

"But, but, but. Enough *buts*. I hear one more *but* from you and you're getting a buzz cut. All you're allowed to say from now on is: 'Yes, King,' got it?"

"…I'll give it my best effort, King."

"And give me your phone. Unlock it first."

"…You're taking my phone…?"

"Yuuko, hand me the clippers."

"Here you go!"

"…Sir, yes, sir!!!"

I grabbed the phone from Kenta's trembling hands and immediately started looking through it to see what kind of apps he had. There was nothing there that came as any kind of a surprise to me. I sighed with disgust.

"Kenta, starting tomorrow, you are forbidden from using Twitter, 5chan, and that goddamn school gossip site. No posting, no scrolling. In fact, don't even look at them. Got it?"

"But those apps are about fifty percent of what sustains me! How long until I can use them again?!"

"Until you learn how unproductive it is to trash-talk people on the internet that you don't even know. But to say thanks for introducing me to those light novels you like, I'll lend you some mainstream novels. Make sure you read them carefully."

"Mainstream novels? They're so hard to read, though…"

"Don't be a wet blanket. You can learn a lot from reading someone like Raymond Chandler. Any hard-boiled fiction, in fact. Really cool, popular guys are driven by more than the desire to be popular. A man should learn about philosophy and aesthetics. But I warn you now, if you leave my books lying open facedown on the floor or dog-ear the pages, I will murder you with my bare hands."

"I...I would never do that to a book. You don't have to worry about that with me."

"I'll also give you a list of movies and TV shows that feature cool male protagonists. You should sign up for one of the streaming services. But you don't need to just consume everything I tell you to. You should find your own heroes to emulate. Even light novel protagonists are fine. Just find someone to use as an example."

"A hero to emulate, huh...? I'll have to think it over."

*I guess that wraps up everything for now.*

*Snip-snip.*

Yuuko had a very serious, un-Yuuko-esque look on her face. Kenta, meanwhile, seemed on edge and was staring at his own knees. He clearly wasn't sure where to put his eyes. It wasn't like he was ever going to get a second chance at being this close to Yuuko. He could at least have made the most of it.

*Snip-snip, snip-snip.*

The sound of the scissors was almost rhythmical.

It was a strange evening.

Here we were, Yuuko and me, two of the best-known kids in the school. Hanging out with Kenta, who was almost completely off everyone's radar. Yuuko was cutting his hair while I was teaching him how to live. A series of strange coincidences seemed to have led us all here. Or perhaps it was a series of bad decisions that had led us all here.

It was definitely a strange sort of miracle, though. Like finding a golden ticket in the very first candy bar you ever bought with your very first allowance.

Yuuko had gotten the clippers out now and was cleaning up the sides.

"All done! What do you think, Saku?!"

"Hmm. From a disgraced samurai to a hippo emerging from the water with weeds on its head. It's an improvement, at least."

"Hey!"

"Uh…"

It wasn't really Yuuko's fault. She didn't have much to work with.

"Let's work on your frame, okay, Kenta?"

When Yumiko got home from shopping, she made a serviceable yet still comforting meal of curry rice for us all. We agreed to stay for dinner before we headed home.

Of course, Kenta had his curry served over a bed of cabbage. And we made him pick out all the potatoes. Simple carbs, after all, were not part of the diet plan.

# CHAPTER THREE
## Let the Mutual Understanding Commence

The day after I managed to coax Kenta back to the real world, I arrived at the Yamazakis' at seven AM sharp. The man himself was pacing around in the living room, already wearing his school uniform. It looked like he was all ready to go. His eyes were bloodshot, as if he'd been too nervous to sleep much last night. Or at all.

"'Sup? Looks like you didn't get much sleep, huh?"

Kenta turned to look at me. He really did have a "That time I got reincarnated as a hippo" kinda panic.

"G-good morning, King... I couldn't sleep, thinking about today..."

"So I see. Ah well. If I were in your shoes, I'm sure I'd be nervous, too. But we have a whole hour until we get to school. Let's chat and see if we can get you prepared psychologically."

"Huh? It only takes twenty minutes to get to school."

"Yeah, by bicycle. But starting today, you're walking. It's only about four miles. Should take around an hour. Actually, I'd prefer it if you ran, but you're so out of shape you're liable to bust a knee. Now give me your phone."

Kenta handed it over meekly. I grabbed it and started tapping.

"I'm downloading this running app I use myself. You can set it for walking, too. It gives you goal distances and times, so use it to keep your pace. It also records your movements. You're going to send me a screenshot of the results page every day. No chance to slack off, get it?"

"…An hour? Th-that's kind of a long time…"

"It's a good pace for burning fat. You'll soon get used to it. Anyway, it's only walking. If you walk seven, eight miles a day, you'll easily manage to bring your fitness levels up. By the way, I already walked like six miles to get here just to take you to school, and now I have to walk four miles back. So quit complaining."

"…I'll grab my stuff, King."

✳

After I said hi to Yumiko, we left the house together. The path through the rice fields didn't have that same springlike "Ah, the joys of youth" vibe with Kenta like they did with Yua and Yuuko. Eh, it is what it is.

"Last night, you got me all fired up with that talk about three-dimensional boobies, but overnight I think I cooled down some… And now I wonder if maybe I was right, that it's going to be too tough for me…"

As we walked, Kenta began whining.

"Also, I took a look at that training plan you messaged me with last night… It looks like torture, but I guess I can give it a go… It's just…"

The basic plan of action I had set up for Kenta went like this: morning weight lifting followed by a protein shake. Lunch and dinner would be tofu noodles, plus chicken soup with a ton of veggies. No other food. And for drinks, only water, tea, black coffee, and black tea without milk or sugar.

By the way, tofu noodles are a super-handy diet food; you can buy them at any convenience store. Like the name indicates, they're mostly made of tofu, so they're low-carb while still being filling. And they give you a good hit of protein for only around a hundred calories per meal. Perfect. The rest of the nutrients come from the veggies in the soup. I gave Yumiko careful written instructions so she knew what to cook for Kenta.

For the weight training, I was going to have Kenta do a thirty-minute fitness challenge catered toward total beginners. If I threw him in at the deep end with a hard-core training routine, he'd probably injure himself. A beginner's course would be more than challenging enough for someone who usually avoided all physical activity.

"Just relax. I calculated everything based off your height and starting weight. Just do what I tell you to do, and weight loss is assured. Anyway, I'm not trying to make you skinny. We just need to get you back to where you were before you started skipping school. The things I really want you to focus on are your social skills and your communication skills."

Kenta nodded obediently.

"But I haven't been to school in three months. I don't even know how I'm supposed to walk back into the classroom..."

"Well, don't worry about that, because hardly anyone even knows who you are. Look, to be honest, you don't even register on anyone's radar. You're lucky that the new school year just started, and you've already been assigned to a whole new class. This way, nobody even missed you, and I can assure you there's zero gossip going on about you not coming to school."

"I...I kinda knew that, but hearing you say it all out loud makes me feel like crap..."

"That said, there's a few students who've realized we've got an empty desk in class. So technically, that does count as a rumor, but nothing too serious. I do think there's a few kids who were in your class last year as well. But it's not a problem. We'll just play it by ear. Today, at any rate, you'll be with me, Yuuko, Yua, Kaito Asano, Kazuki Mizushino, Haru Aomi, and Yuzuki Nanase. All the members of Team Chitose. So you can try to develop your social skills with us."

"Wow, those are all the most popular kids in our grade. Everyone in school knows their names… You really are the king, King. But to be honest, I'm not confident I'm gonna be able to hold a conversation with kids like them…"

"You've got it wrong. These are all the popular kids who I can vouch for personally. No matter how awkward or dorky you act, they'll be fair to you. None of them will try to put you down or look down their noses at you. There's not a bully or a jerk in the whole bunch. Think of this as a training level. No 'game overs.' Just relax and give it your best shot."

"…Feels more like I'm being thrown straight to the final boss."

"Good. Once you've conquered the final boss, you can handle the slimes and goblins with ease."

We were strolling along. I was feeling fine, but Kenta was already starting to huff and puff a little.

"S-so I guess I should make sure not to mention anime or light novels, right? Otherwise, they'll think I'm gross."

I was kinda impressed—not everyone can maintain such a tiny voice when they're out of breath, too.

"You really are an idiot. Why would you have to hide your interests? Popular kids and otaku aren't all that different, you know. Besides, what else have you even got to talk about, hmm?"

"But…I'm not confident I can read the room… What if I say the wrong thing?"

"I hate that expression. *Read the room.* It's just a way people have of trying to suppress individualistic expression."

"Yeah, but it's true… If I want to be popular, I need to know how to gauge the mood of the group, right? And fit in?"

Kenta was looking up at me quizzically.

"Just forget about reading the room altogether. It's far too broad a guideline to be of any use. I told you that there are different types of popular kids. Stop making assumptions. Don't look at us all and think we're a bunch of pretentious jerks with some kind of hive mind. Use your own judgment; don't just rely on your own preconceptions."

I don't know how it is in adult society these days, but in our school, there's a crazy amount of labeling and categorizing going on. All of it is so cynical and negative.

For example, *pretentious*. That word originally came about to criticize people who act better than others, but now it's thrown at anyone who actually puts effort into bettering themselves.

I'm not here to excuse people who diss the first category, either, but putting down people in the second category doesn't sit well with me especially. It's just jealousy, the whole crabs-in-a-bucket mentality. You slap a label on someone so you can mock them and try to drag them back down to your level. All so you can feel better about yourself even though you're not doing anything to improve your own lot in life. I think that's a pretty pathetic, meaningless way to live.

I continued.

"For example, it's definitely important to be careful not to say things that would upset someone else who's maybe feeling down or sensitive about something. But holding back your opinions just 'cause you know they differ from the majority, or hiding the things you're into because they're not mainstream, or putting too much stock in the whole adage about how *the nail that sticks up gets hammered down*… I think that's making a huge mistake. Everyone's an individual and should feel free to be themselves. It's so much more interesting if everyone allows themselves to be unique, right? So assert yourself. Say what you believe is right, talk about the things that excite you, and own it."

I paused for breath, turning to look at Kenta.

"People who get the wrong idea about that and focus only on blending in—eventually, they'll blend in so well they might as well not be there at all."

*     *     *

Well, in my case, I read the room first, and then I use that to figure out how best to present myself. But that concept seemed a bit beyond Kenta.

"Being mindful of others and living your own way… Those are two separate things. Is that right?"

"Yeah, more or less."

"Well, can't you teach me some basic techniques for conversation?"

"If I taught you them now, you'd only panic and get it wrong when the time comes, and I'd have to remind you anyway. So we may as well wait."

"Whatever you say, King."

*

8:10 AM. Kenta and I were standing in front of the classroom for Year Two, Class Five. Through the window in the door, I could see that the other members of Team Chitose were all in attendance already. Homeroom started at eight thirty, but Kura was often late, so usually it was more like 8:35. In the twenty-five minutes we had available, Kenta's fate would be set.

"K-King… I'm sorry, but my stomach hurts all of a sudden. May I go to the nurse?"

"Oh, quit whining and get it together."

"It's the first day, so perhaps I should just take a quick peek and then leave…come back tomorrow…"

"Listen to me, Kenta. If you're really going to change, then this is the moment. It's all a mental game. All you have to do is make up your mind and take that first step. Then your life really will begin to change."

Kenta seemed to be ruminating over what I was saying.

"But the people who tell themselves: 'I'll change when this happens or when the timing's right…' They're kidding themselves.

The right time will never come. You'll just keep on making fresh excuses. And your initial enthusiasm will fade. You're just putting things off until one day you die. But if that's how you want to live, then be my guest."

"So if I decide to change right now... Then just making that decision will mean I've started changing already?"

I smiled. "Exactly. Come on; it's time."

I slung my arm around Kenta's shoulder and opened the door. "Morning, all!"

Kaito, Kazuki, Haru, and my other classmates all turned toward us. Instantly, question marks popped up above each of their heads. Metaphorically, of course.

"This is Kenta Yamazaki—he hasn't been in school since January. I, Saku Chitose, have convinced him to finally come back and join our class. A round of applause, everyone!"

...Clap, clap, clap.

Several people clapped hesitantly, prompted to do so by the energy in my voice. But it was clear they didn't really know what to make of the odd couple who had just waltzed in. They were all exchanging looks that basically said, "Who the heck is that?"

It goes without saying that Kenta was more bewildered than any of them. And alarmed. His lips were flapping soundlessly. It was as if he wanted to say, "King! Are you sure you meant to say that just now?!"

Ignoring him, I continued.

"And just FYI, the reason he hasn't been coming to school is that the princess of his otaku group—the object of his affection—hooked up with the group's prince instead of our boy Kenta. Yikes. I know I wouldn't have been able to come to school again if I knew my classmates found that out about me. So be extra-nice to him, okay? He's still mentally fragile."

Kenta had gone as pale as milk. He was gazing at me in absolute horror.

"K-King?!" he hissed. "Are you in demon mode right now?! Did you really have to say all that? No one knew about my situation, but now that you've told them, I'm going to be the biggest joke in class!"

"Exactly. Just roll with it and watch what happens."

…

…

"Aw, Chitose, you shouldn't have said all that. Don't worry, as a class, we'll all agree to pretend we never heard it. Let's just rewind and go back to two minutes ago, okay?"

It was Nanase who broke the awkward silence.

Then everyone in class began to chuckle.

As if on cue, Kazuki leaned in and started talking to Kenta like they were old buddies. "Saku, our resident airhead, tends to put his foot in his mouth sometimes, doesn't he? It happens more than you think. Kenta, you should head on in and take your seat, before Saku exposes any more of your personal secrets."

Kaito grinned and started joking around to keep the mood light. "By the way, this otaku group princess… Is she real? Like, a cute girl who actually likes anime and stuff? Does she cosplay for you? You got any pictures? I need pictures, dude."

Haru laughed and jumped in, too. "Geez! Just ignore them, Yamazaki. But seriously, though, how cute are you? You couldn't come to school 'cause you were heartbroken? Aw! You know, if Kaito was going to quit school every time he got shot down, he'd never be able to come to school again! He tries it on everything in a skirt and strikes out every time!"

Haru's bright smile and teasing tone helped to lift the general mood of the class even higher.

"King, what's going on…?" Kenta blinked at me in confusion.

"I told you—you're gonna be a joke. That will endear everyone to you way more than it would if you tried to hide the truth and acted all shady about where you've been. It's better to make fun of yourself and invite everyone else to join in. Wear your weakness with pride, and it'll make everyone feel more at ease around you."

I clapped Kenta on the back as I muttered this to him, sotto voce.

"But don't be all tense about it. Act like it was no big thing. Be matter-of-fact about it. Go on."

Kenta took a deep breath, and then in a tremulous yet determined voice, he took a step forward. "Ah yeah, well, she was really cute, though. She would always share her nuggets and fries at McDonald's. And she'd offer you a sip of her soda and stuff. She lent me a handkerchief at summer Comiket, and she said I didn't even have to give it back afterward. She was super kind. That's why I fell for her."

Kaito immediately responded to that.

"Oh, I totally get it! She sounds like a real nice girl. Any guy would fall for that type. What do you think, Haru?"

"Uh, what? You boys are so naive. I mean, maybe she gave away her fries and soda because she was on a diet. And the handkerchief thing… I mean, if I lent *you* a towel, Kaito, I sure wouldn't want it back!"

"What?!"

"'Cause it would be all stinky from your sweat! I'd rather you buy me a brand-new one than give the same one back!"

"But I thought girls liked the scent of a man's sweat?!"

Kaito and Haru had picked up Kenta's conversational ball and run off with it.

And Kenta was looking stricken.

"What's up?"

Kenta mumbled sadly as he watched Kaito and Haru continue to joke back and forth.

"I…I guess I look like I stink, after all…"

Ah, I see, so that's how he took that.

"Haru isn't the type to diss someone based on how they look. Anyway, she said it to Kaito, not you. Giving him a hard time, to her, is like saying good morning or how are you. It's just her way of being friendly. It shows familiarity. You wouldn't want to hang out with someone who didn't have any capacity for in-jokes or banter, would you?"

"There wasn't any banter or in-jokes in my otaku group…"

"That just means everyone was too scared of offending the others or hurting someone's feelings. And they didn't have enough confidence in themselves to expect that others wouldn't turn on them eventually. It takes time to get to know people, sure, but a little good-natured teasing and banter brings people together. Does it look like Haru and Kaito seem afraid of offending each other?"

"No… They look like good friends."

"Right. Banter forms strong bonds. It shows that what's between you is strong enough to handle being tested a little. It's real communication, no walking on eggshells or blowing smoke up each other's asses."

Kenta still didn't seem fully convinced, so I continued.

"You want friends who get all red in the face and offended just 'cause you teased them a little? You want friends who only speak in trite platitudes? Does that sound like a good relationship to you?"

True, it's a fine line to walk, between banter and bullying. A lighthearted joke, coming from a popular kid, might end up being taken as a serious jab by an unpopular kid.

Of course, you should be careful not to presume. But if you get too hung up on hurting the other person's feelings even a little, you'll never get anywhere.

You have to think about the intention behind the words. Is it kind, or is it malicious? It's good to work on cultivating the ability to tell the difference.

"You heard Kazuki call me the resident airhead just before, didn't you? If I got all butt-hurt and started yelling 'Who are you calling an airhead, asshole?!' would that retroactively make Kazuki a jerk? Just 'cause of the way I took it?"

Kenta rubbed his chin thoughtfully.

"...No, I'd think you were the one who couldn't take a joke."

"See? Unpopular kids tend to let their own insecurities color every interaction they have. I mean, straight-up bullying is always a dick move, but sometimes a person really is just trying to playfully tease, and the other person misunderstands and blows everything out of proportion. Remember what I said about the fundamentals of making conversation?"

"You said it's about trying to get to know the other person... and wanting them to get to know you."

"Precisely. If you get to know them well, you'll be able to tell whether they're trying to put you down, or if they're just teasing you in a loving manner. It's a mark of trust, the ability to identify that key difference. When it's friendly teasing, the best thing to do is tease right back."

"But...what if they really are trying to be mean?"

"Then you crush them. Don't worry, I'll be there to back you up if that happens." I clapped him on the back again, a little harder this time.

"Go on, try teasing Kaito and co. But think loving teasing. Loving teasing."

Blinking rapidly, Kenta took a step forward, toward the rest of Team Chitose.

"I...I have a feeling my sweat stinks less than Asano's at least."

"Aw, man! My sweat has floral top notes! It's a complex bouquet!"

Grinning, Haru picked up the conversational ball that Kaito passed and threw it back. "Chitose and Mizushino may be all right, but you, Kaito? You're the typical sweaty, stinky jock!"

Kenta seemed to have gathered together some courage.

"I actually, uh, have this cologne that's supposed to resemble the scent of teenage girls..."

"Really, Kenta? Let me get a sniff of that later!"

"Ew, you guys are too much! If you wear that stinky cologne to school, I'll hose you down in the schoolyard!!!"

There, they were playing a good game of conversational ball. The two of them had naturally stood aside a little, making a space in the Team Chitose circle for Kenta.

Yuuko reached out and poked Kenta in the chest. *Stop that.*

"Kentacchi, later on I'll show you how to style your hair with wax."

Yua was smiling kindly at Kenta, too.

"Yamazaki, sorry I couldn't come yesterday because of club practice. I'm glad to finally get to see you in person, though! Will you lend me a good light novel sometime?"

"Thank you both, I—"

"Aw, no need to thank us! Welcome to Year Two, Class Five! Welcome to Yuuko Hiiragi's Angels!"

"Exactly. Welcome to the class!"

Kenta blinked, blushing as these two beautiful girls welcomed him.

I debated kicking him in his nasty little ass, but I managed to control myself.

\*

"All right, guys, take your seats."

It was 8:35 AM, and Kura entered the room right on cue. His gaze flicked briefly over to Kenta and me. Giving me a quick "Seems you succeeded, then," kind of look, he headed on over to take up his position behind the teacher's lectern.

"I'm gonna take the roll call."

Everyone took their seats, chirping "Present!" as their names were called.

Haru Aomi, Kaito Asano, Saku Chitose, Yuuko Hiiragi, Kazuki Mizushino, Yuzuki Nanase, Yua Uchida...

"Kenta Yamazaki."

"P-present! I haven't been to school since final semester last year, but I'm back now. I'm, uh, Kenta Yamazaki. Y-Yuuko cut my hair like this for me. And Kin...er, Chitose said I look like a hippo emerging from a pond with weeds on my head. It's nice to finally meet you all!"

Kenta had taken it upon himself to stand up and introduce himself to the class.

I grinned to myself.

*Not bad, not bad, Kenta. You learn fast.*

There was an awkward pause of about three seconds before the class erupted in laughter.

Standing up to introduce himself in the middle of roll call was a dorky move, the kind of move that highlighted an inability to, as they say, "read the room." But at the same time, he'd name-dropped both Yuuko and me—and even made a joke. Everyone in class therefore felt comfortable giving him the laugh he was fishing for. I don't really like it, but I can't deny that name-dropping a popular kid's name is always effective. By letting everyone know that Yuuko had cut his hair, and that I had been there to witness it, he went from potentially being seen as a greasy shut-in to a lovable goofball character instead. The whole class seemed to make up their minds about him in an instant, quickly adopting him as one of their own.

After harboring all that jealousy and resentment toward popular kids, Kenta seemed to know better than anyone how useful it could be to borrow the popularity of others. Overall, his bold move had paid off, and it made him look self-secure and even masculine in the eyes of the class.

"Oh, I see. Well, take it easy until you've settled in. And if there's anything you're not sure about, see our class president. He'll take care of it."

"Kura! What have we told you about neglecting your duties as an educator, hmm?!"

*

At lunchtime, we sat down at the usual table. Over the course of a week, it had become "our" table. Of course, Kenta was invited to eat lunch with us.

"King, everyone's staring at me..."

"Stop looking around. Just be cool. Act like you belong. I know we're all good-looking, but there are tons of popular kids who aren't conventionally handsome. Pretend you're one of them."

"But I can't eat while I'm being stared at like this..."

"Who cares about them? They don't matter. They can't do anything for you, and they can't take anything from you, either. They've got no skin in this game. Focus on the people who are willing to share their precious time with you right here, right now."

Tremulously, Kenta pulled his lunch out of his bag. Yuuko's eyes widened.

"What's that, Kentacchi?"

"It's...tofu noodles and chicken vegetable soup..."

Haru whirled around. "Whaaat?! Based on your size, you need more food than that, Yamazaki! You need to eat carbs, or you won't have enough energy!"

"Er, I'm actually on a diet. King said I could eat only this."

"King? Oh, you mean Chitose. Are you doing calories in, calories out? You have to exercise, too, you know!"

"King's made up a training plan for me. I never usually exercise, but he said he's taken that into account."

Kenta showed Haru the training and diet plan I sent him on

the LINE app. Haru leaned in to see, oblivious to the closeness between Kenta and her. Kenta, meanwhile, blushed.

"Whoa. Chitose, this is devilish. The poor guy doesn't even have an athletic background, and he's been in the house for however long, but you still have him doing hard-core workouts like this?"

I lifted my chin and put my hands on my hips, trying to look regal.

"Lowly Subject Haru. In this world, there is much happiness to be found in ignorance. Simply trust in the words of the king, and the way will become clear."

It was cool, though. Sure, if I had Kenta doing three laps of the butterfly stroke in the River Sanzu, that mythical boundary between life and death, he would crack. But I wasn't that cruel. In fact, I had spent a lot of time balancing my diet and workout plan. He'd survive.

By this point, though, Nanase and Yua had taken an interest in Kenta's lunch, too.

"Dieting!"

"Good for you!"

"Well, butter my biscuits, keepin' mah weight steady's hard 'nuff, and here y'are a-fixin' t'lose a whole barrel! Sounds right awful, it does!" (Translation: It takes all I've got just to keep from gaining, so to see you doing all that and actually trying to lose major weight! You must be having a terrible time of it.)

"Y'cain't jus' diet in secret'n show up outta the blue all skinny-like—'s kinda sneaky, if'n y'ask me. Y'gotta come out'n say it! We better keep up, y'all!" (Translation: You're right, Yuzuki. But for me, I feel like dieting in secret and then showing up one day suddenly having lost weight… There's something sneaky about that. It's better to be up-front first! We'd better step up our game, too!)

Ah, they were doing that exaggerated Fukui accent thing again today. The retro version.

"But what made you want to start dieting, Kenta?" Kaito leaned in, looking curious.

"Uh… I want to show the girl who rejected me what she's missing, I guess."

"Ooh, are we talking about our love lives?" I said. "Yesss! Tell us everything, from start to finish, come on!"

Kenta shot me a look. I nodded in a "Knock yourself out" kind of way.

"Er… Well… I was in this otaku hobbyist group. We met via social media. We would hang out on weekends to talk about anime, light novels, stuff like that…and we went to Comiket together and other events and stuff. There were three boys, including me, and one girl."

"That's not many… I was picturing a bigger group somehow."

"I guess there's bigger groups in the major cities, but we're in the sticks of Fukui, so there's just fewer people in general."

"So anyway, you fell for this girl?"

Kenta nodded. Kaito and the others were all listening intently.

"Her name's Miki. You write it with the characters for *beauty* and *princess*. And she really *was* like the princess of our group. Of course, she can't hold a candle to any of the girls sitting at this table… But otaku girls with even half-decent faces are super rare. We treated her like she was an idol."

"Does she cosplay?" Kaito seemed really interested in that prospect, for some reason.

"Oh yeah. I mean, she was always in cosplay when we met up."

Smiling, Kenta began naming some female characters from anime. Ones who even I had heard of.

Kaito leaned in, eyes wide.

"Really?! Okay, okay, I'm picturing it…'cept in my mind, I'm seeing Yuzuki and Ucchi in cosplay instead…"

""Jus' geddidout!!!"" (Translation: Just get it out, in the Fukui dialect. Though whether this was said to encourage Kenta to continue with his story or was just them telling Kaito to erase his mental cosplay imagery, I can't say.)

Those two were really quite the pair.

"Well, we weren't that close at first. It's obvious I was the worst-looking of the three of us guys, but one of the guys who was kinda average, like Miki—he became like our group leader. So she talked to him a lot more."

Kenta took a sip of water before continuing.

"But then all of a sudden, it seemed like we were talking more and more. Not alone, but like, in a group setting, she started talking to me, and like I said before, she would offer me some of her soda or fries or whatever. And she started responding to stuff I said in our LINE group chat…"

"Wow, it sure sounds like she was into you. So you asked her out?"

"I started to think that maybe…there was a chance. And I already knew I liked her. So I took the plunge and invited her to meet me at a café…and told her I wanted her to be my girlfriend. But…"

Kenta swallowed and hesitated, and I jumped in.

"She told him: *'Excuse me? Are you delusional? I would never date someone like you. Don't you even realize what your own social status is? Loser!'*…"

Kaito and the others all gasped in horrified indignation.

"What?! Is she crazy?! What's she talking about social status for? She was in the same nerd group you were! And who cares about social status when it comes to romance? Hasn't this bitch ever heard of Romeo and Juliet?!"

Kaito slammed his fist down on the table as Haru rolled her eyes.

"I agree, Kaito, but when a meathead guy like *you* references Romeo and Juliet, it's just painfully obvious you've never even read a single Shakespeare play."

*Romeo and Juliet were also from* "two households, both alike in dignity," *but whatever.*

Kenta chuckled a little. "That's not all, though," he said. "She was already dating the dude who was the leader of our group. She'd used me to make him jealous so he'd fall for her, since her other attempts weren't working. That's why she was chatting me up. I guess it worked for her..."

Kenta trailed off, clearly reliving the painful memories.

"...After that, they made a new LINE group chat without me, and they made fun of me and my reaction there. Actually, right after I asked Miki out, the leader and the other guy popped up out of nowhere and started saying stuff like *'Have you ever looked in the mirror, loser?'* and stuff... I guess it was my fault for getting the wrong impression, though..."

"No, it wasn't!"

Kaito slammed the table again, bubbling over once more. Now everyone in the cafeteria was looking at us.

"You were totally sincere! How dare they just take a giant crap on your feelings?! What a small-minded bunch of jerks! Hey, Kenta... Call them out this weekend! I'll kick all their asses!"

Kaito looked ready to grab Kenta's phone and dial up his ex-otaku buddies right then and there.

Kazuki put a soothing hand on his shoulder and tried to calm him down. "Just take it easy," he said. "...Let's put all the hot-headed machismo stuff aside and really think about this, okay? Seems to me the only thing to do is to become the best man you can be and make this girl eat her words. After all, isn't that why Saku has taken you under his wing, Kenta?"

"Yes. I know I've been a weak loser...but I'm willing to try."

Kenta smiled shyly, and that was when I knew he'd be fine. He'd get stronger, now that he'd really owned up to how weak he'd been.

Haru interjected then, putting her hand down in the middle of the table.

"You are *not* a weak loser, Yamazaki! *They're* the losers."

Nanase nodded, putting her hand down on the table on top of

Haru's. "I actually agree with Haru for once. If you follow Chitose's instructions and do your best, you're sure to become the best you can be. Then you can stick it to all of them. Okay?"

Kazuki and Kaito both slapped their hands down on the pile.

"Yeah, you have to rise above those jerks and become the better man. If you need any help with your training, you can come to me anytime, Kenta."

"Same for me. We'll leave the finessing up to Saku, but if there's anything we can help you with, don't hesitate to ask. In exchange, you can lend me some choice titles from your otaku collection..."

Haru rolled her eyes and smacked his hand.

Yuuko and Yua also put their hands on the pile.

"You'll be fine as long as you just follow Saku's instructions," said Yuuko. "Saku will never let you down, Kentacchi."

"But maybe lay off the whole 'harem slut' thing. Sooner rather than later," Yua added.

They both grinned. I noticed that Yua's free hand was clenched in a fist. Hope she didn't plan to use it. Meanwhile, Kenta was sitting there looking like all his dreams had just come true.

"...There ya go. Training level over. It was easy, wasn't it?"

I was the final one to add my hand to the pile. After hesitating for a second, Kenta finally placed his hand on top.

"Thank you for having my back, everyone... Was that the right thing to say, King?"

I grinned.

Then we all raised our hands in the air, cheering as one.

There, now it was official. He was endorsed by Team Chitose.

*

"...So what was that whole song and dance about?"

"Ah, you caught me."

After lunch, we were on our way back to the classroom when

Kazuki pulled me aside. Just like Nanase did last week. My luck was all over the place, it seemed.

"You weren't exactly being subtle. Look, I don't discriminate, but I do differentiate. That kid just isn't the type that belongs in a group like ours. Sooner or later, he's gonna realize that, too, suffer a massive inferiority complex, then have a complete breakdown."

"Listen, I just forgot to explain things to you beforehand. I wasn't trying to pull a fast one on you. I don't have the energy for that."

I gave Kazuki a brief explanation of the situation.

"Honestly, there's a ton of other routes you could have gone down that didn't involve him having to hang out with us. You could have gotten him hooked on Ucchi or Yuuko, used them as bait to bring him back. Or you could have just shamed him and lectured him into returning to school. This way…it just causes the most inconvenience for everyone, Saku."

Kazuki almost seemed annoyed with me or something.

"Dude, I thought about all that. But it just didn't seem right. It didn't fit with my aesthetic."

"Your 'I am so great, and everyone loves me' aesthetic?"

"Yeah. But it doesn't sound as cool when you say it like that…"

Kazuki sighed deeply. "All right, all right. Whatever. If that's what you need to do to feel good about yourself, then fine. You could have just said you felt bad for him and wanted to help him out of the goodness of your heart."

"Well, I don't. I only want to do it to boost my image. You don't get an opportunity like this every day. I wanna be Saku Chitose, the class president who takes care of business and helps the teacher deal with his little problem student."

"Right, but no one in class, no one in our group even, knew what you were doing. You want to show how superior you are? At least make sure people understand what the hell is going on.

Otherwise, what's the point of even doing it? Your actions are completely illogical, you know."

Kazuki trailed off then and shrugged. His grin said he was willing to let all this slide.

"Have you ever turned down anyone's request for help, brah?"

Man, he was pissing me off. Don't "brah" me. You're a Fukui country bumpkin like the rest of us.

I hoped that one of his fangirls stole his change of underwear during training so he had to walk home stinky.

"I don't help out everyone I see who's in trouble. Only the people who come directly to me."

"So that means you assist everyone who asks you. You act like you're such a cool guy, but you're really a regular old Good Samaritan. And you're so sneaky about it. Why can't you just be more honest? Drop the tough-guy act. Maybe you'd have a few less enemies if you did that."

"Ah, shut up, asshole. Don't try to label me! Anyway, you're always bending over backward to get people to like you, too. Can't you see the irony, hmm?"

I was getting annoyed with this conversation, and I wanted to change the subject.

"I'm nice when it suits me. But you seem to have this Kenta kid fooled. No matter how nice you have us all act toward him, the social hierarchy still stands. You think he can change that just based on his tone of voice, his conversational skills, or what seat he takes at the cafeteria? Too bad, the social structure has already been solidified by this point. Second year is way too late to change that."

"…Yeah, probably."

Social structure this, social hierarchy that.

I'm so sick of it all.

I knew Kazuki himself didn't really care that much about things like that. He was just speaking in broad terms here. But the school hierarchy in this Podunk Fukui town…had deep roots.

Kazuki kept on doggedly. "If he had any knack for this stuff, he'd have dealt with his issues himself. Locking himself in his room, avoiding school, and making excuses… That kind of thing just proves where his position in society ought to be."

"I'm not arguing with you there." I meant it, too. "What do you think of Kenta as a person, though, Kazuki?"

"Honestly? I don't mind him. He's pretty funny. I wouldn't mind being casual school pals with him."

I knew there was a *but* coming, so I stayed silent and waited for it.

Kazuki sighed.

"But…I don't really want to hang out with him every day, like how I feel about you, Kaito, Yuuko, Ucchi, Yuzuki, and Haru. He doesn't have that spark. He may be a novelty and a source of amusement now, but it's going to get old fast."

"Yeah, I know. I agree totally."

I made that clear to Kenta himself, after all, didn't I?

"But just picking something and setting your mind to do something… Don't you think it's kinda…cool and 'hard-boiled' of me?"

"I have no idea what you're talking about. I never do. Anyway, I prefer soft-boiled eggs myself."

"Okay, let's use your metaphor, then. You've got this runny egg in front of you… Don't you wanna throw some soy sauce on that bad boy? Improve it some?"

"I usually cut off the tops and sprinkle on some salt, myself."

"Let's try another example. Say Yuuko and I were drowning in the sea, which one would you save?"

"Yuuko, obviously."

"Even if the waters were filled with crocodiles and piranhas?"

"If the waters are filled with crocodiles and piranhas, you're both on your own. I'll light a candle for you sometime. If I remember."

"…So that's where you fall, huh?"

∗

After school that day, I gave Kura a basic progress update up on the roof. Kura had only asked me to get Kenta back to school, so I guess it would be more accurate to call it a final report. Everything I was doing from this point forth was optional.

After hearing me out, Kura said, "You definitely went about this in the Saku Chitose way, didn't you?"

"What do you mean by that?"

"OTT and overdramatic. Doing it for the look of it. You're like a titty bar waitress in her thirties, wearing a school blazer and pretending she's in her teens."

"Are you trying to start trouble with me, sir?"

Kura cackled and blew a stream of Lucky Strike cigarette smoke out of his nostrils.

"Perish the thought. But I like a brazen titty bar waitress in her thirties who pretends to be a teenager for the laughs, rather than one in her twenties who almost seems embarrassed that she's no longer in her teens. Being considered a hero is mostly nonsense, just meaningless optics. Unless you've got the skills to unleash a powerful surprise attack when the moment calls for it."

"Meaningless optics?"

Kura narrowed his eyes. Maybe smoke got into them. I couldn't read his expression.

"Not that I'm blaming your methodology. Getting sidetracked and taking the long route is where the real spice of life is to be found. After all, sometimes we have to move ahead faster than we want. While you're young, you should take time for detours. Focus too much on getting to adulthood in the most efficient way, and you'll end up an efficient adult with little in the way of character. You'll end up versatile, functional, and entirely replaceable."

"If only Kazuki were here to hear this."

"Never mind him. He's different from you. He's the type to seriously consider whether a detour would mean something to him or if it would simply be a waste of time. Whether that's the right decision doesn't matter. He'll end up like a mass-produced, consumable product."

"Yikes, imagine a world flooded with mass-produced Kazukis."

I slurped down some of the iced café latte I'd bought at the nearby convenience store. Thinking back over my spat with Kazuki earlier, I suddenly realized I wanted to get Kura's opinion on something.

"Can I ask you something, Kura?"

"There's still four days until payday. I've only got twelve bucks in my pocket. Can't lend you what I don't have, kid."

Kura pulled a crumpled note and two coins from his suit pocket to show me.

"Geez, next you'll be borrowing from us. But listen, Kura. What do you think about social hierarchy?"

"Hmm, that's an unusually abstract question from you."

Kura fell silent, sucking down his cigarette for a while before speaking again.

"To answer in equally abstract terms… Social hierarchy is inevitable. It's our cross to bear, as human beings."

"Our cross to bear, huh?"

"Living life your own way is flowery rhetoric that sounds good, but there aren't many people out there who can go their own way in the society and times we live in, with the backgrounds we come from and the paths that are open to us. Most people never make the effort to recalibrate their moral compasses and social altimeters to try to understand what the inner landscapes of other people are really like."

The tip of his cigarette let off a crackling sound as it glowed red.

"So instead we simply observe others and ask ourselves if what they're doing is the thing we should all be doing or not. We want to drag everyone down to our level so we can reassure ourselves we're in the right. We can't relax unless we do that. Rather than strike out alone and risk failure, it's better to fail as a group, relying on the safety and security of the herd. That's how we live our lives, like herd animals."

Kura stubbed out his stump of a cigarette in his pocket ashtray, then immediately lit up another one.

"But every now and then, you encounter people who are making their own path, people who never stop to wonder if what they're doing is what's normal or right. People like you, and Mizushino, too."

It sounded like Kura was actually choosing his words thoughtfully for once.

"But people who are making their own path, not wondering if they're in the right... That doesn't mean they actually *are* in the right, now, does it?"

I remained silent, listening for the rest.

"When people come across someone like that, there's a range of ways they react to them. If they feel like that person is coming from the same place as them, they'll follow. Then you have the blind sheep who follow anyone who looks confident. But you also have those who simply observe, as well as those who seek to distance themselves as much as possible, claiming that person is simply misguided. Those differences lead to the construction of a social hierarchy. Only the ones in the lead get to set the standard that everyone else is supposed to reach."

"...Somehow, I feel like your moral compass is more righteous than any other adult's I know."

"No one's got a completely righteous moral compass. Certainly not you kids. We have to decide for ourselves what morality means to us. That's all we have to go on."

How did I get to this point, again?

The thought seemed to come out of nowhere.

My compass was pointing right up at the sky, probably.

Toward the moon... The moon I reached my hand up to that day...

Then Kura yawned, distracting me from my nebulous thoughts.

"Incidentally, I don't really care whether I'm right. I'm not headed in any specific direction anyway. I just go with the flow, wherever the tide takes me. As long as the direction I'm headed in has booze, cigarettes, and titty bars, I'm fine with that."

"Replace *titty bars* with *women*, and you'll sound fifty percent less asshole-ish."

I decided to stop thinking about the heavy stuff any further.

"Good job, though. It looks like you're planning to stick with Yamazaki for a while longer. But from here on, you're on your own, okay?"

Kura got to his feet with a "Hup!"

"You didn't even give me any guidelines or advice to begin with."

"I pointed you at the kid and gave you a simple instruction, and I thought that would suffice. Which it did."

I got to my feet as well, swiping the dust off the seat of my pants.

"You'll do anything to pass the buck, won't you? I think it's scandalous on the part of a so-called educator. Once your paycheck comes in, you should take Kenta and me to lunch to say thank-you—"

"Whoops! Almost time for my private session at the gentleman's club!"

"Get back here, old man. It's not even dark yet. And you've only got twelve bucks."

"Listen, Chitose. You have something far more precious, far more valuable than money. You might not understand it right now, but someday…with the wisdom of age…"

"Don't think you can distract me with some sappy 'Youth is worth more than money' talk."

"…Ah, hello? Yes, I'd like to book a private room with Hitomi tonight at nine PM…"

"Hey! Are you seriously booking a call girl right now?!!!"

*

I sent Kenta a quick message saying "*I'm done*," and he instantly responded with "*I'm waiting by the school gates.*"

I made sure I had all my stuff and then headed out of the school building. I could see Kenta standing by the school gates with his back to me. I already told him I'd walk home with him today, so we could go over his progress so far.

"The heck is wrong with you, man? The school gates? Why couldn't you wait in the classroom? Meeting by the gates—are you a schoolgirl with a crush on me or something?"

"Ah, I just thought this would be the easiest landmark to meet at… I mean, I figured this way I'd be able to catch you if you forgot and tried to go home without me…"

"Forget the schoolgirl with a crush; you're actually just a stalker. You could have just called me if it came to that."

Kenta's eyes widened, as if the thought had never occurred to him. Shaking my head, I started walking.

"So how did it go? Your first day back at school?"

"Uh, well. This probably sounds overdramatic, but I have to say…it was the kind of day that made me want to rethink my entire life up until this point…"

"You weren't getting baptized in the Ganges River or anything.

You keep saying stuff like that, and you'll be easy prey for cultists and Ponzi schemers."

"No, no, I really mean it, though. It's like, wow, what kind of tiny, sheltered world have I been living in all this time, you know?"

"Oh yeah? …What do you mean, specifically?"

"Honestly… Popular kids are *nice*. No one tried to put me down, and none of them did any backstabbing or bitching about any other kids, either. They were super nice and welcoming even though I inserted myself into their group out of nowhere, and I look like…this. Everyone's so…open-minded and earnest, and they even took my side when I told them about my personal problem… I mean, really, one day with them was already way more uplifting than all the times I spent with my otaku hobbyist group…"

Hearing Kenta say all this made me feel really good about dragging him out of his otaku den and pushing him back into the real world.

I'd been a little concerned about the possibility that exposing Kenta to popular kids might backfire and lead him to develop an inferiority complex, but it seemed like he'd really warmed to us. Good—that meant I could cut him loose sooner, and he'd be fine on his own. At any rate, the chances of him wanting to retreat to the safety of his bedroom seemed to have dropped dramatically.

"What about your conversational skills? That's what you were worried about."

"I can't say it went smoothly or anything, but I managed to get through it! I asked questions like you said. And I tried to open up about myself, too, and find points in common. Communication, making conversation… It's a legitimate skill, isn't it?"

"…In other words?"

"I know you kept telling me it's all about wanting to get to know the other person, King… But when I actually put those things into practice, the words just started flowing. I guess all I need is practice! The reason I always sucked at making conversation was because I got hung up on my own insecurities... I didn't care to get to know others, and I feared them getting to know me then rejecting me..."

"Well, yeah. If you're only using your conversational skills to find out about someone else's interests, but you're not actually interested in them, then it's like trying to build a secure castle out of papier-mâché. It's not the conversation that's the objective. It's improving relationships. If you're not sincere, the other person will be able to tell."

"...Before I met you, I don't think I even thought that hard about sincerity. I was like, how do you make yourself seem sincere?"

"Good. Then at least you were questioning it."

Kenta nodded, smiling. It looked like a great weight had been lifted off his shoulders over the course of the day.

"I guess I've realized that complaining all the time and making excuses won't ever lead to any kind of personal growth..."

In only one day, Kenta's mindset had progressed this much. I was genuinely pleased to see it.

"...That's one of your good points, Kenta." I threw that out there as a casual, offhand remark.

"...One of my good points? What makes you say that?"

"You've got the ability to recognize where you've gone wrong and have taken steps to correct it. Until now, you've been way too entrenched in otaku culture. Of course, I'm not saying you have to abandon that mindset completely. It's one way of seeing the world, after all. And I'm not saying that popular kids are always in the right."

Kenta didn't seem to realize I was trying to give him a compliment here.

But that was fine.

One day, Kenta would look back on this and be able to feel proud of how he'd grown.

Figuring there was no need to say any more on this topic, I changed the subject.

"By the way, Kenta... What did you think of the other members of Team Chitose? Who would you date if you had the option?"

Kenta blushed. "Wh-what?" He flailed. "...Wh-why would you ask me something like that, all of a sudden...?"

"Oh, relax. It's a totally normal topic of conversation among kids like us. I'm ready to cheer you on, as long as it's not someone I'm interested in myself."

"Y-yeah, but... Uh...okay, then. If I had to pick someone...if I absolutely had to... You won't tell her, will you? Okay, if I had to pick someone...it would be—"

"Oh, let me warn you first that Yuuko and Yua are already on my list. Sorry about that."

"...Th-then, what about Nanase?"

"Sorry..."

"Aomi...?"

"Hate to inform you..."

"Then there's no one left for you to cheer me on with!"

"Not true. You still have your pick between Kazuki and Kaito. Lucky you!"

"Aw, man..."

\*

That weekend, on a sunny Saturday afternoon, Yuuko, Kenta, and I all met at the entrance to the Lpa mall. Kenta was in his school uniform as instructed, and Yuuko and I were wearing our regular clothes.

"King, Yuuko... Thanks for giving up your weekend time for me." Kenta's eyes kept darting about.

"No worries. This is actually a date between Yuuko and me,

and us helping you pick clothes is kinda like if we were at an amusement park, and we wanted to go into the haunted house."

"That's right!"

"...Is the sight of me trying to improve my appearance really such a monstrous thing to you guys?"

Lpa was filled with little kids and their parents, junior high schoolers, high schoolers, college kids, grown-ups, old folks, the whole spectrum. I guess it was the weekend and all, but didn't they have anywhere else to hang out?

"By the way, Kentacchi, have you lost a little weight?" Yuuko prodded Kenta's chest and belly as she spoke.

"Uh, y-yeah. I've been weighing myself every day, and I've lost four pounds."

Kenta was as jittery and nervous as ever, but I guess I could give him a pass today.

"Wow, you really must have been feeling the effects of staying inside all day. Four pounds in one week—that's amazing! And you've even mastered how to style your hair with wax, like I showed you at school! Good job!"

...I take it back.

Yuuko was wearing a light, off-the-shoulder top with short-shorts. It was the kind of outfit that could look a little trashy, but she made it elegant with her sophisticated rose-gold necklace and pinkie ring—and her little leather shoulder bag. The top's exposed neckline offered the faintest suggestion of cleavage, especially if she leaned forward. It was designed to kill a virgin instantly.

I leaned in to whisper in Kenta's ear.

"Listen here, Kenta. Sometimes a man has to rise to the occasion, you know what I'm saying? And then other times, he needs to show serious self-restraint. You dig me?"

"S-s-stop it! You're just making me even more aware of it! I was busy trying to steel my mind and count backward from a hundred, but now you've distracted me!"

Kenta whispered back to me, his face constricted.

I grinned and kept whispering.

"If you drop your wallet on the ground, maybe she'll pick it up and give you a bird's-eye view."

"Stop it, King! Don't say stuff like that!"

Yuuko tilted her head curiously as she observed us both. "What's up?"

""Ahem!""

Frowning, Yuuko continued with what she'd been saying.

"Well, I was about to say that if you go changing any more, Kentacchi, you'll lose all your Kenta-ness! I won't be able to pick you out of a crowd!"

"Huh?"

I slapped Kenta on the shoulder. "Well, that's why we're here. To give Kenta a new style. And with his diet starting to take effect, it should be easy to spruce him up and make him presentable, at the very least."

"For me, dressing up is about as difficult as making conversation… But I brought all of my savings with me today! I didn't end up using any of my New Year's gift money this year, what with being stuck in the house and all."

Kenta whipped out his wallet, which was attached to his pants with a chain. It was covered in studs, with what looked like the design of a cross. Time (and money) was of the essence today, so I decided to just pretend I hadn't seen it.

"Today we'll be buying new glasses, some tops, pants, shoes, and a bag… The whole set from head to toe. Yuuko, where should we start?"

"Hmm, I think glasses first. It takes time to have them made up, and once we've got the right look for his face, that'll guide us when choosing the rest of the outfit!"

"Okay, let's start there."

*

We headed into JINS, the eyewear store, and we all started looking through the selection for some glasses that would suit Kenta.

"Personally, I feel most comfortable in this style of glasses…"

""No.""

Yuuko and I were unanimous. The glasses Kenta had picked out were similar to the ones he was already wearing. They had thin metal frames.

"Those kinds of glasses are the standard type, but few people are actually suited for them. Maybe a really hot actor or a smart businessman in a nice suit could pull them off, but they're too severe for your face. They just make you look geeky. Look, try them."

Kenta put on the glasses and stared at himself in the store's mirror. "Oh yeah, I see what you mean," he mumbled.

"See? It's obvious, isn't it?"

Then I took the glasses off Kenta and put them on my own face.

"…Man, I really *am* hot. I look cool and studious in these."

I took them off again and passed them to Yuuko.

"Man, I really *am* cute. I look like a hot teacher!"

"You two are messing with me."

Kenta put his selection back, then accepted the pair Yuuko was holding out.

"If you want to look like a cool guy, you should go for a thicker black-plastic frame, I think! Here, try this Wellington model."

"Hmm, I don't know… They do look cool, but I feel like they look better on guys with more masculine faces…like, with some stubble. Kenta's got pretty subtle features, so these might stand out too much. I think the Boston model would be better."

"King, what's Wellington? What's Boston?"

"In layman's terms, the ones that have more of a squarish shape are the Wellingtons. The ones that are more rounded off are the

Bostons. Your old glasses are more square, I'd say. Anyway, try the ones Yuuko picked out, and let's see."

""Nah...""

"Wow, that was fast!"

Kenta tried on the Bostons, too, but those didn't have that winning quality, either.

"You're right, Saku, the glasses stand out way too much. They say, 'I'm trying to stop being such an otaku, so I just bought black frames to look cooler.'"

"Right? Well, there's only so much that can be done. But those won't look good on me, either. My facial features are too delicate."

I took the glasses from Kenta and tried them on as I spoke.

"...I take it back. They look good. Damn, I'm so hot I can pull off anything. I look like some tortured, genius artist."

I took off the glasses and handed them to Yuuko. "Ooh! They look cute on me, too! I look like a young actress, secretly carrying on a clandestine relationship with you, Saku!"

"Can you two please stop?!" Kenta sighed, replacing the glasses Yuuko chose. "Look, I've been wanting to ask... Is there some reason I can't just wear contacts? Usually guys who are trying to cast off their otaku pasts just switch to contacts..."

Kenta took off his old glasses and looked at us expectantly with his bare face.

"You know, I thought about it, too, but your face really needs some oomph to it. Glasses actually work in your favor. They're a must-have fashion item, I'd say, at least in your case. They draw the eye, and the right frames make your bland face look ten times more interesting. But you're lucky. You don't have to jazz up your school uniform to look cool; you can get the same effect with a single piece of eyewear."

"...I see. I've been wearing glasses since elementary school, but I've always hated them just 'cause they're a sign that my eyesight is bad..."

"Then that's all the more reason you should stick with glasses. They're like one of your features now. I bet you've never even thought of them as a fashion accessory before, have you?"

As I was talking, I picked up a pair of glasses I'd noticed earlier.

"These are the ones I recommend. Round frames. See how circular they are?"

"What? No way... That's totally out of his range! It makes him look like he's trying too hard to be fashionable!"

Yuuko's reaction was immediately negative, which rubbed off on Kenta.

"Er, are those even fashionable, though? They look like the ones worn by old literary masters..."

"Nope, unlike your weird cowboy-wannabe check-lined denim, these are what people with actual fashion sense wear. You're not a hot, cool guy, unfortunately. You're neither hot nor cool."

"You don't have to repeat yourself!"

"But you've fixed your hair and started to slim down, so there's still hope for you. Your face is kind of plain, but it's not unpleasant to look at. And I have more good news for you. These days, there's such a thing as having 'hot-guy aura.'"

"I thought that was, like, ironic. Like a joke."

"Hmm, sometimes it can be used as an insult. But you see it all the time these days... A guy whose face is kinda 'eh,' but for some reason the girls all go crazy. Like those actors and musicians who other guys would call mediocre-looking, but they have girls going nuts over them. Let me give you a few examples..."

I proceeded to reel off a list of currently popular male celebrities.

"...Oh yeah, I've wondered why some of them are popular with girls. It's like, with that face? Seriously? ...It's like if they had one bad haircut, they'd look like a total dork."

Yuuko was offended. "Hey! I like all those guys! I don't know what you're talking about, either? Every one of them is handsome!"

"See, even a girl of Yuuko's caliber is into them. I don't get it personally, but eh. Anyway, what I'm saying is that we need to work on getting you to project a hot-guy aura."

Kenta still didn't look fully convinced.

"…And I need round glasses? For a hot-guy aura?"

"Precisely. If Yuuko and I, with our gorgeous faces, were to wear these glasses, it would be almost obnoxious. Like, look at us! We're beautiful! We can wear dorky glasses just for the fun of it! But if a guy with plain features like you wears them, it looks kinda endearing. It's also why I chose that hairstyle for you, with the unruly curls on top."

I put the round-framed glasses on myself.

"…Ah, darn it! I've done it again! These look great on me, too! I look like an old literary master! Old-school cool! They should pay me to model these!"

I took off the glasses and handed them to Yuuko.

"…Whoa! It's like, why? Why doesn't this store just hire Saku and me for its promotional posters already? If we were the models, its profits would skyrocket!"

"You sure were right about it being obnoxious. I think we're done here, thanks!"

All jokes aside, I returned the glasses to Kenta. "Go on, try them on."

Nervously, Kenta put on the glasses. I noticed Yuuko's eyebrows shooting up.

"Hmm… I'm not sure about this, you guys…"

I ignored him and spoke to Yuuko. "What's the verdict?"

"…These work! These really work on you, Kentacchi! I actually had to do a little double take just then! Wow, Saku, you have the best eye for this kind of thing!"

Well, yeah. I had already been on the store's website before coming so I could familiarize myself with their product lineup. Roundish, thin frames so as not to erase the benefits of his neutral features. But with a subtle tortoiseshell pattern to add a pop of style.

How could Kenta fail to be won over after being praised on his looks by the prettiest girl in the school? Still, he hesitated, shifting back and forth.

"King...are these really okay?"

"Yeah. At least, better than your old ones."

I gave Kenta my best "I'm hot and I know it" grin.

★

"Seriously? You've gotten hooked on walking, and you want to start night running now? You're choosing neon rainbow? You want to make sure you stand out in the dark? All right, Rudolph, why don't you guide the sleigh tonight, then? All the other reindeer won't be laughing now! Why don't you go stand on the shore so passing ships can use your glow to navigate? You'll be the star everyone's wishing on now!"

"King...please, calm down..."

Once we put in our order at JINS, we were told that we were in luck. They had the right item in stock, so we only had to wait an hour to have them made up. In the meantime, we were at the shoe store, choosing new shoes for Kenta.

This time, Yuuko and I both remained silent at first and let Kenta choose whichever shoes he thought were cool. But once we saw what monstrosities he'd picked out, I hadn't been able to stop myself from giving him a severe roasting.

"Don't even think about buying something like that unless you've got the natural style needed to pull it off! No! Bad!"

"But I thought... I thought that might be good to have a little pizzazz... Mix things up a bit..." Kenta looked down at the sneakers in his hands, crestfallen.

"Those are too much for someone like you who's a total newbie at fashion. I'll explain this in detail while we're picking clothes, but don't fall into the trap of thinking that flashy equals fashionable. You need to rein it in, dude; you need to rein it all the way in."

"But if I go too plain, won't I just look dorky still?"

"No. Plain is good. For sneakers, you should go for some Adidas Stan Smiths, like the ones I'm wearing. Or the Adidas Superstars. You could also go for some Nike Air Force 1s, some Converse All Stars, or Converse One Stars. Or some New Balance 996s or Vans Authentics... All these are classics; they've been popular for decades for a reason. People have been wearing them for years, not just because of the brand name, but because they've stood the test of time. Try to memorize this advice. It goes for shoes, clothes, bags, wallets, watches, and all other accessories, too. Always go classic."

"I've got so many pairs of All Stars, in different colors! They're all the same design, just the colors and patterns are different. Today, my outfit is kinda showy, so I went neutral on the shoes. See? High-tops in off-white!"

Yuuko hiked her leg up in the air to show Kenta her sneakers.

"Yeah, and I'm on my third pair of Stan Smiths in a row. And I've got a few pairs of Authentics, in different colors and patterns, too."

Kenta looked at our feet, his expression solemn.

"Oh, I see. Yes, now that you mention it, King, Yuuko, all your stuff seems to be brand staples... Can I have a few more minutes to browse?"

Kenta went off for a bit, then came back with a pair of New Balance M996s in navy.

I nodded in approval.

★

Kenta changed into his new shoes on the spot, and we picked up his completed glasses. Next, we headed to MUJI to pick out some tops and pants.

"Are you sure MUJI is the right place to go for clothes? I never really saw it as a clothing store..."

"Uniqlo might have worked, too. But Uniqlo has too much

stuff with patterns and mascots. I don't want to have to roast you again, dude. MUJI's safer."

"Is this related to what you said earlier, about flashy not always being fashionable?"

"You're getting it, you're getting it." I picked up a plain white-linen button-down shirt. "Kenta, what do you think this is?"

"It looks like an organic cotton type of white shirt."

"What do you think of it?"

"Uh… It's nice. Simple. It's not super cool or anything, but it definitely doesn't look dorky at all."

"So why not wear something like this? It's already a million times better than your own dorky clothes."

"Yeah, I know… But are you sure that's the kind of thing I need?"

"That mindset of yours stems from fear. Fear of true fashion."

I put the shirt back and went over to take a seat on one of the store's display sofas. Yuuko sat down on my right, and Kenta sat down on my left.

"Fashion's just another hobby, like hiking, cycling, reading, or video games. But if it doesn't appeal to you, it doesn't appeal. Can you ever see yourself getting excited about clothes in the same way as light novels or anime? No. Does hearing a hiker rave about the splendor of the mountains make you immediately want to become a hiker? No."

"You're right. I can't see myself getting into fashion anytime soon."

"Yuuko and Kazuki, now, they live for fashion. That's where they spend their money, and they spend their time keeping up with all the latest trends. Yuuko, can you ever see yourself spending money on mobile games or anime merchandise like Kenta does?"

"Nope, no way!"

"…See? Your light novels make it sound like you've got to become a fashion maniac just to get a girl to look at you, but nothing could be further from the truth. I mean, yeah, fashionable guys tend to get extra points with the girls. But that's just one factor, like being good at sports or being super well-read. To be frank, if you don't see yourself getting into it as a hobby, then there's no reason to focus on it that much."

"B-but hold on… I'm confused. Didn't you bring me shopping today to make me fashionable?"

I got up off the sofa and turned to face Kenta. Then I pointed my finger right between his eyes, like a home tutor imparting a very important lesson.

"Let's break it down. In this world, you have your Yuukos, who love keeping up with the hottest clothes, bags, what have you, and planning outfit combinations. Then, you have your Kentas, who dress badly because they simply don't care and don't put any thought into their outfit combinations or even how well their clothes fit."

Kenta nodded obediently.

"Now, it's impossible to make one into the other. But what we can do is meet halfway. We can make you into someone who cares about his appearance and wants to show off a little personality without becoming a fashion slave or even having to spend that much time or money. Now, Kenta, take a good look at what I'm wearing and tell me what you see."

Kenta looked me up and down. I know I told him to, but it sort of gave me the creeps to have him scrutinizing me this way.

"Huh. You're actually not as fashionable as I thought…?"

"…Watch it, Kenta. For a second there, your head looked like a soccer ball just begging me to kick it. But you're right. The truth is: I don't care about clothes or fashion at all."

Yuuko frowned, piping up. "He's right. Saku never ever agrees to come shopping with me. He's always like, 'You look cute in anything, so just pick whatever.' No interest whatsoever!"

…Oh, she already figured me out.

Incidentally, let's discuss my outfit today. I was wearing my

Adidas Stan Smiths, Gramicci jeans, a white Champion T-shirt with a chest pocket, and my G-SHOCK GWM5610 wristwatch with the black-and-white display. Plus, the same silver necklace and ring that I always wore. And my backpack, which I also used for school, the black Gregory one. That was all.

"And I didn't dress down today for your benefit, Kenta. This is what I always wear, all year-round. Whatever the season, I usually wear some kind of hiking wear for pants, with a plain shirt or T-shirt or polo shirt and maybe a parka on top. My watch and jewelry are the only ones I own. And I didn't choose them to look cool; I just happen to like silver accessories. Even if gold is more in fashion these days. See?"

"Huh. You wear your clothes like they're super fashionable, so I just assumed they were… So you're telling me I could dress like you, too?"

"Yes. All you have to do is pick out some basic pants and shirts. Look at me. Do I look dorky to you?"

"No, no, you look like a king… In fact, you're so confident you just come off as being super well-dressed…"

"Ah yes, good answer, Kenta, good answer! You've summed up my aesthetic nicely. My goal is to make whatever I'm wearing look good, rather than relying on it to make me look good, if you follow me."

I put my hands on my hips and puffed out my chest.

"So you don't need to worry about choosing 'cool' or 'stylish' items of clothing. Just stick with a look you like. And since planning outfits doesn't excite you, just pick basic, staple pieces that can all be mixed and matched to work together. If you pick classic pieces, then you can always buy the same ones again if they wear out, and stores will be less likely to stop selling them as fashion trends move on. I also recommend choosing good quality accessories that you can use for a long time and make them into your personal touchstones. That's why it's better to save your money for a really decent bag, wallet, and what have you."

"I like that! I like that a lot! So I can look like a man of taste, right?"

"Right, right. What do you think, Yuuko?"

"Uh, I'm not sure... I'm not like you at all, Saku. I always want to be wearing something different. And I want to be the first one to wear all the new trends! I feel like every time I buy a new bag or shoes, I'm discovering a new side of myself. And I love spending ages getting dressed up to see you, Saku... Choosing something super cute and a little bit sexy, you know? But then I also love experimenting with more boyish, casual, cool styles when I hang out with Ucchi!"

That was Yuuko to a T.

"Right, well, that's the thing about clothes. As Yuuko points out, they tell a story about who you are and who you want the world to see you as. There's this fashion genre that's super popular lately called normcore."

Kenta furrowed his brow. "Normcore?"

"Yeah. You know how Steve Jobs was known for always wearing the same outfit? New Balance M992s, Levi's 501s, and an Issey Miyake black turtleneck. And then there's Mark Zuckerberg, who created Facebook. He always wears the same gray T-shirt. Those guys didn't want to have to think about what to wear every day, so they gave themselves a uniform to free up thinking space for more important stuff. Kinda cool, right?"

"...Yeah, that does sound kinda cool."

"Normcore is a portmanteau of the words *normal* and *hardcore*. It involves consciously choosing clothes that are functional and undistinguished. Now, I'm not saying you have to devote yourself to pursuing whatever the definition of 'normal' is..."

Like, yeah, sometimes a majority of people feel the same about something, but if you ask a bunch of people what normal is, you'll get a ton of different answers.

"Personally, I like to stick to basic, staple pieces, but I also like mixing in relaxed athletic wear and cool accessories, too. And

Yuuko's style is influenced by her personality. To get a bit more extreme, if you really feel like punk is your personal style, Kenta, then I don't have an issue with that. You need to decide for yourself what feels the most natural."

"I see…"

"But you don't have to have it all figured out from the beginning. Just tell me, what kind of clothes would *you* like to wear?"

Kenta looked back and forth between Yuuko and me in silence. I could practically see the gears turning in his head.

"Honestly, I don't really want to stand out in the crowd. I'd prefer to look polished, rather than sloppy. Only, I don't want it to be too obvious that I just walked into a store and picked up only white shirts and brown chino pants."

"All right, Yuuko. Shall we do this, then?"

Yuuko bounced up off the sofa.

"All righty! I think I've got a good mental picture of what we're aiming for! Do you feel comfortable leaving it up to us?"

"Y-yes. Thank you…"

Kenta stood up, facing Yuuko and nodding his head politely to her.

"Let's go with button-down shirts. They'll look good with the round frames Saku chose for you. They'll make you look individualistic, like a liberal arts student! But we don't want anything that wrinkles easily or looks too synthetic. Let's go with organic cotton shirts. Maybe in navy, to match your sneakers."

"Right, I wanted to ask about…how to choose colors?"

"Uh, if you stick with complementing colors, you should be okay. You don't like anything too bright, right?"

"Nope. I can't really see myself wearing anything red or, like, yellow…"

"Okay, then let's stick to black, white, and navy. Any combination of those would look okay! You can't go wrong with those. Oh, but no white pants. That will only make you look like a playboy. Anyway, Kentacchi, since your sneakers are navy, we can't go with navy pants. We need some balance. Maybe black pants would be better?"

"Hold on a sec," Kenta said, tapping down everything Yuuko was saying into the Notes app on his phone.

"But just remember not to wear the same color on the top and bottom. If you buy black, navy, and white tops, then the bottoms should be brown or khaki. We should probably start by choosing the pants, since our options there are limited."

"I'll leave the order up to you, Yuuko, but should I choose slim-fit pants or baggy ones?"

"Hmm… I think some looser pants, and maybe a more fitted top? Something with some stretch, for easy movement and a low-key kinda vibe. If you don't have any specific preferences, I recommend pants that are tapered at the ankle. Shall we go see if we can find some?"

Yuuko led Kenta over to the pants section. I followed along behind.

"See, what about some of these?"

Yuuko picked up several pairs of pants off the rack and thrust them at Kenta.

"I think I like…the brown, the black, or the gray…"

"Oh, gray would be good! They'll go nicely with your navy sneakers. And gray is so much more chill than white. And not many people go for gray pants, so your selection will look like a deliberate fashion choice! Now, what about shirts?"

Kenta went back over the notes he'd written in his phone.

"Er…maybe those organic-cotton button-down shirts you mentioned earlier? In navy!"

Yuuko nodded and went to grab some shirts.

"Okay, now it's time to try them on!"

"What? No, I don't think I need to do that. It's kind of embarrassing."

"Don't be silly! You can maybe get away with buying tops without trying them, but pants absolutely must be tried on first! Now, hop to it!"

Yuuko grabbed Kenta's hand and dragged him to the fitting rooms. Kenta had this look of awe on his face, as if he was thinking, *I'll never wash this hand again!*

*

""Wow!""

Yuuko and I both gasped as Kenta emerged from the fitting room.

"What do you think?"

Kenta had the same nervous energy as a hamster that had been taken out of its cage. He looked himself up and down in the mirror, chewing his lip.

"Before we give our opinion, what do *you* think?"

"I feel...awkward. But I think I look kinda cool? Like, I could go to Starbucks in this outfit."

"Yeah. All you need to do is lose a few more pounds, and you'll have that hot-guy aura we're after."

"Wow, Kentacchi! You look totally cool! I'm not just saying that, either! You're bound to find a nice girl now!"

Yuuko seemed really excited, for some reason.

"Oh, you've gotta wear it home! Excuse me! Staff person! He wants to wear this home! Can you ring us up? Oh, and can we get a bag for his school uniform?"

Yuuko marched over to the cash register, ignoring Kenta, who was still standing there looking awkward.

"All right, the only thing left is the bag. You've got that dumb junior high schooler bag with the long strap that hangs down to your butt. You still have money?"

"I was expecting us to buy more expensive stuff, so I actually still have around thirty thousand yen."

"That should do it. If you like shoulder bags, though, you should go for something canvas. I think that would suit the hot-guy aura style you're going for."

I tapped around on my phone before showing Kenta a few pics I found online.

"They look good, but I was thinking of mixing it up a little…"

"In that case, why not choose athletic wear like me? It won't look too dressy, so it'll be a good match for your casual clothes. Plus, they're practical and will last you a good while. For backpacks, I recommend the Arro by Arc'teryx, and if you want a combination backpack/shoulder bag, you should go for the Mystery Ranch's Invader or the Outsider."

I showed Kenta some more pics.

"Hmm. They all look good… But what's this one with the little bird-type logo?"

"That's the Arc'teryx symbol, the archaeopteryx. So you like that one? Let's go and buy it after this, then."

While we were talking, Yuuko finished paying with the money in Kenta's ridiculous wallet. Somehow, she made that awful thing look stylish in her hand, like a studded Gucci purse.

She handed the wallet to Kenta and jumped right into our conversation, like she'd been listening to us.

"Hey, let's go to Starbucks first! Why not? This is where you'll be meeting your old friends again, right? Let's go and do a practice run!"

"Sounds good. We can role-play, see how it might go."

By the way, I know Starbucks is just another coffee chain in the big cities, but in Fukui, Starbucks is *the* place for high school kids to gather and flex on each other. Things have relaxed a bit recently, but not so long ago, it was the kind of place where only popular kids had the required level of social privilege to be seen drinking coffee there.

"Oh, then let me buy you both coffees, to say thanks." Kenta jumped right in with the offer.

"There's no need to thank us. I'm doing this for my good-guy optics."

"He's right, Kentacchi. Today was fun! You don't need to make up for anything!"

"Oh…you guys…"

"But since you offered, I'll have a matcha Frappuccino, with extra chocolate chips and extra whip cream. And an apple crumble pie."

"And I'll have a Starbucks latte with an extra shot of espresso and a clubhouse sandwich. You got enough to cover that, Kenta?"

"…Is it too late for me to rescind my offer?"

"Hey, you wanted to thank us, right? Consider us thanked!"

"Right, right!"

"You guys are always bustin' my balls!!!"

*

At the counter, Kenta flubbed his words and asked for a "ground" latte instead of a grande. I offered to take over and order everything myself with his wallet, but Kenta blanched at that. Eventually, we made it to a table with our food and coffees.

"So have you made any plans to meet your old friends yet?"

"Yes. Saturday, two weeks from now. The first day of Golden Week vacation. But…to be honest…I'm scared. Until I met you guys, they were the most popular kids I'd ever spent any time with. Look, this is what happened when I messaged Miki on LINE…"

Kenta opened up his LINE app chat to show us.

Huh? I thought you left our group when I turned you down? So you couldn't make any other friends and came crawling back, huh? Still, whatever, sounds fun. I'll invite Ren and Hayato, too.

I see, I see. Not a very nice response, now, was it?

"I'm already feeling down about the prospect of meeting them… By the way, Ren is Miki's boyfriend. And Hayato's the other guy in the group. I'd really prefer to meet Miki alone, but I guess they all want to have a good laugh at me…"

Ren and Hayato. They already sounded like good-looking guys. I pictured them outperforming Kenta in every way.

Yuuko slurped down some of her matcha Frappuccino with her straw.

"I don't really know the situation, but what do *you* want to do, Kentacchi? Do you wanna walk in there and give them all a good slap in the face?"

"Of course not! Nothing so dramatic. I just want Miki to think to herself…you know…'Maybe I made a mistake.' That's all. If I could just make her regret how she treated me, that would be more than enough…"

"Oh really? I thought you were going to invite Miki to duke it out on the banks of the riverbed. Mano a mano, y'know?"

I remembered someone saying something like that recently…

"If all you want to do is make Miki regret her words, then that should be easy! Excuse me! Barista? Would you mind taking a photo for us?"

Yuuko flagged down a passing barista and handed over her phone. Then she went to stand behind Kenta, who was on the other side of the table. I went to go sit down next to him, immediately figuring out what she was up to.

I hunched down a bit and put my arm around Kenta, and Yuuko put her hands on Kenta's head, before placing her chin on top of her hands.

"…Wh-whoa! A photo?" Kenta was taken aback and hadn't processed what was going on yet.

"Just relax! Okay, we're ready!"

*Flash, flash.*

Yuuko asked the barista to take two shots, just in case. Then she retrieved her phone and scrutinized the photos. "All good. Thanks so much!" The barista smiled and walked off.

"Look, look, Kentacchi!"

Yuuko put her arms around Kenta's head from behind to show him her phone screen.

I was prepared to jam my straw right up his nostril if he dared take advantage of this and lean his head back.

"Is this...really me?"

"Yep, it's you, Kentacchi! What do you think?"

"I hope you guys don't get offended if I say this, but...I look kinda like I actually...belong? With you?"

"You know, when we first met you, you were sooo snotty and mean to us both! I thought you were a total stain on society, a lazy pig who—"

"Yuuko, stop. I know, I know. I admit to it all. But please don't say any more... I'll be crushed if you do."

"But now...you really *do* look like one of our group. You should work on your smile, though, and you still need to keep up your diet. But you could totally be the plain-looking guy in the popular group who has the hot-guy aura!"

Yuuko threw him a peace sign.

"Anyway, yep, you really do look like you belong standing alongside Saku and me! So no problem. But you know, our support can only take you so far. You're gonna have to do the rest yourself."

Then Yuuko patted Kenta's head.

"But...I had no idea changing would be this easy. I've barely done anything except come back to school..."

"That's not true at all." I shook my head. "You made the decision to come back to school, and you worked hard to get along with everyone and keep up your diet. Now you've even got new hair and a whole new wardrobe. Of course, this isn't enough to become truly popular. But you've made great steps, Kenta. The future looks bright."

"Do...do you really think so?"

I grinned. "Listen, Kenta. What's the most important thing when it comes to making a change?"

"Er...having friends to rely on, like you and Yuuko?"

"That's only one part of it. The answer I was looking for is: 'willpower.' You've got to have that determination to do it, no matter what setbacks come your way. And never give up. You approach it like that, and success is assured, no matter how long it takes. Skills come with practice, but motivation is something you have to find for yourself."

"I think I'm starting to understand. I guess I just have to keep doing my best, right?"

I grinned wider.

"Right. If you keep going, you'll become who you want to be at some point. That's all there is to it... Simple, right?"

Kenta nodded vigorously.

"I'll keep running every day, for the next two weeks! I'll make sure to rise above those jerks in my otaku group! I'll do it for you, King...and you, Yuuko...and for Uchida, and Mizushino, and Asano, and Nanase, and Aomi...to honor your assistance! And because...because..."

Kenta trailed off, seemingly having difficulty getting the words out. He took a deep breath, then whispered it.

"Because you're my friends."

"If you're gonna say it, then *say* it. Otherwise, it's just weird."

"Yeah, that was very lame of you, Kentacchi!"

"Sorry, sorry; forget I said anything!"

Ah, I love messing with him.

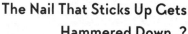

The following Monday, I arrived at school earlier than usual. After accompanying Kenta on his daily walking exercise for a while, I'd gotten into the habit of waking up early.

I wouldn't have minded getting up early to meet a cute girl, but it was kind of depressing getting up at the crack of dawn just to be met with Kenta.

Yawning hugely, I headed toward the classroom. Then I realized I could hear raised voices coming from inside.

"Why don't you tell us, then? We're your classmates, aren't we? Why is someone like you hanging around with Chitose's group?"

"Uh... Just... King came to my house after Mr. Iwanami asked him to..."

"King? King? What's that about? That's hilarious! Is that what you call Chitose?"

That short exchange was all I needed to hear to know instantly what was going on. I peered into the room through the window in the door.

I knew it. It was the exact scene I'd been picturing. Kenta and Yua were surrounded by five other classmates and being interrogated. There were three guys and two girls. The guys were the same ones who'd been giving me the death glares on the first day of class.

It looked like the other members of our group hadn't made it to school yet or were otherwise busy with morning sports practice. I couldn't see any of them except for Yua.

"Let's not interrogate him... Why not get to know him first?"

Yua put her hand on Kenta's shoulder, trying to stick up for him.

"We don't *want* to get to know him. Anyway, it's him we're talking to, not you. Why don't you butt out, huh, Uchida?"

Yua blinked as one of the girls started getting snarky. The girl had a trashy look about her.

"Um, but Yamazaki and I were talking first before you came over here..."

"Yeah, I know. But neither of you two really fit in with Chitose's group, come to think of it. You're sort of dull and boring, aren't you, Uchida?"

Yua shrugged and smiled.

"Heh... I know I'm a little on the dull side. I guess I'm just part of the gang to give them someone to play off for a little light comic relief..."

Kenta butted in, even as Yua was trying to defuse the situation.

"N-no! When you first came to my house, I thought...she's definitely one of the popular kids! You're pretty and vivacious, Uchida!"

One of the guys snorted at this.

"To a shut-in, school-no-show like you, any woman would look like a goddess. But wait, are you saying Uchida went to your house, Yamazaki? So that means you started coming back to school after getting a crush on her, hmm?"

"N-no... That's not what happened..."

Yua looked back and forth between them.

"It was Saku who convinced Yamazaki to come back to school. All I did was help a little."

The trashy-looking girl responded to that.

"You know, Uchida, the other girls all call him by his last

name. Chitose. Why do *you* call him Saku? Don't you realize how obvious you're being?"

"Um… I guess I've never really been aware I was doing that… I guess I'm, like, his sidepiece? Hee-hee."

Yua was trying to lighten the atmosphere by making a joke, but the trashy girl snorted in disgust. "Ew, gross," she said, curling her lip.

Ah, man. A bout with these types might be a little tough for them without backup.

"Okay, Buddy A, Sidepiece B, I need your help with something."

I turned to address my other friends, one of whom had attached himself to me and the better-smelling one, who I wished had attached herself to me.

"Ah yeah, I was expecting them to come and start trouble sooner or later. I just never imagined it would be over Kenta. Still, I knew from the first day that they would have beef with our group. I could feel it in the air."

…So said the one still draped over me, Kazuki.

"Captain, if I'm to take on this duty, I want a promotion to Wifey A."

…So said the sweet-smelling one, Nanase. Why couldn't she be pressed against my back right now?

"Hmm, I'll consider it. Ready to provide backup, troops?"

"All right. Not much else we can do, now that they've started it. But let's keep it friendly, okay? Otherwise, they'll just come back to harass Kenta and Ucchi again while we're not around."

"Right, let's try to smooth things over without any bloodshed."

∗

So we headed on into the classroom.

"Mornin', Kenta, Yua."

I ignored the other five for now and called out to my friends.

"…G-good morning, King…"

"Saku… Mizushino… Yuzuki… Good morning."

Kenta and Yua both looked visibly relieved.

Kenta had clearly identified the danger in this situation right away. I wasn't sure how long the bullies had been at it, but I knew Yua would have stuck with Kenta and been by his side throughout.

The situation, though, was extremely annoying to me.

Just when I'd managed to get Kenta moving in the right direction. This kind of thing could be enough to have him scurrying back to the safety of his room.

"Hey, Chitose, Mizushino, Nanase. We were just having a chat with your new friend here."

One of the guys spoke up first. He seemed to be the leader of this little group.

I'd noticed them on the first day of class. The five of them were a pretty standout group of popular kids in first year.

I took in their unbuttoned shirts, rolled-up pant legs, and the heavy makeup on the girls. Popular, hmm… It would be more accurate to say they were a group of trashy kids. Fukui still has that countryside delinquent youth subculture thing going on, so that's another way to describe them. Even in an elite school like ours, there's always a trashy element. Still, fashion is a matter of taste. Just 'cause I thought they looked trashy, didn't mean I had the right to judge.

"Uh… You're all in our class, as I recall… Right?"

A little diss, to start things off. Just to let them know that they were barely on my radar, even though they had already revealed that they knew my full name. Hopefully, that'd be enough to piss them off—make my job easier.

The ringleader guy pushed back his long bangs with irritation. He'd shaved his eyebrows down a little, and you couldn't exactly call him handsome.

"That's kind of a low blow, Chitose."

I see, I see.

I hadn't spoken to him before, so he hadn't really registered with me, but it was clear that he was more significant a character than the Rough Guy A role I'd cast him in. It looked like I had to try harder if I wanted to crush this little rebellion of his.

"By the way, we played against each other in the prefectural finals in junior high. I was a pitcher for Youkou Junior High. The name's Atomu Uemura."

Of course, I remembered that we had played against Youkou Junior High. But it *was* two years ago. I couldn't remember this guy, or even his name, at all. I tilted my head to one side and shrugged. Atomu continued, sounding pissed.

"You little genius prodigies are all the same. Everyone saw you as the standard to beat, but you were only interested in yourself and how well you played. I figured you got into this school just so you could have a shot at the Koushien National High School Baseball Tournament, but no… You immediately quit baseball and started hanging around with girls."

"Sorry, but I don't tend to focus on the past all that much. Anyway, Atomu, if you were so good in junior high, how come you didn't join baseball last year?"

After all, I did keep up with baseball, at least during the first year of high school. And I was pretty sure Atomu hadn't joined up in the middle of the year.

I smiled facetiously. Atomu, too, smiled facetiously.

"…Continuing with baseball into high school seemed like a waste of time. No one cares about trying to go to Koushien anymore. It's lame."

Kazuki interjected just then, grinning in a sharklike manner.

"Well, soccer is the big sport nowadays, isn't it? Koushien isn't the dream anymore. Now it's the inter–high school tournament or maybe trying for the U-17. But enough sports talk. I actually *do* know the name of that cutie standing next to you. We've chatted before, right? Nazuna Ayase?"

"What, you remember me? That's so sweet! Mizushino, Chitose… Aren't you embarrassed to be seen with them? C'mon, come hang out with us."

Nazuna looked really happy all of a sudden. And her face was already noticeably attractive. She glared at Kenta and Yua.

Then someone stepped around me, walking farther into the room.

Mmm, someone who smelled good.

"Whaaat? Am I that embarrassing? I had no idea! Perhaps spending too much time focusing on sports has robbed me of my natural femininity? Yikes!"

It was Nanase who had stepped forward, deliberately misinterpreting Nazuna's diss to include herself—and overreacting in a theatrical manner.

"Uh…no… I didn't mean you…"

Well, of course not. Nazuna was cute, sure, but she was nowhere near the level of top-class girls like Yuuko and Nanase. Nanase had used Irony, and it had been supereffective. Also very in-character for her.

"Never mind that…"

Atomu stepped forward and put his arm around Kenta's shoulder. Kenta froze immediately, eyes darting about as if unsure as to what exactly was happening.

"Chitose. You've been buddying around with this kid lately, right? But just look at him. He's not the kind of guy you'd usually find hanging in a group like yours. What is this, a pity thing? Or did Kura force you to be his friend?"

"No. We're just regular friends. Last weekend, Yuuko and Kenta and I actually all hung out at Lpa."

Okay, yes, Kura had given me the initial push, and I had felt sorry for him. But everything I said was true.

"You've gotta be kidding. Who'd want to be seen at the mall with an otaku like him? What do you even talk about?"

"We talk about the light novels we've been reading recently. Kenta recommended me this great one: *I'm a Huge Otaku, but the Slutty Girls Are All Up on Me?!* I've actually just finished it, so I could lend it to you if you'd like?"

Atomu, Nazuna, and the other members of their group stared at me like I had two heads. It was pretty funny. Sadly, though, it seemed they weren't willing to get on board.

"Give me a freakin' break, Chitose. And listen here. Your group's pretty well respected in this school. But stop letting riff-raff join. The other girls were pretty pissed when you let Uchida in. They felt shortchanged. Just be aware that you're lowering your social stock value with all these bad decisions you keep making."

Atomu suddenly got Kenta in a headlock and started giving him a vicious noogie.

"Ack! I'm only a temporary member of..."

I raised a hand to stop Kenta.

"If my 'social stock value' goes down over something as simple as being friends with Kenta, then so be it. At any rate, we don't care about the social hierarchy. We just hang out with who we choose to hang out with. That's all we need to enjoy high school."

"Spare me. You all walk around the school with these shit-eating 'We're so popular' grins on your faces."

Nanase interjected then. "You're wrong. We just hang out with people we like and feel comfortable with."

Then she put one hand on my shoulder and the other on Kazuki's.

"I find Chitose, Mizushino—and I guess, Kaito—way more attractive and fun to be around than any other guys. And any-way, if hanging with Yamazaki brings down our social stock, then that'll be a good opportunity for your group, right, Uemura? You can climb the social ladder right to the top, if it matters that much to you."

Nanase turned to grin at me, then at Kazuki. It was a calculated move to make sure that Atomu knew he hadn't registered on her radar as a guy at all.

For all the tough-guy front he put on, Atomu was still a high school boy. Being ignored and described as 'any other guy' by a beauty like Nanase…that had to sting.

As if on cue, Atomu started scowling again.

The way Nanase phrased things, it sounded like she was mocking this group for not already having managed to be the most popular group in the school. But she'd done it in such a subtle way, a way that would make them look like jerks if they got mad. She was good.

"…Whatever, you just want to surround yourself with hot guys. You're such a slut," Nazuna spat.

Instead of backing down, it looked like she was going to go head-to-head with Nanase now, in an effort to defend her wounded pride.

"Really? But I don't pick my guy friends based on their looks. I just happen to get along with guys who've got handsome faces. But if you really want to become friends with hot guys, why don't you just try talking to them in a normal way, hmm, Ayase?" Nanase smiled, so full of confidence.

"I never said that… I don't even know what you're talking about…"

But everything Nanase was saying was common sense. Nazuna didn't have a leg to stand on. That's when Kazuki spoke up again.

"That'd be fine with me. And, Atomu, I have nothing against you. We're all in the same class, so we should stop this silly fighting. And, Nazuna, I'd like to be friends with you, too."

There was no way Kazuki would ever want to be friends with kids like this. He was always the peacemaker and hated fuss of any kind. In fact, he was the steadiest member of our group. But he always made sure to avoid associating with people who would cause drama or reflect badly on him in any way.

He was just sticking up for Kenta, here. As a favor to me.

Kazuki's plan was calculated. He knew the group would reject his offer of friendship, but continuing to seek a fight with us after Kazuki had been so magnanimous... That would make them look like jerks in the eyes of the entire class.

"You know, I hate kids like you who've never had to deal with any hardships in life. I prefer to hang with kids who know what the real world is like. And y'know, have actual emotions. But listen, Yamazaki... You can cling on to Chitose all you like, but remember your place. Don't go dragging him down with you."

Was this guy actually decent, or wasn't he? What a complicated fellow. As Atomu, Nazuna, and the other still-silent members of their group turned to leave, I spoke up.

"Hey. One last thing. Yua might be on the plain-and-boring side, sure. But she's boring the same way packing materials are when you ship something. She's like...bubble wrap."

"...Saku, can we speak later?"

I ignored Yua and kept talking.

"You can ship something super valuable and expensive, but if it gets scratched or broken, it'll be worthless. You need soft padding to keep it safe and maintain its value. And when you need some entertainment, you can take it out and pop all its little bubbles."

"That's meant to be a compliment...?"

Yua was looking at me with exasperation.

Atomu's group turned and walked off silently.

✳

After school, I took Kenta to Hachiban Ramen, the ramen joint near our school.

Hachiban Ramen is a ramen chain that was originally established along Ishikawa Prefecture's Highway 8 but soon spread to the entire Hokuriku region. It's considered soul food for Fukui people, along with our iconic katsudon. It's not particularly mind-blowing or anything, but for some reason, I always find myself going there. Whenever the holiday rolls around, and everyone comes back to their hometowns in Fukui for Golden Week, Obon, or New Year's, the TV channels are choked with commercials for Hachiban Ramen. They've got this slogan: *It's gotta be Hachiban.* It beats me why someone who lives in Tokyo, which has more amazing ramen restaurants than you could dream of, would want to eat Hachiban Ramen whenever they're back in Fukui. But they do. Weird, huh?

I ordered a noodle set without soup. Upon my recommendation, Kenta had the salt-flavored veggie ramen without the ramen (so in other words, vegetable soup).

"That was tense, back in the classroom this morning, huh?"

I dumped a ton of vinegar and chili sauce on my ramen and mixed it up in the bowl. Most people order the veggie ramen, but I think this is way better.

"Popular kids are scary as heck."

Kenta looked completely downcast. Aw, man. I knew he'd been picked on by popular kids in the past, but he'd probably never been singled out so aggressively.

Still, it could have been a lot worse. If I'd shown up even a few minutes later, or if Yua hadn't been there, then things could have ended in disaster. Kenta could have been scared off popular kids for life.

"Ah well, I had a feeling that group would be coming for us all sooner or later. They've just been biding their time waiting to strike, ever since our group claimed dominance the first day of school. You were just the convenient excuse they used to start trouble. It wasn't anything to do with you, really. Shake it off; that's my advice."

I slurped my noodles.

To be honest, I think the only reason they didn't come for us right away was because I'd been named class president on the first day of school. We seized the initiative, and it took them a while to recover.

Kazuki was totally right—they just honed in on Kenta for an excuse to start shit with us. I was going to have to keep a closer eye on the Team Chitose members. They could handle themselves usually, but I'd let the rival faction get the jump on us this time.

I didn't want to make a big deal of it, but I was painfully aware of the fact that Kenta was suffering because of our issue, not his.

"King, I remember you saying that being popular was like playing on hard mode... I think I'm starting to get that now. It's not just the unpopular kids who are jealous of you; it's rival groups, too... Man, if confrontations like that happened to me every day, I'd completely crack."

"It's not like all popular kids are dueling it out for supremacy or anything, though."

"Oh yeah, I noticed you guys didn't really fight back. You kind of killed them with kindness and took the moral high ground."

Kenta was eating his vegetable soup with an expression of dissatisfaction.

"All right, this is a teachable moment. As I've said, there're all kinds of popular kids. You've got your 'natural-born' popular kids, your 'self-made' popular kids, and then a hybrid variant in between."

"Okay, so which members of your team are which?"

"For example, Yuuko is a natural-born one. A hundred percent. She's the type who can go straight to the top on the strength of her personality alone. Conversely, Yua is a self-made type. She didn't stand out at all in first year, but then one day she struck up a conversation with our group, and she started to change, little by little, in both appearance and personality. That's the example I want you to strive for, Kenta."

"I see. But I would have thought Uchida was a natural-born popular kid…"

"Kaito and Haru are both natural-borns. They belong to the jock subdivision. You know, standout sports stars always achieve a level of fame throughout the school, don't they? And then Kazuki, Nanase, and me, we're the hybrid types. We have the natural-born talents, sure, but the difference is that we're *aware* of them. And we control our images very carefully."

Kenta seemed to be considering all I had to say very carefully, too.

"Eh, but to be honest, it's not like the lines are drawn in stone. Yua's a self-made popular kid, yeah, but she always had the talent. She just cultivated it. And Yuuko certainly puts a lot of effort into her clothes and makeup. I'm just giving you a broad overview here."

I filled our empty glasses with water before continuing.

"What I wanted to get through to you is that, among the popular kids, you also get this variant that's always striving to put others down to elevate themselves."

"…You mean like Atomu and his group?"

"Precisely. In that group, you've probably got your usual mix of natural-borns, self-mades, and hybrids, but what unites them is this desire for dominance. They're always trying to prove how cool they are by dunking on others."

Kenta's chopsticks paused as he turned to look directly at me.

"Like what happened today. They attack other popular groups, most specifically, that group's weakest link. That's how they demonstrate their superiority to others. Or maybe they're just checking to make sure they're still popular. They're a mess of insecurity, you see."

"I know—I've had to put up with enough of that in my life so far. But I've never been attacked so directly before today…"

Kenta gazed across the restaurant unseeingly, as if reliving the events of this morning. He looked so forlorn that I almost felt like throwing the kid a bone and telling him to go ahead and order some *gyoza*.

"But I've never seen your group try to flex on anyone or show dominance, King. How come you guys don't do that?"

"There's two main reasons. The difference between our group and groups that try to claim dominance is that we don't *care* about being popular. It's not how we define ourselves. Being top of the school hierarchy isn't something we consciously think about, nor strive for."

"Objection! You're totally lying, King. You're always going on about how popular you are, the hottest guy in the school, blah, blah, blah."

Kenta pointed his Chinese soup spoon at me accusingly. Hey, didn't your mama teach you not to wave utensils at people?

"Of course, being on top of the hierarchy is pretty sweet. We always have our table in the cafeteria, and there's tons of other perks like that. But we were never aiming for any of those things. They're just part of our reality. We're just enjoying our school life. If I'm really being honest, I wouldn't care about being considered popular as long as I could continue hanging out with the same group and having fun together." I finished up my noodles and wiped my mouth with a napkin. "Anyway, popular or not, I'd still be hot. That's just a fact."

"So...you're saying that other people have all just decided you're popular, King, and you've just been living your life?"

"It may sound conceited to say so, but...yeah. But for those other kids who are desperate to climb the ranks, their whole high school life is all about that. They think that popularity means they've won, and that the unpopular kids are just losers. They don't know what else to be, if not popular."

In fact, Atomu's group was a pretty good representation of Kenta's prior concept of popular kids.

"So then, how do you evaluate yourselves?" Kenta leaned in with interest.

"You either evaluate yourselves based on what others think of you or what you think of yourself. I'm the latter. As I said before, it doesn't matter what others think. You should just try to be a version of yourself that you like. Atomu and his gang totally evaluate themselves based on others' opinions. Comparing themselves to others, to see where they fall in the hierarchy. This guy is above me, this guy is below me, always thinking about dumb stuff like that."

"...And that's why they try to challenge other kids?"

"Yeah. Whenever they get a chance, they'll go on the attack, trying to see if they can't bring the other party down a peg or two. And elevate themselves into the bargain. That's the whole reason why they do it."

"Yeah, that Uemura guy kept talking about social stock value, but you just talked about friendship."

Huh, so Kenta had actually taken in the conversation. I'd thought he was too busy freaking out. I raised my eyebrows at him as he continued.

"But how should I handle that kind of popular kid? I should argue back, right?"

"You should follow the example we already set. Don't engage with the enemy. But try to meet him on a level playing field. If you try to one-up him, you'll be locked in an endless war, and he'll be loving it. Just see him as a member of a different tribe that you want to peacefully coexist alongside. And if he gets too unreasonable, you shouldn't be afraid to walk away."

Besides, jerks like that would just keep on at it indefinitely. You had to knock them back when they encroached on your turf, sure, but if you weren't careful, you'd spend all your precious youth dealing with them.

And there was no need to waste one's precious youth on stupid stuff like that.

"Changing the subject, Kenta... God, carbs are *so* good. They make you feel glad to be alive!"

"Hey! You're one of them, after all! You're trying to one-up me right now!"

*

After I walked Kenta home, I headed back along the riverbed path in a chilled-out mood.

I found my thoughts returning to the morning's events. It was lucky I'd shown up to save Kenta's butt, but if I'd been too late, he might have gotten freaked out about being in social situations again.

I was relieved to see he was still good. But it got me thinking about things I didn't usually think about.

Jumping in to save somebody else was all well and good, but if I didn't learn not to take responsibility for his life, the weight would soon become unbearable.

After everything I've told Kenta...how I've been acting like this wise life-coach, sensei-type figure toward him... It would all come to nothing if he wasn't able to rise to the occasion on the day of reckoning and stick it to his old friends. If he failed... after everything I'd done to build him up...I'd be responsible. It would be even worse than if I had just left him alone in the first place.

But a part of me was whispering that it wasn't *all* on me, and it wasn't *fair* to blame myself. I wasn't the one who started this. Kenta had wanted this. And if he did mess up in the end, then that wouldn't change the fact that both Kenta and I had done our best in our own ways. I had to draw the line. He wasn't my responsibility. I was just helping him out a little. Right?

But another part of me was screaming that this really *was* all on me. I was the one who accepted Kura's mission. Maybe I should have said no in the first place. I was just too prideful to turn down the request. I wanted to be Saku Chitose, cool guy who can take care of business. So the results of that, whatever they might turn out to be...they *were* on me. All of them.

I felt like Kenta's success or failure would make or break me. And then what was to become of Saku Chitose afterward?

I sighed deeply.

*...WHAP.*

I felt something strike my back, hard.

"'Sup, Chitose?! Why you only heading home now? I thought you were part of the go-home club?"

I turned to see Haru, standing there with a sports bag slung over her shoulder along with her schoolbag. Her smile made all my self-deprecating thoughts of a few moments ago disappear in an instant.

"I accompanied Kenta on his walking workout. Walked him all the way home. By the way, that hurt."

"Oh, don't be such a big baby. Gotten soft since quitting baseball?"

"You didn't need to punch me. You could have just said hello like a normal girl. Anyway, how was club practice?"

The sun was starting to get low on the horizon, but it was still pretty early for Haru to be out, considering that basketball club practices often ran right up until seven PM, which was as late as they were allowed to run.

"Our coach had something to do and couldn't stay for long, so we just did some simple shooting drills and called it a day. I hate to waste the opportunity to work out, so I was thinking of heading to Higashi Park and doing a little solo training. You busy, Chitose? Wanna join me?"

"I just got done walking seven miles, and now you want me to work out with you?"

"Just walking? Pah! That's nothing. Anyway, if you're going to spend all this time with Yamazaki, you owe me some quality time, too."

"That's like commuting to school by bicycle every day but then suddenly being forced to compete in the Tour de France."

"Oh, quit your bellyachin' and hop on, Chief."

Haru hopped back onto her blue GIOS hybrid bicycle, gesturing for me to hop on behind her. I noticed it didn't have the footrests that granny bikes like Kaito's have. *So I'm supposed to just find somewhere else to put my feet, am I?*

"Let me hold on to your shoulders."

"Of course. I'd like to see you try to stay on hands-free. You should join a troupe of Chinese acrobats if you can do that."

I took hold of Haru's shoulders and carefully rested my feet on the wheel's outer hub, being careful not to obstruct the wheel itself. The bike lurched to the side a little as we started off, but Haru soon corrected it.

"You're lighter than I thought, Chitose. This is way easier than when I give rides to Kaito."

"Not sure if I should take that as a compliment on my slender figure from a pretty girl or as a slight on my build as an ex-athlete…"

Haru pedaled smoothly as we rolled off. In just one month, I'd ridden double with Yua, Yuuko, and now Haru. Man, I really was living that high school boy dream, wasn't I?

Haru's shoulders were narrow and feminine but also strong and slightly muscled. It was clear she was having no problem hauling my weight. I felt slightly unmanned at first, but I was sorely tempted to give myself over to her athletic charms.

"You can lean on me a bit more, Chitose; I can take the weight."

It was like she was reading my mind.

"I can't lean on a girl. I'll have to surrender my Man Card."

"You know, you'd be boyfriend material if you didn't say things like that all the time."

"But that's part of my charm. It's part of what does make me boyfriend material, isn't it?"

"Hmm, I guess it depends on the girl."

Becoming Haru's boyfriend… Now, that would be a challenge. She's tough to scoop up, like a goldfish at a summer festival booth. The shiny gold one is too fast, and you're left going after the boring black-and-white ones with the bulging eyes instead.

★

After about five minutes of hybrid bicycle riding, we arrived at Higashi Park, which is located close to Fuji High. We got off the bike, and Haru immediately whipped off her skirt. I almost had a heart attack. Of course, she was wearing shorts underneath. And another T-shirt under her school blouse.

…I'd be lying if I said I wasn't a bit turned on all the same.

"Let's start with some light stretching to warm up our muscles. Would you mind pushing on my back?"

Haru plopped down on the ground and stretched her legs out in front of her.

"Yes, Mistress."

I went around behind her and pushed against her back with all my might. Her back felt warm enough to me already. I could feel her body heating up my palms through her shirt.

"Mmn."

"Wow, you really are flexible."

I was trying hard not to focus too much on her bobbing ponytail and the exposed nape of neck below it. I realized I was touching her bra strap, and I quickly moved my hands to a different spot.

"Having supple muscles is vital when it comes to playing sports. Why are you frowning?" Haru twisted around to look at me.

"…Am I frowning?"

"You are. You keep making this pained face. You do that sometimes."

"Is that why you invited me to work out with you? To help me loosen up?"

"Nope, this is totally unrelated. I prefer to work out with people who are going to put their back into it."

"Oh yeah, that so?"

Haru spread her legs wide, and I proceeded to push on her back as she stretched over first her right leg, then her left. She went all the way down, so far down that it was almost comical. I could smell the fresh scent of her deodorant.

"You know how the coach gives us a quota of points to try to reach during midseason games? And they're all like 'I know *you* can do it' to motivate you. How does that make you feel, Haru?"

Haru snapped her legs together and bent forward to touch her toes. I pushed on her shoulders and put my weight into it. Her legs were so long and smooth, and slightly shiny. So different from my own hairy legs that it seemed impossible to believe we belonged to the same species.

And uh, all this stretching and posing… It was getting dangerous.

"Hmm, it does make me feel motivated, I guess. I wouldn't want to let the coach down, after they've shown such faith in us."

Haru got to her feet with a "Hup!" Then she pointed to the ground. "Your turn," she seemed to be saying.

"But what if you failed to hit that quota? What if you lost the game? …Ow-ow-ow, hey!"

"Yikes, Chitose, you're so stiff! You've really been slacking off since you quit baseball. Hmm, if I failed, it would be because of my own lack of effort. I'd apologize to the coach and just try harder next time."

Not only was she digging into my back with the heels of her hands, but she was also pressing her chest against my back. Maybe she was used to being this hands-on with the other girls on her team, but surely she hadn't forgotten that I was a guy here? I wondered if she did the same thing when she practiced with Kaito... Huh, wow. I should *not* be thinking these kinds of thoughts right now.

"So you'd just keep trying, without feeling like your pride got hurt? Ouch, ouch, quit that!"

"Chief, you need to loosen up! In more ways than one. It's up to the individual to decide how much effort they want to put into something, right? If I felt that badly about being in the club, I'd quit. Right now, I'm happy to continue like this. Why did you quit baseball, Chitose?"

"...I got sick of having to keep my hair so short."

"Aha, I see. You're trying to dodge the question."

I got to my feet and put my back against Haru's, linking arms with her. Then I bent forward as far as possible, lifting Haru on my back.

"Guhhh! Ugh! But you played with such focus. I can't imagine you quitting over something so superficial. I hope this isn't out of line for me to say, but I can tell how much sports meant to you."

"It was pretty superficial, yeah."

We switched, and this time she lifted me on her back.

"You're not willing to talk about it, then? Guhhh!"

"You're gonna snap my back at this rate! I feel like one of those golden fish ornaments you see on castle walls whose heads are bent back to their tails!"

Haru had lowered her head almost to the ground, and I was bent so far back I was almost upside down.

"...There, all done."

Haru stretched out her arms and legs briefly before heading over and opening up her ball bag. Pulling out her basketball, she went to the concrete court and began to dribble.

"If baseball went wrong for you for whatever reason, there's always basketball, Chief! If you train up a little, I bet you could make the team regulars!"

"I'll think about it, as long as you agree to stretch with me every day."

"Sorry, I'm not interested in boys who are less skilled than I am."

"You shouldn't underestimate my athletic prowess."

Haru didn't comment on that one. "Come on, play a game with me. We can't use the hoop since those elementary schoolers are using it. So how's this? You manage to dribble past me, and you get one point. I manage to dribble past you, and I get one point. Let's see who can get to ten points first!"

"How do we define *dribbling past*?"

"Let's just wing it. If neither of us can agree, we'll restart the round. Okay? I'll even let you go first."

I grinned. Only Haru would come up with a set of rules like those.

"Bring it on."

I retied the laces of my Stan Smiths, pulled off my jacket, and rolled up my shirtsleeves. I was a jock at heart. A little challenge was all it took to get me fired up.

I remembered the excitement I used to have before baseball games, and I felt a pang of regret, mixed with nostalgia.

I grabbed the ball and began dribbling, crouching low.

Haru crouched low as well, her eyes on me.

"The loser has to answer any question the winner poses, okay?"

"Why? What are you planning to ask?"

"Well, what I want to *know* is why you quit baseball. But what I'll ask is: How come you were frowning earlier?"

"I already told you: I wasn't even frowning."

"Nuh-uh, I saw it. I make a point to always try to read my opponent, even in the midst of a game!"

"...Tch. All right. If I win, do I get to ask you something dirty?"

"Are you insane? Why would you ask something like that? But whatever, ask anything you want. If, by some miracle, I happen to lose, then I'll answer anything."

"All right, I'm in. And also, the loser has to buy the winner something from the hot food section at the convenience store."

"Okay, Chief. I'm ready for you; show me what you got!"

I quickly faked her out, making her lunge to her dominant side while I zipped past her with ease...

✳

"...I've bought what you asked for, Mistress Haru."

"You sure took your time! That's five minutes I've been waiting."

"What are you, some sort of demon? Making me rush to buy snacks after that ferocious game we just had. I'm exhausted."

I had lost pathetically. Haru was just plain better than me. I'd only been able to get five points. And I'd only been able to get them by using my size and strength to shove Haru out of the way.

Now I knew why Haru, who was on the short side for the basketball team, was considered such a valuable player. She sure was fast. Of course, I could outrun her if we were running in a straight line. But she was nimble. She dodged, ducked, and turned on a dime. I was only able to fake her out that one time.

"Ah-ha-ha, you're so funny, Chitose! You let your guard down, underestimated me, and let me get five points past you! Your natural athletic abilities don't amount to much, huh? Kaito's more of a challenge than you, by far. Now, to enjoy my spoils!"

"Hmph. I wasn't on top of my game today; that's all."

"Sure, sure, if that's what you need to keep telling yourself!"

"...Anyway, that last point? I still call foul."

"Oh, drop it already."

Haru expertly put her ball away in its case, handling it with incredible ease, as if it were a part of her.

"Now, you haven't forgotten the other part of our agreement, have you?"

"Listen, I'm fine. I wasn't frowning, and there's nothing wrong. I was just thinking about stuff; that's all."

"Now, now. Tell Auntie Haru everything."

I felt like Haru had played me. But it was my fault for accepting her challenge. I couldn't really complain about it now.

"...Tch. Remember I told you about how I've been helping Kenta out?"

"Yeah, you've been making him cooler so he can get one over on his old friend group, right?"

I nodded. "Yeah. I've been kind of conceited, making him think I had the answers he needed, but now it's like...what if the plan fails? Just when he was getting back on his feet. If he ends up crushed again, it's going to be on me this time. How am I supposed to deal if that happens?"

"Ah, so that's why you were asking me about point quotas and stuff..."

I hate complaining and whining. Especially when it's me doing it in front of my friends.

"I'm the one who came up with this plan. It's on me to make sure it works."

"Chitose... I don't really know what you want me to say right now..."

Great, just what I didn't want. Pity.

I wasn't looking for reassurance, really. I just wanted to know that somebody out there understood how I felt.

I guess I was paying the price for losing our little basketball wager.

I should just try to laugh it off.

"You really are a dumbass, aren't you? Lighten up!"

...*Huh?*

"What, don't tell me you think you have to be perfect all the time? I thought you actually had a real problem! Quit whining!"

I blinked at Haru. I wasn't expecting her to say something like that.

"…What? I *am* perfect, though."

Haru reached over and grabbed my nose.

"Do you want Haru to pull off your perfect little nose, then? Listen, Chitose. You're the coach. Yamazaki's your player; he's the one out on the court. You get it?"

"I don' geddid. Dad hurds."

"If a coach's star player screws up on the court, does the coach blame himself? Sure, maybe a little. But he shouldn't. The mistakes of the player are the responsibility of the player. Messing up during a game, in public, that's the risk we all take when we play competitive sports. Do you get that, Chitose?"

…Hmm, she had a point.

"Yamazaki chose you as his coach based on his own decision. And he made the choice himself, to step out onto that court! I know he was prepared. So whether he ends up succeeding or failing, he's the one who should either feel good or bad."

Haru let go of my nose but kept on talking.

"Saying it's all on you… That's downplaying his hard work. It's disrespectful! And let's say you screwed up during a baseball game, how would you feel if the coach was like 'Oh, it's all my fault, Chitose!' …Huh?"

"…Yeah… That'd be hard to take. That makes it sound like all my failures *and* my successes, too, just belong to the coach."

Haru grinned.

"Yep. It's like, gee, Coach, why don't you just play instead of me, then? But the job of a coach is to guide. To have faith in the players! And to help them out when they come up against a wall and don't know what to do next. And then, if they fail…to help lift them back up!"

I was starting to feel a little ashamed of myself now.

Without realizing it, I'd begun to view Kenta as beneath me.

I got so caught up in my own position that I stopped thinking about his.

...I preached to him about trying to get to know how others think and feel, but then I went and did the exact opposite myself.

Haru leaned in again and pinched my cheek, a little too forcefully.

"Get down off your high horse, Chitose!"

She smiled bright as the sun, and it was almost too much.

⋆

We relocated to the park's swing set. I handed Haru her bottle of Pocari Sweat electrolyte drink and her hot dog on a stick, and then I took a bite of my own fried chicken.

Afterward, I popped the lid of my bottle of Royal Sawayaka soda, a Fukui staple, and chugged it. I was thirsty, and it tasted amazing. It's this sweet green soda that tastes like someone dumped a bunch of melon-flavored shaved ice syrup into fizzy water. Ever since I was a kid, whenever I got the urge for something carbonated, I always went for a Royal Sawayaka.

"Wow, Chitose. I haven't drank that since I was a kid."

"Right? Remember how it used to come in a glass bottle instead of a plastic one? And you could buy it from the candy store."

"Oh yeah! And you'd get a dime back if you returned the bottle to the store."

Haru slathered her hot dog in ketchup and mustard and then shoved it into her mouth.

...Oh man, that is hot, especially from a girl you don't usually think of doing hot stuff. Why doesn't she realize the implications? Not that I'm about to point it out.

I looked around, noticing that dusk had settled all of a sudden. I hadn't worked out this hard in ages, and the cool breeze rolling off the river felt good on my sweaty skin. Haru looked shadowy and indistinct in the gloom. I guess I looked the same way to her.

The swings creaked.

The elementary schoolers who had been shrieking and playing in the park were gone now. They were probably home already, waiting for their dinners to be dished up.

"Hey, Chitose… This park used to be the city-run baseball field, didn't it?"

"Yeah. I never got to play here, though. They repurposed it into a park before that."

"It's pretty, isn't it?"

"It is."

I couldn't tell if Haru was trying to tell me something or just offering commentary.

It was kind of nice, sharing the silence of a place like this and noticing its beauty together.

"Haru, thank you. I feel a lot better now."

"You don't have to try to come up with some fake reason why you lost our wager. You're so neurotic."

"…Sorry. I'll reform."

"You know, you're so much cooler earnestly chasing after a ball rather than strutting around trying to pretend like you're so cool and that you know everything all the time."

"Really?"

"Well, that's what I think at least. I can't speak for others."

Haru stood up on the swing and started swinging. I followed suit.

"…All right, well, I want a rematch," I said. "Let's see who can jump the farthest."

"I think that's why that railing is there? To prevent people from doing that?"

"Who cares? We're athletic. The loser has to… I know—the loser has to divulge their one biggest weakness. I don't want to leave things like this, with me being the only one who's opening up here."

"All right, you're on. But I should warn you: I'm lighter than you. I have the competitive edge."

*Skreek, skreek. Jangle, jangle.*

We both leaped off our swings, flying into the air across the twilit park, our shadows leaping behind us.

The first star of the evening was already twinkling in the sky.

I wished I could reach it.

I was aware of Haru, airborne by my side. She was colored in an indigo hue, her skirt fluttering up, her shorts visible, her ponytail streaming behind her.

I wanted to leap higher. This wasn't high enough for me. I wanted to vault high into the sky, so high that no one would be able to reach me.

I wanted to reach a place where I wouldn't have to rely on the kindness of a friend to prop me up…where I wouldn't have to rely on anyone at all.

✳

That evening, I got an unexpected phone call.

It was from Yuzuki Nanase.

We messaged on LINE plenty of times, but this was the first time we would be speaking over the phone.

I tapped the answer call button.

"Yeah, it's me."

*"And it's me. What's the status update?"*

"Just like you predicted. I have to say, though, this job doesn't sit right with me. It's beneath me, frankly. It's like if I had to undo a bra clasp within the space of three seconds. I only need one and a half."

*"You get sloppy when you're feeling overconfident; that's your problem. I know you're good, but you overlook the small things. You thought the bra clasp was on the back, but it was a front-hook bra all along. In this line of work, you gotta consider the variables."*

"I'll check out the back in zero-point-five seconds. Then with the remaining second, I'll move around to the front. Easy. You want to test me?"

"*...No, thanks. I'd hate to lose a valuable man at a critical moment like this.*"

Nanase dissolved into laughter, bringing our role-play to an end.

I was playing the role of the hard-boiled hit man who let his guard down and needed the intervention of the busty lady who had employed him to kill her husband. Nanase really held up her end of the role.

After we finished chuckling, Nanase got serious.

"*Hey, Chitose. You free to talk now?*"

"Hey, Nanase. Sure, let's chat."

After all, hadn't we made plans to talk more, that first day of school?

There was an odd sense of distance between Nanase and me. We'd been on conversational terms since first year, but I'd never gotten close to her like I had with Haru. We were friendly, of course. But it was like we were only showing each other our surface levels. Nothing deeper.

That reminded me—I needed to thank her for helping out that morning.

"You really came in clutch this morning, Nanase."

"*Don't mention it. But why did you decide to help out Kenta Yamazaki in the first place?*"

"...Kura asked me to. He and I have a 'You scratch my back, I'll scratch yours' type of deal. I do some favors for him, and he lets me get away with whatever I want."

I had the feeling it wouldn't be the greatest idea to come up with some sort of dumb lie in front of Nanase. She'd see through me in a second.

But Nanase seemed to see straight through me anyway.

"...I see. That's a very plausible-sounding reason. Yeah, it's smart. When you don't want to tell the whole truth, just stick to the surface facts and obfuscate the real details. That'll get the job done."

"What you're saying is very complex, Nanase. Are you saying I have some other reason?"

*"Are you asking me?"*

"Doesn't every good cheesy rom-com involve a woman helping a man discover his true self?"

Nanase replied without a hint of blushing or dishonesty. *"You're not a rom-com lead, though. You're Saku Chitose."*

"...And you're Yuzuki Nanase."

*"Oh, good. I was right, then."*

"...I don't like it when people try to read too much meaning into things."

*"Well, every good rom-com starts with a misunderstood bad boy."*

Man, she was tough to spar with. She was way too intense, just like Kazuki. The both of them really needed to kick back and enjoy life more.

Nanase cleared her throat.

*"Can you at least tell me why you chose Yuuko next after Ucchi, when you went to try to convince Yamazaki to come back to school? I mean, why wasn't it me?"*

"Oh, are you feeling left out?"

*"I just thought it was a little...unexpected."*

"I like being in charge, rather than being the one taken for a ride, I guess."

*"Hmm, I'm down to be taken for a ride, you know..."*

"Oh good, I'll swing by to pick you up sometime soon!"

Nanase giggled. *"...Too bad, though. I was really hoping to get you in my debt, Chitose."*

"You don't need me to be in your debt. I'm always willing to lend a hand to a cute girl. Even more so if she's a girlfriend of mine."

*"Oh, that's good to know. Well, since it's clear that I am one of your girlfriends, I guess I'll have to ask you a special favor sometime soon."*

"Hmm, so even the great Nanase needs a favor every now and then, huh?"

*"Yeah, like for example, maybe you'd consider...being my boyfriend? Or something like that."*

"Ah, I love a surprise attack."

*"Just kidding. Hard to get out of character after all that top-tier role-playing earlier."*

The teasing nature had gone from Nanase's voice. I guessed this session of baiting each other was over.

I lowered my tone to match hers.

"Yeah. We'll be embarrassed tomorrow morning when we see each other face-to-face and remember this conversation."

*"You're not kidding. I'm already regretting it as we speak."*

Making my voice sound feminine, I decided to tease her by repeating her own words back to her.

"Well, every good cheesy rom-com starts with a misunderstood bad boy."

*"Oh my gosh, stoppp."* I could hear her drumming her legs against her bedspread. *"Anyway, you started it! What was it you said? 'Doesn't every good cheesy rom-com involve a woman helping a man discover his true self'...?"*

"Oh my gosh, nooo!"

I dived onto my bed and started smacking my face into my pillow.

Nanase could hear it over the phone. She let out a very high school girl-esque squeal of laughter.

*"How about we call it a draw before this gets any worse?"*

"Hmm, I agree. No sense in both of us getting hurt."

Talking to Nanase... I had the feeling it would never get old.

I realized she was the type of girl who has all kinds of different sides to her, sides she usually keeps hidden.

I wanted to tease her one last time. "So does yours hook in the front or the back? I have to know, or I won't be able to sleep tonight."

I could hear the sound of cloth rustling over the phone.

Then Nanase spoke in a sultry tone, almost whispering into my ear.

*"In the back, of course. And it's blue. As blue as April skies."*

"...I misspoke. Now I won't be able to sleep tonight."

*"Good. Consider it a taste of my revenge."*

"I see. Then I'll just have to think of more ways to make you even madder at me."

*"Good night, Chitose."*

"Good night, Nanase."

*

Two weeks passed. It was the final week of April, the day before the Saturday Kenta was due to confront his old group. Kenta and I were getting changed into our sports clothes for fifth-period gym. The girls always used the locker rooms in the gym, but we guys couldn't be bothered and usually just changed in the classroom.

Kazuki and Kaito had already headed out to the sports field.

"...Maybe it's just me, but I feel like these last three weeks have passed in a flash, huh, King?" Kenta sounded somewhat downcast.

"Well, yeah. We've done so well and made so much progress since that first day I gave you those assignments. Time tends to fly when you're busy."

"Yeah, but... I know, but... I was picturing more defeats, then being encouraged by cute girls, and more heartwarming scenes like that..."

"I'd never come up with such a flawed plan. I've set everything up so you should be able to succeed without having to strain yourself too far. If you don't like my plan, though, then feel free to go it alone from now on."

"Was it really all your plan? Some of your old-man Dad jokes reek of Kura, you know what I mean?"

"Hey, know where to draw the line. That comparison offends me."

I took another look at Kenta, who was in the middle of changing his shirt.

"By the way, man, you've really trimmed down. And you've gained muscle, too."

"Uh, I guess, yeah."

It wasn't as if he'd suddenly sprouted six-pack abs or anything, but nobody could call Kenta fat anymore.

"And you've gotten totally comfortable talking with popular kids, right?"

"Well... I've just been copying you and Mizushino, when you talk to Nanase and the other girls... I've tried to memorize your speech patterns."

"So then, what's the problem?"

"I just don't feel like it suits my personality..."

"Look, as I've said before, this is my harem rom-com story. Who wants to follow the story of Sidey McSide Character? Why don't you try to crowdfund your own novel if it matters that much to you?"

"You've started comparing everything to light novels now, King."

It was true; I'd been borrowing all kinds of light novels and anime series on Blu-ray from Kenta during the time we'd been hanging out.

"Anyway, tomorrow's the big day. Do you think you can pull it off?"

"Well... We've done all we can, I think we can safely say. I just have to try not to screw up while I'm there. I'm sure it'll go all right in the end... Oh, I almost forgot."

Kenta pulled out his phone and showed me the lock screen.

"I'm thinking about sitting at the same exact table. I just feel like it'll help me stay calm."

He had the pic of Yuuko and us at Starbucks as his phone's lock screen.

"I know it's standard to set pics of you with your friends as your lock screen, but this is kinda creepy somehow... Why do you feel the need to gaze at my face every time you wanna use your phone?"

"...Er, King? Why are you covering your chest with your sports clothes...?"

\*

We finished changing our clothes, then put on our outdoor sports shoes and headed to the sports field. Incidentally, here in Fukui, we call our indoor sports shoes and our outdoor sports shoes indoor sneaks and outdoor sneaks, but they don't do that in other prefectures, they just call them shoes. It was embarrassing in baseball club when one of us slipped up and called them sneaks while we were playing games against teams from farther away.

Fuji High gym classes usually consist of two classes at a time, and they're held separately for boys and girls. Classes One to Five, the humanities-focused classes, have more girls and fewer boys, and Classes Six to Ten, the science-focused classes, have more boys and fewer girls. So to balance things out, they mixed up the classes in second year so the humanities and science kids were teamed up for gym. We're Class Five, and we're teamed up with Class Ten. Today's gym session was to be a friendly game of soccer.

I met up with Kazuki and Kaito and returned a wave from Yuuko, who was over in the nearby tennis court. Just then, Atomu and two other guys walked up. They were both part of the group who had been hassling Kenta and Yua the other day.

Kazuki let out a sigh under his breath, audible only to me.

"Hey, Chitose," said Atomu. "A normal game sounds too boring, so why don't we make it interesting? Losers have to face a punishment."

He slung his arm around Kenta's shoulder, grinning. Why were these "ambitious" popular kids always so touchy-feely?

"Sounds good. I like a good wager."

Kazuki and Kaito had no objections, either.

"Your team has to consist of Mizushino, Asano, this guy here, and you. My team will consist of these guys and me. The short-haired guy's name is Shuto Inaba, and the big guy here is Kazuomi Inomata."

The names seemed to mean something to Kazuki.

"Oh yeah, I thought I recognized you. Inaba, the captain from Michiaki Junior High. And, Inomata, you were the goalkeeper. Hearing your names sparked my memory."

"Long time, Mizushino. I think the last time we met was at the district tournament, wasn't it? But we actually recognized you last year, by the way."

The short-haired Inaba seemed friendly, but his eyes were cold.

*Kazuki, I seriously doubt you're only just recognizing these guys.*

Inomata was tall and well-built. And he looked angry.

"I sure haven't forgotten how you got four goals past me in one game."

"Oh really? That kind of thing barely registers to me. I don't tend to remember little details of old games like that."

So Atomu's group had two soccer players in it. That was probably why he'd suggested this game. Maybe he'd even rope in Class Ten's current soccer club members as well. But no need to worry.

I had Kazuki, and this was just gym class. No need to worry about balancing teams down to the player.

Kaito was already stretching, and he seemed totally into it.

"So what's the punishment going to be? Let's make it something really nasty."

"Okay, the losers have to hop around the entire school grounds like bunnies. While the girls are still outside for their class, of course."

That was Atomu's suggestion. It sounded suitably embarrassing, as far as a punishment goes. But I had one concern.

"…Hold on a second. The only ones who should have to do the punishment are me, Kaito, and Kazuki, right? And you three. There's no need to get the others involved in this. And I doubt Kenta has the physical strength needed to bunny hop around the entire school grounds."

Atomu nodded his agreement. I knew it. His real target was me and my group all along. He had no real interest in Kenta.

"And while the losers are hopping, they have to yell 'Monkey! Gorilla! Chimpanzee!' at the tops of their voices. That will make it a real punishment."

"Excellent suggestion, Chitose."

✳

Once gym class got underway, we were told to split into four teams. First off, the other two teams played against each other while Atomu's group and mine watched.

Once that was done, we were up.

We ran out onto the field and faced off against each other. The gym teacher had okayed our little wager. "Good; that'll spice things up," he'd said about our suggestion.

As I'd predicted, Atomu's team was comprised of soccer club members and other jocks. My team, however, was kind of a mishmash.

Kenta turned to me, his voice tremulous.

"…King, are you sure you want to be doing this?"

"Don't look so worried. It's just a bit of fun, so let's enjoy it. And keep your eyes peeled, 'cause we're gonna pass to you as well."

"No, no! I can't! I really suck at ball games! In fact, all sports! I can't control my body… It just goes all over the place! And I certainly can't control a ball! I can't even play catch properly with my hands. So I know for a fact I can't do it with my feet! Why would you even ask me to do this?!"

"Just relax. I'm not expecting you to become the MVP of the game or anything. And anyway, we're the ones who accepted the game and the risk of having to do the punishment. You don't need to worry, whether we win or lose. So just chill and try to have fun with everyone!"

Kazuki leaned in, backing me up.

"He's right, Kenta. If the ball comes to you, just pass it to Saku, Kaito, or me. If that's too difficult, just kick it any way you can."

Kaito was jumping up and down on the spot with impatience.

"Kenta, just stay out of the way of the ball if you're that worried. But this is gym class! You have to participate. Don't overthink things too much."

"I already told you, I can't… Before my grandmother died, she warned me never to lay hands on a soccer ball! Otherwise, uh, I'd fall under the family curse!"

What a crazy excuse. Kenta was really reaching.

"Your grandmother's right. You lay hands on it, and that'll be a handball."

I ignored Kenta, who was still blithering on, and turned my attention to the kickoff. Atomu and I did rock-paper-scissors to decide who had the honors. I won.

As soon as the whistle blew, I passed the ball to Kazuki. Immediately, Inaba and the other two soccer players on their team closed in. It looked like the others weren't marking anyone in particular. Kazuki pulled off a subtle feint and kicked the ball without passing it to another player. I'd seen Kazuki play in soccer games a bunch of times, but I always marveled at how the ball seemed to bend to his will.

"Kenta, head to the goal and wait there."

I called out to Kenta, who was just standing there. Reluctantly, he began trotting across the field.

Kazuki kept looking this way. I ran into an area of open space and received a pass with a light touch.

"Great!"

I trapped the ball, dribbled, and then Atomu seized the opportunity and closed in on me. He was athletic himself and managed to put a lot of pressure on me. I kept him from stealing it, thanks to a technique Kazuki had taught me once when we were messing around, and passed to Kaito, who was wide open.

"You're not going for the goal, man?"

"This is just gym class. I'm more focused on having fun with everyone and fostering teamwork."

"Pfft. Whatever."

Kaito's dribbling was sloppy, but he was rushing up the right side. He was really just kicking the ball ahead and running after it, but he was fast enough that they couldn't keep up.

"Kazuki!"

Once he got in front of the goal, he passed the ball without giving it any air. Kazuki pulled off a kick feint and let the ball roll past him and toward me. I had run up on his left side.

Our trap had resulted in only Kazuki, Atomu, Kenta, and me being in range of the goal. I passed to Kenta, who was again just standing there.

"Go for it!"

I tried to pass the ball as gently and cleanly as I could. By the way, this was just a gym class sports game, so we weren't using the offside rule or being too picky.

My pass was pretty much perfect, rolling straight to Kenta's feet. Naturally, he was unmarked. Even the goalkeeper hadn't been paying any attention to him.

Kenta's face went dead serious all of a sudden, and he drew back his leg to kick the ball straight into the goal...but he missed the ball entirely and performed a spectacular idiot fall flat onto his back.

It was the most graceless, hilarious fall you'd ever seen. The ball rolled slowly past the goal, bumbling its way over the grass.

"PAH-HA-HA-HA!!!"

Everyone was cracking up. Kazuki, Kaito, and I were all laughing, too, of course.

"Hey, Chitose, are you guys even trying? That otaku's a liability; put him on defense!" Atomu yelled across the field, loud enough for everyone to hear.

"Kentacchi, that was so funny!"

We could hear Yuuko yelling over from the tennis court. It sounded like she'd been watching.

I ran over to Kenta and gave him a hand getting up.

"That was great, Kenta! So funny! You're a genius. You and I should team up and head for the global stage...the comedy stage, that is."

"I *told* you I couldn't do this..."

Kenta was half crying as Kazuki and Kaito jogged over to join us.

Kaito thumped Kenta reassuringly on the back. "Shake it off, Kenta! I admire your gumption. Anyway, sports is all about having fun. Keep it up!"

Kazuki smiled at Kenta as he seized the opportunity to impart some soccer advice.

"In all seriousness, based on my knowledge, it's totally fine to pass behind you rather than choke under the pressure when you're near the goal. Also, it's hard to kick a moving ball as a beginner, so it's better to trap the ball first, then reposition yourself for the kick. Also, when you kick, you should use the flat of your foot or the ball of your foot rather than your toes. It gives you better control over the ball."

Kazuki was always sort of cool and aloof, but when it came to soccer, he turned into an impassioned sportsman. It was clear he wanted Kenta to enjoy the game as much as he did.

But Kenta's expression was dark with embarrassment, and he looked completely disheartened. It was clear he didn't know how to find any fun in a game like this at all.

✳

After that, we enjoyed a pretty good game of soccer. Even Kenta managed a few passes. You could still tell that Kazuki had played soccer before, but he seemed to be holding back for the rest of the game. Conversely, Atomu's group kept the less athletic players back defending their own goal, and they had their seasoned soccer players go on the attack. As a result, they managed an easy lead.

"Heh, you front like you're some amazing player, but you're all talk today. What the heck are you doing? Why won't you play properly? You asleep out there? …Pisses me off. But whatever. Get ready to hop, bunnies."

"Cool your jets. We're just playing for fun today."

Still, the score was eight–one in their favor. And there were only five minutes left. We were going to lose—and by a large margin. You can't make a comeback in soccer under these kinds of conditions. Baseball, maybe.

But so what?

Atomu's group was clearly trying to signal superiority as athletes by winning this game. But Kazuki, Kaito, and I really were just playing for fun. If we actually took it seriously, though, it would have been a much closer match.

But what benefit was there in that, for us?

I had already dropped out of school sports. And if I did want to show superiority, it would be during a real tournament. Not some dumb gym class. There was no need to show off during a friendly match. No, a tournament was the time to do it. What was the fun in dominating a fun game and leaving the other, untalented players no opportunity to touch the ball or enjoy the game at all?

After all, a game's no fun unless the whole team plays together. Atomu's group and my group saw the punishment attached to this game in completely different ways. For them, it was a way to shame us and signal their own superiority. But for us, it was just a way to make gym class even more entertaining.

"You need to stop hanging around with that otaku; he drags you down." Atomu sneered at me.

"Don't be a jerk. Kenta's cool. You'd better watch out for him. He might overtake us all someday."

"Yeah, right. Like that's ever gonna happen."

Actually, I was serious. Yeah, looking at Kenta's basic specs, he was nowhere near the level of any of us. In fact, he was overwhelmingly mediocre.

But there aren't many people out there who decide to change themselves and actually follow through with it. I certainly took longer to turn myself around.

It seems simple enough, looking at it from the outside. Just make a decision and then follow through. But it's so much harder than it looks. That's what makes it so beautiful when someone actually does it.

Kenta kept giving it his all during the game. Every time he got the ball, I could see him trying, and failing, while attempting to implement Kazuki's advice.

"Saku, show us something good!"

The girls seemed to have wrapped up their gym class already. I could hear Yuuko calling over from where the girls were packing up their equipment.

"If you manage to turn it around, I'll treat you to a bowl of Hachiban's!"

*Nanase, you do realize that's impossible, right?*

"Put your back into it, boys! You're a disgrace!"

*Sorry, Mistress Haru.*

"You can do it, Yamazaki!"

*Yua's always so sweet.*

All right, maybe we could put our backs into it for the last few minutes. I signaled to Kenta.

"Pass to the king."

Kenta kicked the ball vaguely my way, and I had to chase after it. Atomu did, too, but I was faster.

"Come on, Atomu. Let's play for real, now."

"...Tch."

I turned to Kenta. We made eye contact.

*Come on, Kenta. Join in. Do it in your own way; that's fine. Just give it a shot. Try to stand alongside us.*

I dribbled to the left, then sped ahead. Atomu was hot on my heels. He even grabbed the sleeve of my sports shirt, but I shook him off and ran even faster.

Kaito was running up the midline. I passed to him with the instep of my right foot.

"Nice pass, Saku!"

Kaito pretended to shoot, but it was a feint. Instead, he passed to Kazuki on the right side. While he was doing that, I found a gap and broke for the goal.

Kazuki was being marked by three players, but he managed to evade them, shooting across to me.

"...Go for the goal, Saku!"

Atomu was closing in on me. I thought about a direct volley, but Atomu was on the side of my right foot. And the keeper, Inomata, had positioned himself in the way of my potential shot.

I chested the ball, then kept it up on my knee. Atomu was closing in on me, pressuring me. I had to turn my back on the goal to avoid him.

"Oh, this is gonna be good."

Kneeing the ball up into the air, I flung my leg backward and blindly kicked the ball straight down the field behind me.

*PWHOOSH!*

Inomata grasped for it, but the ball hit the back of the goal net. Yuuko, Nanase, Haru, and Yua all screamed with delight.

"Saku!!! That was *so cool*!!!!"

"Nice shot, Chitose!"

"Yeah!!!"

"Nice pass, Yamazaki!"

I landed hard on my butt, and it kinda hurt. Actually, it hurt a lot. But I had to pretend it didn't. I had to be cool.

Don't try this at home, kids!

"Where'd you learn to do a bicycle kick like that? Not in baseball club, that's for sure."

The goalkeeper, Inomata, jogged up, frowning.

"I may not be a seasoned soccer player, but you shouldn't have underestimated me. Backbends, backflips, dunk shots, double-clutch, heel lifts, bicycle kicks. I practiced all kinds of flashy sports techniques in elementary school and junior high. I was a jock, you know."

"…Man, you're a real asshole, you know that?"

I looked up. The sky was wide and blue, like the ocean.

The final whistle blew, marking our defeat.

★

"Okay, Kazuki. Okay, Kaito. Let's keep the energy high, all right?"

My two pals both chirped "Yes, sir!" from either side of me. Then we got into formation.

"Monkey!"

"Gorilla!"

"Chimpanzee!!"

Hop, hop. We began our bunny jumping.

"Monkey!"

"Gorilla!"

"Chimpanzee!!"

Yuuko, Nanase, Haru, Yua, and the other girls were all watching us, cracking up with laughter.

"Oh my gosh, my sides are splitting!"

"They're so cute! Look at them hop!"

"Someone take a video of this, quick!!!"

Inaba, Inomata, and those guys started off jeering and heckling us, but they began cracking up, too, when they realized it was ridiculous to take something like this so seriously. Out of the corner of my eye, I could see that Atomu was talking to Kenta again, no doubt giving him a hard time once more.

But this was fine.

This was *good*.

Gym class is pointless, so make it fun. And this time, it was. Also, a game with some kind of penalty attached tends to come with an element of risk, and that makes it all the more entertaining. Rather than shoving someone down to avoid the penalty, why not enjoy the thrills of victory and the sting of defeat together?

We knew that our "social stock price" wouldn't be affected by losing the game or by our having to perform a punishment. As long as we could get everyone laughing, we'd still come out on top.

"Louder, louder! Let's have the crowd chant with us now! MONKEY!"

""""Gorilla!!!"""""

"""""""CHIMPANZEE!!!""""""""

Our voices, and the voices of the crowd, rang out across the dry and dusty sports field and disappeared on the wind.

*

After school, Yuuko and I were waiting in the classroom for Kenta. We had arranged to walk home with him so we could talk strategy for tomorrow's big meeting. But Kenta had been called to the staff room. Apparently, he was slow catching up on all the work he'd missed, and Kura had given him a ton of extra homework. The others had all gone off to club practice.

"Man, today's gym class was *so* funny. You guys looked so cute hopping around, Saku."

"Heh. Man, I managed to make all the girls swoon even while hopping like a cute bunny."

"Uh, no. You were a total lame-o through the whole game. Except for that final shot. Those other guys creamed you."

"...Blame it on Kenta."

Yuuko giggled. "All right," she said. "...But Kentacchi was pretty funny, too. I saw him try to kick the ball, miss, and fall on his butt, like, five times."

"The guy's got the coordination of a baby goat. I wouldn't even trust him to ride a bicycle. We lost at least ten chances at goal because of him."

"Uemura and Inaba and those guys were really making fun of you. Said you were nothing, just all talk."

"Hmm... I think I'm done with Kenta's antics. I should consider cutting him loose from Team Chitose sometime soon."

"He's really become a fairly normal guy lately, though. He doesn't have that comic appeal he had at the beginning."

While Yuuko and I were joking around, I started thinking back. Kenta really had come a long way. Yuuko calling him a normal guy... That was actually high praise, based on where he'd started from.

Tomorrow would mark a whole new chapter in his life, I was sure of it. At least, I really hoped so.

"Ah, Kentacchi!" Yuuko called.

I turned to see Kenta standing in the doorway of the classroom.

"Did ya get reamed out by Kura?"

I called out to him, but Kenta just stood there, hands clenched into fists. Yikes, he must have been given a ton of homework.

"Hey, we waited for you. The least you can do is buy us a couple coffees for the walk…"

"…Are you seriously trying to act like nothing happened?"

Kenta's voice had a strangled quality to it.

Yuuko and I exchanged glances. We both looked like we should have little *?* marks floating over our heads.

"…Like, what happened?"

"Don't bullshit me!!"

"…Like I said, what are you…?"

"Shut up!!"

Kenta was yelling. It finally registered that he really was mad.

"You and Yuuko were just bad-mouthing me and laughing about me, weren't you?! This is exactly what Uemura told me after the soccer game! He said you've all been making fun of me from the start!"

I can't deny that we've had a few laughs over Kenta. That's a fact. But it's not like we were talking about him behind his back or purposely making fun of him, though. And we certainly didn't say anything we wouldn't also have said to his face.

"Kentacchi, you've got the wrong idea. We haven't—"

"Yuuko." I shook my head, cutting her off.

Getting up from my chair, I headed over to the doorway to face Kenta directly.

"Continue. What next? Are you going to drag out the trauma from your otaku friends again?"

"…I knew something was up as soon as gym class started! You know I don't have any sports ability, but you still kept passing the ball to me and the other kids who suck, too! You wanted us to screw up so you could all have a good laugh at our expense!"

"I passed to you because that's what you do during a game. It's called teamwork. It wouldn't be a very fun game if only the talented players kept possession of the ball. And we laughed because we're your friends. Besides, everyone laughed at *us* while we were doing the bunny hop, right? I kept telling you that gym class is about having fun. I just wanted to make it an enjoyable game for everyone."

"Don't lie!" Kenta trembled, clearly not used to confrontation. "You shouldn't have dropped the act, if that was really your intention! You say you wanted to have fun with 'everyone,' but no, at the end you just had to abandon us so you could show off how cool you are! Pulling off that goal with that trick shot... You're just as bad as Uemura! You two are the same!"

"...I'm not going to deny it. We wanted to enjoy ourselves, just as much as we wanted you guys to enjoy yourselves. And why are you excluding Kaito, Kazuki, and me when you say 'everyone' like that? You're saying we should hide our skills the whole time and just focus on propping up you nonathletic kids?"

Kenta slammed his fist against the door.

"You shouldn't have roped me into it in the first place! Do you have any idea how terrifying gym class can be to unpopular kids like us?! All we can do is pray the ball won't come our way! It's so much easier for us to just hang back and stay out of trouble! It's only athletic, jock jerks like you who think it's fun to get a chance to handle the ball!"

"...I tried to give you all advice. So did Kazuki and Kaito. I mean, look at how much you improved by the end of the game, compared to the beginning. Don't you find fun in learning new skills...?"

"..."

Kenta seemed to be having trouble picking the right words. Perhaps what I was saying had hit home somewhat. But he had gone too far in his anger to back down now.

He started yelling again right away.

"...So I improved a little? So what?! I'm still only around to make you guys look better! You talk like you're so generous and kind, but you're just another one of those shallow popular kids who's always trying to dump on other people to get to the top! You have no idea what it's like to be unpopular! Oh, let's pass the ball to the poor loser, give him a taste of what it feels like to belong! Your entire existence revolves around trampling on other people, all of you!!!"

"I'm...sorry."

I hung my head, honestly feeling bad. Maybe Kenta was right. Maybe we projected our own feelings onto the other kids in class. We thought that a game where we didn't get to touch the ball was a waste of time, no fun at all. And we honestly believed that it's fun to learn new things. That's why we tried to give advice like that.

None of us had any idea how our actions could end up hurting others. How many other people had I hurt in my life, just from not understanding that? This time, I was in the wrong. Irrefutably so.

But Yuuko shook her head over what I said, addressing Kenta instead of me.

"Hold on, Kentacchi. I think that's enough. You really think Saku is like that? After spending all this time with him? You think he's the kind of guy who likes to laugh at your failures behind your back? You think he passed to you just to see you screw up, so he could show off how athletic he is in comparison?"

I thought Yuuko was being a little harsh. She took a deep breath and continued in a kinder voice.

"Listen. Saku has been doing all this out of a genuine desire to help you. He's been willing to stick with you to the end, hasn't he? Can't you see that?"

Kenta grimaced, all kinds of emotions fighting it out on his face.

Kenta had a lot on his plate. Atomu trying to psych him out, his feelings of trauma over what happened with his otaku hobbyist group, his own feelings of inadequacy after a lifetime spent being unpopular, his anxiety over the impending meeting with his old friends tomorrow... All of it combined just ended up making him explode.

I felt sorry I hadn't been able to predict this outcome and give him more support before it came to that.

"It's all right, Yuuko. I tried to explain it to him. How the difference between bullying and friendly teasing lies in how comfortable you are with each other. I guess he wasn't comfortable enough with me yet. So I should have known where to draw the line… I'm really sorry, Kenta."

Kenta's eyes filled with tears as he stomped over to his desk to grab his schoolbag. Then he stomped toward the classroom door. I called after him.

I may have failed as a life coach, but I still wanted him to know I was rooting for him.

"Kenta! Give it your all tomorrow. And I hope it turns out okay."

But Kenta didn't turn around. He just walked out.

*

"…Are you sure you want to leave things like this, Saku? Kentacchi was totally wrong about everything!"

After that, I decided to walk Yuuko home. She lived about a fifteen minutes' walk away from Lpa. It was pretty far from school, but I didn't want to be alone for some reason.

"…It's all right. It was only supposed to be a three-week thing, after all."

"What are you going to do about tomorrow? Are you going to go and see him off?"

"No. I doubt he wants me to come, either. We only started hanging out on a whim. This seems like as good a time as any to call it. Things are fine like this. Starting tomorrow, we'll go our separate ways again."

"If you insist, I won't say anything more about it…"

National Highway 8 went right through this area, so it was sort of Fukui's industrial sector hub. Just a few roads off the highway, though, and it was all rice fields as far as the eye could see. We had opted to take one of the little dirt roads through the rice fields to avoid the heavy traffic of the highway, even though it added a few minutes to the journey.

An empty can went rolling across the ground.

As we walked along, we were the only two people in sight.

The rice fields were filled with water now, and they reflected the setting sun. An April breeze sent ripples across the surface of the water.

A crow cawed from somewhere far-off. An old man in long boots puttered past us on a beat-up scooter.

"Hey, Saku... These past three weeks have been kinda fun. Usually, there wouldn't be much to find enjoyable about convincing some random classmate to come back to school, but it's kind of made me think that...these are the days we'll be looking back on when we're grown-ups, you know?"

"Yeah. I guess this will end up being one of those memorable events that sticks out after all. A once-in-a-lifetime type of deal."

"But I guess it's over now. I hope Kentacchi's reunion with his old friends goes well."

There was a peaceful quality to Yuuko's voice that went perfectly with the stillness of the coming sunset.

"It'll go okay. We've taught him well over the past three weeks."

"Well, *you* have, Saku. You don't have to act so bashful and try to make it sound like it was a group effort."

"It was. After all, you've helped out a ton, Yuuko."

"Yep. I've been your ride-or-die girl. It was only because I wanted to be close to you, at least at first. Partway through, though, I started wanting to cheer our Kentacchi on for real. I see him as a friend now. But if you hadn't started the whole life-makeover thing, I sure wouldn't have gotten involved. I mean, I was pretty much convinced he would never be able to change..."

Yuuko smiled softly.

"But that's the difference between you and me, Saku. I guess that's what it takes to be a hero, huh?"

I guess twilight makes everyone start feeling sentimental.

I hoped that ten years from now I'd be able to look back on this moment, recall the words Yuuko had said to me, and smile.

"You make me sound so much better than I really am. I just wanted to look cool in the eyes of people like you, and Yua, and the rest of our group. I wanted you to think, *Wow, Saku really is awesome.* But that's how I ended up hurting Kenta's feelings. I'm no hero. I'm just a popular kid from a hicksville country town who wanted to look cool."

"Yeah, well, I don't want my heroes to act like they know they're heroes. The truly good people are the ones who are never quite sure how good they really are."

"Don't. Don't put me up on a pedestal like that. I can't handle the pressure. If I fall, you're just going to lose all faith in me in a second, you know?"

"You won't fall, Saku. You're strong, and you're good, and I like you. A lot."

"…Hmm, not sure I can really trust your taste in men."

"Oh, now, that stings. I have excellent taste! I've spent a lot of time with a lot of people, ever since I was small."

It wasn't like Yuuko to get so philosophical.

"Well, I'll try to believe you, then. As much as I can."

"Good. Because my feelings won't change. Maybe not ever."

We reached Yuuko's house. She turned to me, smiling.

"Want to come in for some tea? I don't think my parents are home yet, though…"

"Maybe another day. When the timing is…special."

*Bye. See you.*

We waved our good-byes as the dusk deepened.

# CHAPTER FIVE

This is the story of Kenta Yamazaki, aspiring ex-nerd, as he approaches the biggest crossroad of his life so far.

I, the aforementioned Kenta Yamazaki, approached the Starbucks step by precious step, as I went over all the things King had told me in my head.

I couldn't sleep a wink last night. I knew that I was in the wrong. King and Yuuko had given me so much over the past three weeks. They all had... But in the end, I'd thrown it back in their faces.

What a fool I was.

I didn't need Yuuko to remind me what a great guy King really was. Did I trust him? Absolutely. In fact, there was no one else in my life I could trust more. But I was still so caught up in my nerd-persona complex, so poisoned by the things Uemura had been saying to me... I felt like shit about myself, and I wanted to blame someone else. So I tried to act like I was the wounded party, and King had even apologized...to me.

*"If you get to know them well, you'll be able to tell whether they're trying to put you down, or if they're just teasing you in a loving manner."*

\*　　　\*　　　\*

I remembered King saying that to me. It seemed like such a fundamental thing. But I had forgotten it. My identity as an unpopular, bullied nerd ran too deep.

I felt sure that, even now, King was blaming himself. Probably thinking he'd failed in earning my trust, like he said yesterday in the classroom. Which he hadn't! King hadn't done anything wrong. I was just…being a brat.

King could do everything. That was probably why he felt so responsible for me. He probably felt like he could solve any problem anyone was having, as long as he caught it in time. Otherwise, he blamed himself. No doubt he was taking my cruel words to heart, even though I had just thrown them out there in a fit of self-directed frustration.

After what I'd done, I knew there was no way back to King's side.

All I could do now was try my best to show how much I'd changed. To honor the effort King and his group had made for me over the past three weeks.

…I started thinking back on my first meeting with King.

I found myself smiling.

Reflecting on it now, he'd made a terrible impression on me when he showed up and started talking to me through my door. Bringing a cute girl along with him, acting so superior. "Oh, shall I help you out, poor misguided little shut-in?" He was the personification of everything I hated about popular kids.

I figured he'd soon give up once he'd made his point with the "Look what a great guy I am" shtick. But then he busted through my window and barged into my room. What a lunatic. Talk about overkill.

I chuckled to myself.

So much had happened since then.

I still felt weird wearing the glasses, clothes, and bag King and Yuuko had picked for me. Like I was wearing a costume. But when I looked at myself in the mirror at home, I actually managed to forget for a moment that I didn't have any friends anymore. I liked what I saw.

The new look wasn't just proof I'd become less dorky and more popular-looking. It also represented the times I'd shared with King and his group.

To be really honest, I didn't care about Miki anymore. And my desire for revenge, my hope that I could make Miki regret her actions... Those feelings seemed to have disappeared. As if blown away by a strong yet gentle breeze, cast off into some far-off ocean.

*"If you put in the time and effort toward something you're suited toward, then results will follow."*

I was proud of myself now. I was proud of what I'd achieved in the past three weeks.

Today wasn't just about settling my personal score. It was about something so much bigger than that. It was a matter of pride.

...Yeah, King would probably roll his eyes at that.

I was nervous. I kept getting the urge to turn around and run home. But I kept on walking anyway. King had always praised me for sticking to it, at least.

It looked like I really was Sidey McSide Character, just an amusing plot point in King's harem comedy story. I had no particular charms of my own. I guess I was always meant to just fade out of the plot. Actually, that altercation in the classroom yesterday... I bet that was supposed to be my exit scene.

Well, it makes sense. He could be mean sometimes, and he was undoubtedly a cynic and a narcissist, but I'd never met anyone with as big a presence as King's. He was strong, warm, funny, cool. Surrounded by a cast of equally shining stars...Yuuko, Uchida, Nanase, Aomi, Mizushino, Asano. You had to be special to ride with the king.

...These past three weeks... Man, they were fun. For just a

short period of time, King had invited me into his story. He had shown me a world I hadn't realized was possible. But it had come with an expiration date from the start.

I gritted my teeth. I felt like tears might come at any moment if I didn't hold myself together.

Things would be different, going forward.

I had to make something of my life by myself.

I remembered King saying...

"...Take responsibility for your own story, and write it how you want it to be."

This is the story of Kenta Yamazaki, aspiring ex-nerd, as he approaches the biggest crossroad of his life so far.

\*

I could see Miki, Ren, and Hayato standing in front of the Starbucks already. The three of them were looking at Miki's phone, laughing about something. Maybe she was going over my LINE group messages and laughing at me. I felt my heart sink.

Gathering my courage, I walked right up to them. Miki and Ren lifted their heads and looked at me, but they didn't seem to recognize me as the person they were waiting for. They turned away from me and continued their conversation.

Miki was wearing a gothic Lolita outfit today.

"...Sorry, have you been waiting long?"

I spoke up, trying to keep my voice as steady as possible. My throat felt dry already. I couldn't wait to get an iced latte in my hands.

The three turned to me in annoyance.

*Why is this guy talking to us?*

*How rude, interrupting our conversation like this.*

*What an annoying jerk.*

That's what their eyes were saying. I could tell. I would have thought the same thing myself, three weeks ago.

Then Miki's eyes widened.

"Er... Kenta?"

"Oh... You've forgotten what I look like already? Ouch..."

It was obvious my makeover had knocked them off-balance.

Once they realized it really was me, Kenta, Ren's whole attitude changed.

"Seriously? That's you, Kenta? The heck are you wearing? You doing your big high school makeover? You're a year late, you know? Oh man, you're hysterical."

I had to admit that Ren looked pretty cool. Even though the way he was trying to dunk on me to make himself look better was the embodiment of everything I hated about popular kids. He was another one, just like Uemura, who acted out of a sense of deep insecurity. Kinda sad.

I knew that, but his words still stung. "Ah, no, it's not like that, exactly..." I tried to laugh it off, at first.

Then I remembered King saying:

*"It's better to make fun of yourself and invite everyone else to join in."*

"...Although, you're not totally wrong. After being rejected by Miki, I was pretty shocked. I couldn't even go to school for a while. But now I'm over it, and I'm trying to get along with everyone more and make friends like popular kids do. What do you think of my new look?"

But their reaction wasn't what I was expecting. Ren looked stunned. Was it because I was doing my best King impression? We went to different schools, so he couldn't have known I hadn't been able to attend school for a while. I offered that information myself.

Now Hayato spoke up, his lip curling in derision.

"You couldn't go to school? All because a girl rejected you? Man, that's pathetic. This isn't a light novel, you know. There's no way a cringey loser like you could ever become popular in real life. Right, Miki? Right, Ren?"

I was sure he was trying to drag me back down to my prior position. Thanks to King and Yuuko, I'd started to feel okay about myself lately. I'd even managed to start projecting a bit of hot-guy aura. They had to have noticed. They were so hyper-aware of popularity and the social hierarchy. That was why they were acting so unsettled.

It was sad they had no idea that, in this world, sometimes stuff does play out like a light novel. There's a real-life OP hero even more unrealistic than the ones in those series.

I could almost hear King saying:

*"Forget the others. Focus on becoming someone you'd like if you weren't you."*

"I know, I know. But I figured, I can't get even lower than this. What do I have to lose? So I thought I should give it a try."

Right. Even though King, Yuuko, and the other members of Team Chitose had so many natural gifts, they still did their best every day to maintain their own high standards. I didn't have anything worthwhile to begin with, so how lucky was I to get all this praise just for smartening myself up a little?

I took a deep breath and tried to make sure I wasn't talking too fast.

"Anyway, instead of standing around out here, shall we go and sit down?"

"Yeah. I've actually never been here before... Have you been to Starbucks, Kenta?"

Maybe I was imagining it, but Miki's way of speaking was nicer than I recalled.

"Uh, I've been here once before, yeah."

*Grande, grande, grande. Not ground. Not ground. Grande!!!*

*

I ordered a Starbucks iced latte. The other three said they'd have the same, so I ordered for them all. Then I led everyone over to the same table as the one in the photo I had on my phone's lock screen. We took our seats. Recalling the photograph made me relax, just a little.

Ren leaned his arm over the backrest of his chair and crossed his legs in an ostentatious manner.

"You don't seem used to being in a place like this, Kenta. Most regulars customize their orders, don't you know that?"

Yes, he was right. I remembered how King and Yuuko had added all kinds of things to their orders. But I was so busy thinking about everything else that I'd completely forgotten about that.

*So why didn't* you *customize your order just now?* The words were on the tip of my tongue, but I bit them back.

I could almost hear King now:

*"Dragging down other people won't lift you up any higher. It'll just degrade you until you end up descending to their level."*

"Well, as I said, I've only come here once before. I came for a dry run, to practice inviting you all here today."

Hayato snorted.

"You had to do a *dry run*? He really is a loser, isn't he, Ren? Shame we couldn't just hang with Miki today, just the three of us."

"Cut it out, Hayato."

Everything that came out of these guys' mouths was a put-down.

Why was I even part of this group in the first place? This meeting was so unpleasant.

But this was my own fault—I'd spent enough time with them before to know what they were like. I'd wanted a friend group outside of school, a safe haven where I could share my interests with like-minded people, and I'd waded into the mud with them. So I expected too much of them, and then I got my feelings hurt. I didn't know these people, not really. Not at all.

I could almost hear the King's voice:

*"Now, let's try to understand each other."*

"So how have you all been doing? Have you been to any events lately?"

But Ren remained smug-faced.

"Yep. We have. Since you left, we've actually been able to get together more and more. So thanks for that."

"Oh, that's good. Sorry, I didn't realize I had been holding everyone back so much. Recently, I've been reading a lot of main-stream novels and watching mainstream cinema. It's surprisingly interesting. And I've been getting into lifting weights, too."

Hayato scoffed and joined in with Ren.

"So now you're not just trying to climb the social ladder, you're turning your back on otaku culture as a whole? Ridiculous. You'll never be anything but a loser. You think this is like one of those transformation stories you find in light novels? Look at those clothes and that bag. Someone else picked them out for you; that much is obvious."

"Yes, my new friends from school came shopping with me."

Hayato was turning out to be a bigger douche than I remembered.

He was probably scared of looking like a third wheel to Miki and Ren after I left the group. So he was trying hard to make them seem like they had this great three-way friendship going on.

Miki kept sneaking glances at me. "Kenta... I thought you didn't have any good friends at school? So you made some new friends?"

...This flirtatious manner of hers was what led me to getting the wrong idea about her.

But I guess Miki was just trying to seem like the cute girl. Especially in front of her boyfriend, Ren. If I really wanted to win her affection, I should have just tried harder.

Right, Yuuko?

"Well, a lot's happened. They're not so much friends as, I guess, life coaches? Or a king. Or a crazy demon lord. But they're all really cool. They have a great philosophy on life. I've been far more influenced by them than by any of the light novels I've read, I'd say."

"...Are any of them girls?"

Miki had a sort of wistful look in her eyes. Even though I had broken with their group, hearing about an old friend making new friends isn't always the easiest.

"Some of them are. The guys are super cool, and the girls are really charming. How about you...? Are you and Ren still dating and everything?"

"Uh, yeah..."

Miki looked away, trailing off. Maybe I shouldn't have asked such a personal question, even though I was trying that whole mutual understanding thing. I guess some people don't like to talk about that stuff in public.

"...So do you have a crush on any of these girls?"

But Miki was asking me personal questions now. I guess I became someone people actually want to know about?

"Oh, no. They've all done so much for me, but I haven't been able to offer them anything in return. I'd never presume to have a crush on any of them, not without being able to settle the score first. I mean, maybe, one day, after I'm done working on myself."

It was weird. In response to Miki's question, my mind didn't go toward Uchida as I might have predicted. Instead, it showed me something else. I had this mental image of a clear lake reflecting the sunset. It would soak up the setting sun's rays, offering a warm place to bathe for everyone who reached its shores. I thought about the girl I had recently come to know, whose name was written with the characters for *evening* and *lake*. *Yuuko*.

"Have you...have you forgotten about me? When I got the message from you after so long, I was really kind of excited to see you again..."

...I see.

She was playing the same game as last time. But this time, I could see right through her. She was showing interest in me to bait her boyfriend, Ren, into jealousy. To reaffirm his feelings for her.

But I no longer harbored any resentment toward her. And my desire to make her regret her actions had also dissipated. If she hadn't rejected me like she did, I would never have met King and the others. What could I do to repay them for that?

Perhaps I could prove useful by pretending to still harbor feelings for Miki, to fan the flames of Ren's jealousy?

I had the feeling it would be effective. But I wasn't sure I could pull it off.

Well, I could try being honest with them and try to reassure them that I wasn't interested. Then they could be honest with each other, too.

"It doesn't sound very nice to say I've forgotten you, but I guess I have. I don't have feelings for you anymore, Miki. I've found a better way forward by myself."

...

There was a long silence.

For some reason, Miki's shoulders appeared to be trembling. Uh-oh. Did I say something wrong?

But it was Ren who spoke next.

"Are you for real? This is why you invited us out?"

"…Er, yes?"

"I don't know who gave you the idea, but did you seriously ask us to meet you just so you could get revenge on Miki for rejecting you by flashing your new hairstyle and clothes and lying about all the hot friends you've made? Seriously?!"

I wasn't sure what was going on. I really did make new friends. And I did ask these guys to meet me so I could show them how I'd changed. But why was Ren getting so mad?

"Uh, but I really did make new friends. And I swear I never intended to get revenge. I did have a crush on Miki before; that's true. But I don't see her that way anymore. I guess I just wanted to set things straight with you all. I kinda slunk out of the group without even saying good-bye, you know?"

"Are you insane?! The hell is wrong with you?! 'Oh, I've found cuter girls now, so I don't rate you anymore?!' Y'know, I actually felt a little bad for you, so I decided to be nice! Get off your high horse! You haven't changed at all! You're completely oblivious!" Miki broke her silence and started yelling at me.

I must have said something wrong…

I was shocked, honestly. I was hoping to have a nice discussion, make friends with everyone again, and go home feeling good about myself. I'd really felt like I could do it, after all the changes I'd made…

King and Yuuko seemed to think I'd changed. I thought I had, too. But I guess it didn't look that way to other people…

"S-sorry… Did I say something to offend you? I know you're not interested in me, Miki. I know you're dating Ren. I've never even had a girlfriend, so I know you two live in a totally different world…"

"What? Man, you piss me off! Are you saying Ren and I got together just like that? Like we're both so easy? You're a popular kid now, so you live in a different world from us otakus? You think a new haircut and clothes change anything? We used to be friends, so I'll let you in on a secret... There's a one hundred percent chance your new friends are making fun of you! 'Let's give the otaku a makeover; it'll be sooo funny!'"

Ouch. I wanted to deny it, to tell Miki they weren't like that. But how could I, after I had just accused King and Yuuko of doing exactly that, yesterday in the classroom?

So instead I kept silent. Which gave Hayato the chance to butt in.

"Kenta hasn't realized that. He's too stupid. Us unpopular kids are like toys for the popular ones. Like, they'll dare each other to confess to you as a joke. You think they're your friends? I bet the whole time they were laughing about those dumb round glasses of yours. You know, just like we laughed at you. Miki sent us screenshots of everything you said to her in real time. We practically pissed ourselves laughing. What was it you said, again?"

"Uh, I think it was: 'Until I met you, I had no idea of the beauty of three-dimensional girls...' Oh, oh, and he also said: 'I'll change, so I can treat you right, Miki!' And then he was like: 'I saw you in my dreams again last night, Miki'...!!!"

"Ew, gross! What a loser! Total virgin!"

This was too much. All the pain from that time was flooding back. Why did they have to be so cruel? What was I even doing here, trying to talk to these people? What happened to the new me the confident guy I'd been cultivating over the past three weeks? Nothing I was saying was getting through to these people. This was all pointless.

Man, this is what I must have seemed like to King and Yuuko back at the beginning.

Why did they even bother with me in the first place? I know I wouldn't have.

Popular kids... They're really something else.

If I just kept going, maybe I could be like them someday.

I cleared my throat, which was still painfully dry.

"...Ah-ha-ha... Yeah, thinking back on it now, I was pretty

cringey. Sorry, I didn't mean to upset everyone. I feel like an idiot now; I got the wrong idea about so many things."

"…Why are you trying to laugh this off?"

Ren scowled.

"Aren't you upset? Aren't you mad? If you are, just say it. You can't just pretend like what we're saying doesn't affect you. When people are making fun of you, you can't do anything but laugh along. No matter how much you try to change your appearance, you're still just a sad, friendless loser on the inside."

Ren suddenly leaned forward, bringing his face right up next to mine.

"Wanna know something? Remember when you messaged Miki something like 'You looked cute eating ice cream today lol' and she responded 'Aw, ha-ha, I bet you were thinking dirty thoughts!'…? Well, Miki was with me in my room when she sent that. And my parents were away on a trip. No one else was home. Do you get what I'm saying here?"

Then he leaned in farther, his harsh breath in my ear.

"Laughing over your LINE message was, like, the perfect foreplay for us. We did it five times that night. Thanks, Kenta. I owe you for that."

I felt pain flood my chest.

I couldn't handle this. I could see the whole scene in my mind. My LINE message was a prop in their sex life?

"Ren! Don't tell him *thaaat*!"

"Hee-hee, I stole the girl right out from under you, huh, Kenta? The classic trope! Maybe you'll discover a whole new genre!"

Hee-hee-hee, ha-ha-ha.

I felt like I was all alone in my mind, under a dark-gray sky pouring with filthy, slushy rain.

I could feel the dark water swirl around my feet, threatening to pull me under and drown me in despair.

*…I can't do this, King. There's no way to turn this around. I just*

*want to run home. Lock myself in my room, where it's safe, and no one can hurt me. I want to curl up under my bedsheets, a filthy, soggy, drenched rat of a human being.*

I really was nothing but a gutless, miserable, shut-in loser. That was why I had said all those horrible things to King yesterday. I hadn't changed.

I choked back my tears, trying not to let them fall.

*Don't cry, don't cry, don't cry. At least not until this is over, and you'll be alone.*

*I'm...sorry, King. I'm sorry, Yuuko. I failed the final exam. I won't be graduating after all...*

...I could almost hear the King's voice.

"Now, now, you're forgetting the most important part."

It was like a message from heaven.

The foul rains cleared, and the sun peeked through the heavy rainclouds.

"Answer this, Kenta. What if they really are trying to be mean?"

"Then...then I crush them?"

"Precisely."

A strong hand patted me on the back.

"I've come to watch your back, Kenta. Just like I promised."

I turned around, and he was there. He was really there. It was the king.

A single tear slid down my cheek.

Ah, geez. After all that work I'd done trying not to cry...

\*

"Hmm? I thought I recognized that voice from the table behind me. Hey, Kenta. You could have invited me if you were coming to Starbucks."

I quickly scrubbed my face with my sleeve, erasing my tears.

*It's no good, King.*

*What are you doing here anyway?*

*Why'd you show up out of the blue in a blaze of coolness?*

I was so taken aback by King's sudden appearance that I couldn't speak. There was too much going on.

"Who are these guys? They're not *friends* of yours, are they, Kenta? They look kind of…lame?"

"…Th-these are my old friends."

That was all I managed to say. I think I did pretty well getting any words out at all, under the circumstances.

"Heh. Really? Never woulda guessed. You've really moved up in the world."

King was acting strange today. He was projecting about 50 percent more BDE than usual. It was like he was using his top-class popularity status as some sort of weapon…

But my old friend group seemed twice as stunned as I was. In fact, they looked like they were about to crumble into ash at any second. Miki cleared her throat and spoke in a strained sort of voice.

"Um… Wh-who are you?"

"Uh, I'm Kenta's buddy? Hi, old friends. The name's Saku Chitose. What's up?"

King gave her a dazzling, hot-and-I-know-it smile. If I was a girl, that smile would absolutely slay me.

Ren suddenly pointed accusingly at me, either sparked into action by Miki's simpering or by King's show of superiority.

"Y-yeah, so what? This guy's a real otaku loser. Do you have any idea how many anime figurines he has? He'd only ever whacked off to animated girls, until he met Miki."

"Yeah, I know he's an otaku, thanks. He actually keeps me supplied with all the best and latest light novels and anime series on Blu-ray. And we have plans to go to Summer Comiket together. We're gonna buy as many *dojinshi* as we can fit."

We made no such plans, King!

And who told you about *dojinshi*?! Why are you talking about buying *dojinshi* at Summer Comiket in the same casual way normal people talk about taking a summer vacation at the beach?!

The heck are you doing, King?!

"I actually overheard your conversation just now. Kenta, are you secretly trying to be an actor? Were you doing a script read-through?"

Okay, now I was completely lost.

"An...actor?"

As I blinked at King in confusion, he grabbed my Starbucks latte cup and took a sip. "Huh. No extra espresso this time," he murmured.

King was asserting dominance and flexing all over the place. The rest of us were mere mortals groveling in his presence. Miki had hearts in her eyes as she gazed at the king, but I wasn't even jealous. He was the king.

"Good performance anyway. Uh, now, Ren, was it? Yeah, you were good, too. Your attempt to diss Kenta over his Starbucks order... You really got the part of the pompous love rival down. Full marks, Prince Jiro. The losers must love kissing up to you."

Everyone was speechless as King continued.

"You too, Miki. The way you actually do kinda like Kenta now and then turned on him the instant he mentioned other girls? Classic. Shame Kenta didn't seem to catch that, though. He hasn't gotten that much experience with girls. Still, it was kinda cute how desperate you were to save face. If you weren't Ren's girlfriend, I'd sure like to teach you a thing or two..."

King trailed off, gazing into Miki's eyes.

"Ah, unless the thing about you two dating was also part of the script? In which case, can I call dibs?"

King brushed Miki's bangs aside and touched her chin. All of a sudden, he was giving off waves of sex appeal, which even a guy like me couldn't fail to notice. Ren could only sit there while King was hitting on his girl.

If what King was saying was for real, then I had gotten things completely wrong. Now I could see why Miki and Ren had gotten pissed. Still, while it was a bit late for me to realize this now, I could still feel regret over how I'd handled things.

"Um, well, m-maybe we could exchange LINE info..." Miki was blushing and stammering.

*No, don't fall for it!*

"...Only kidding. I hate girls like you, who flit from one guy to the other. Even if it is just the character you're playing."

King turned away from Miki and focused his attention on Hayato.

"But I have to give the Oscar to Hayato here. Trying to act like the big man in his little otaku nerd group of only four members. You're not even on Sidey McSide Character levels. You're more like Thirdy McWheeler; know what I mean? You hate yourself, so you spend all your energy slinging verbal stones at other people. You played the part of the villainous coward so perfectly, I have to say I was quite convinced. Talk about stealing the scene."

*Mommy, Daddy, there's a demon inside a high schooler's body.*

"Yeah, it was an excellent read-through, but I have to say the best part was when this guy went into cringeworthy detail about his sex life... Pfffft."

Then King cracked up laughing.

"Okay, be real with me, the whole thing was some sort of

meta-commentary on otaku tropes of the day, right? I mean, all the standard character archetypes were included. But you need to keep it grounded in reality; you can't have the nemesis character come out with such a bald-faced lie. The audience won't buy it. Good for a laugh, though, right? Ha-ha-ha!"

"Uh, King? What bald-faced lie?" I had managed to calm down enough to speak a little.

"The part about both his parents being away on a trip. And who does it five times a night when it's their first time? Ha-ha-ha. Your little soldier just keeps poppin' back up, does he? What, did you pray too hard at a shrine for good health? And poor Miki. She's like some modern-day castle you just keep plundering, isn't she? Ah, that must be because you weren't bringing much of a gun to the fight. More of a pencil, huh? Thin, long-lasting, never needs sharpening? Ha-ha, you're a couple of kids."

I wasn't quite following, but Miki and Ren had both turned bright red. I had a feeling King had managed to land a string of critical hits.

"If you two really did cross that line together, that memory would be way more special to you. You'd want to keep it close to the chest, away from everyone else. Sure, you might let your most trusted friends know it happened. But blurting all the details like that? No one does that. So I call bullshit. A fictional tale constructed by a couple of virgins. Was this meant to be some sort of parody of those teen coming-of-age movies or something? Ha-ha-ha!"

*Mommy, Daddy, the demon lord is preparing to take over the world...*

Now the blood drained from both Miki's and Ren's faces, leaving them white. Hayato was staring down at the table as if he wished the ground would open and swallow him up.

"All right, Ren, Miki, Hayato. What do you have to say for yourselves? I've given you my critique of your read-through; any objections?"

The situation had become clear to me now.

King had been here all along, watching and listening to our conversation. Then, when he saw that I was flailing, he had stepped in to save me.

Even after all those horrible things I said to him yesterday.

...How dumb are you, King?

Yeah, I'd figured him out now. King was as dumb as they come. And way too soft. He came to coax me out of my room on a teacher's order and then tried to help me improve myself like some makeover scene from a light novel. Then, like a dog biting the hand that feeds it, I'd lashed out at him. And he was still here, showing up for me, having my back. He had to be dumb, to even be doing that.

But that's Saku Chitose for you.

As the realization hit me, I became covered in goosebumps.

King must have lived his whole life this way...

He was something else. What a ridiculous way to live. I got the feeling I had only seen the surface level of the complex human being that was Saku Chitose.

*"Your entire existence revolves around trampling on other people, all of you!!!"*

My cutting words came back to me all of a sudden. He was just living his best life, but he had to put up with so much from the haters. He never lets it stop him, though.

He could have just cut off everyone beneath him. That would be easier. But he didn't. He stuck up for everyone around him. How many others had he tried to help, who then turned around and stabbed him in the back like I had done?

And yet he kept offering help. Maybe it was for the "optics," like he said. Maybe it was because of mistakes in his past. Maybe it was because he had such a strong conscience and a good moral compass. I couldn't say.

All I knew was that I had none of the goodness in me that he had.

*"Listen. Saku has been doing all this out of a genuine desire to help you. He's been willing to stick with you to the end, hasn't he?"*

*You were right, Yuuko.*
My vision swam with tears.
That's why he is the best. No one else can reach his level.
He's unbeatable.

Yeah, he was the dumbest, bestest guy I knew.

"What the hell is your problem?"
"Hmm?"
"Who the hell gave you permission to come and barge in on our conversation anyway?! Who do you think you are?!"
Ren slammed his fists down on the table and got to his feet. It looked like he'd snapped. He knew that King was on a much higher social level than him, but he was so steamed that he didn't care about that anymore.
"Hmm, I'm Saku Chitose. Most popular guy in my school. You may call me King. Many do."
King gave Ren a sardonic grin.
"Huh?! You wanna fight; is that it?!"
"Hmm, I seem to recall it was you guys who were picking a fight with my buddy here."
King stared Ren down.
Hearing him call me his buddy like that... It made the floodgates open, and the tears started flowing again. Maybe he was

just saying it because of the circumstances, but King still considered me a friend…!

"Mind your own damn business! This is between our group, so just butt out!"

"It *is* my business. I'm his friend. You guys are just his ex-friends."

"Pah! You were probably just amusing yourselves by giving a makeover to an unpopular kid! All you popular kids are the same! You act like being popular gives you a pass to shit on everybody else! You hunt the rest of us down for sport!"

"You're one to talk. What you're doing here is picking on someone less popular than you, within your little otaku hobbyist group. Wow, aren't you the big, cool man?"

Ren looked like he was getting ready to throw a punch. King, meanwhile, just smirked coolly.

"Shut up!! All you popular kids are shallow wastes of space! All you do is laugh yourselves stupid over boring, dumb stuff in the classroom, thinking everyone is watching you, imagining how cool you are! You can all go to hell!"

"So what you're implying is that you otaku are these deep, cultured individuals who simply keep your true natures on the down-low at school? Well, that goes for us popular kids, too. In the classroom, we show our everyday, fun-loving sides. Then, while you sad sacks are sitting in your rooms trolling and writing nasty takedowns on online forums, we're out there doing school sports, working up a sweat, helping out our friends, or chatting with girls late at night on the phone and being a shoulder for them to cry on."

King took a casual slurp of my iced latte.

"What do you expect us to talk about in the classroom? Politics? Current events? You base your assessment of people on what they chat about with their friends between classes? If we're shallow, what does that make *you*? You basically don't exist."

This reminded me of the conversations King and I had back at the beginning. I felt a pang of regret, deep in my chest.

"You should chat with the unpopular kids, too, not just your popular buddies! You act like you're so nice and generous, but you only act that way to other popular kids!"

"Well, let me ask you this. Have *you* ever tried to get to know popular kids or extend any kindness to them at all? You want people to be nice to you—you should start by being nice to others. No, you just expect people to extend courtesies to you that you wouldn't even think of returning or initiating. We're your classmates; we're not your mom. We're not Mother Teresa."

All of Ren's attacks were bouncing off King and getting thrown right back in his face. Like verbal boomerangs.

"Wake up. Groveling around on the floor, hissing up at the popular kids—you're just as bad as the popular kids who sneer down at those below them. Two sides of the same coin."

Ren seemed to have realized he was no match for King. Now he was on the defensive.

"W-well anyway, there's no way a gloomy nobody like Kenta could ever truly be popular. Even if he worked his ass off, unpopular kids never get to become popular. It just doesn't happen. I don't know what your plans were with him, but I can assure you that Kenta doesn't trust or care for your type, either. He's just going along with what you want, preparing himself for the moment when you all turn on him. He hates you for it!"

Ren turned to me, sneering.

"People don't change! People *can't* change! And seeing you try so hard… It's just *pathetic*!!!"

I blinked at him. He was right. I proved it yesterday, with my little outburst. I had no right to keep enjoying the benefits of King's support.

King sighed, not looking at me. Instead, he took a step closer to Ren…

\*     \*     \*

"You're really pissing me off, you know that?"

King took another step closer. And then...

*BAM!!!*
King slammed his hand against the wall behind Ren's head with a bang, boxing him in, getting all up in his face. The Starbucks baristas and the other customers all froze and looked this way.

But King ignored them all. He glared at Ren, who turned his face to the side, grimacing.

I had never seen Saku Chitose get angry. Until now.

"All right, listen up, you miserable asswipe. Kenta has taken a good look at himself and taken steps to get closer to the kind of person he'd like to be. Yes, he's got a long way to go, and some people might have a problem with his new persona. But he's still moving forward regardless. He's promised himself that he'll never go back, no matter how hard it is or how many times he falls."

*SLAM!*
King drove his fist into the wall on the other side of Ren's head.

"Kenta is reaching for the moon. That distant, shining, beautiful representation of everything he wants to achieve. Do you have any idea how hard it's been for him to make that decision and then follow through with it? Have you no respect?"

Then King grabbed Ren by the front of his shirt.

"Someone like you, who never tries to better themselves, just eating and breathing, entrenched in their sad little life while slinging shit at people who are doing better than them..."

King was really yelling now.

\* \* \*

"You have no right to laugh at someone like Kenta!!!"

…I couldn't hold back.

…The tears were flowing, and I couldn't keep the sobs inside anymore.

King was mad. King was yelling. For me.

He was always so happy-go-lucky, such a chill guy. But for me, he was letting his true emotions show for once.

I had never been so encouraged in all my life.

This was King's final gift for me, before we went off on our separate paths.

*Keep going! Don't stop! Don't turn back!*

*Your choices are good ones! Your motivation is solid!*

*Come on; try to match me! You'll get there! Someday!*

That's what King's actions were saying.

I had to honor his gesture. I couldn't flounder anymore. I had to take King's message to heart.

I wanted to remember this moment forever.

I tried to burn the image of King standing up for me into my mind. So I would always have it with me.

And then…

"Aw, Saku! I wanted you to use that sexy wall-pounding move on me, hee-hee-hee!"

A girl appeared all of a sudden, peering at King. She was wearing a knockout of a dress, which exposed her shoulders, back, and a good deal of her cleavage. She looked like a pop idol. Her smile, as always, was radiant.

King turned, and for a moment, his eyes bugged out, and his

jaw hung slack. He looked almost comical. Like a real idiot. This definitely hadn't been in his plan.

"…Yuuko? What…? What are you doing here?"

"Hmm? Well, of course I was going to show up! I was worried about you and Kentacchi, so I had to come see what was happening! No fair leaving me out, boys!" Yuuko turned to the baristas and customers who were still watching us in silence. "Sorry for the commotion! It's all cool now!"

She waved reassuringly, and the tension started to dissipate. Slowly, everyone went back to what they had been doing. The baristas returned to wiping tables and taking orders, and the customers went back to chatting over their coffees.

King and Ren seemed to have backed way down as well, their aggression disappearing.

In fact, King patted Ren on the shoulder before stepping away from him. Quickly, his usual composure came back. Over the past few weeks, I had never seen King lose his cool. It had been an incredibly rare sighting.

Then Yuuko turned to me. "Kentacchi, your curls are always so cute!" she squealed as she dug her fingers into my hair and messed it up. Miki, Hayato, and Ren were just standing there dumbfounded. On top of everything else that had been going on, Yuuko's bombshell appearance and friendliness with me had them completely floored.

"Well, now then, since it seems everyone's said what they wanted to say, shall we put all this behind us and start fresh tomorrow? …Kentacchi, is there anything else you wanted to say?"

Yuuko turned to me, beaming. She sure managed to lighten things up, all right.

I looked at King.

King took a deep breath as if to steady himself before speaking. "This is your story, right, Kenta? Your story of self-improvement.

And we're your supporting characters, the cute guy and girl who show up when you need a helping hand. But this is the final scene. So the hero gets to give a closing monologue."

I knew what I needed to say.

I lost my way for a moment there, but I had won this fight against my old self and arisen victorious.

Like King said:

*"Kenta is reaching for the moon. That distant, shining, beautiful representation of everything he wants to achieve."*

I closed my eyes for a second, picturing that shining light in the night sky. There was a figure standing in front of it, silhouetted against it. The figure of the king.

This was my way of remembering everything that had happened— and my good-bye.

I opened my eyes, turned to my old friends, and smiled.

"I'm...going to reach for the moon. I won't look back, not anymore."

✳

All right, that's enough of the side story of Kenta Yamazaki, aspiring ex-nerd, as he approached the biggest crossroad of his life so far.

Now let's return to the main story. The harem rom-com starring Saku Chitose, popular hot-guy extraordinaire.

"Why did you come?" Kenta sniffed. "You lied."

"I wasn't expecting to. Anyway, I never said I wouldn't come. But remember how I told you it would go well? Of course it would, 'cause you've got Saku Chitose in your corner."

"This again...?"

Now that we were away from the stress of the situation, Kenta wasn't even trying to hide his tears anymore. They were flowing freely. With a lot of snot.

"Can you stop crying? Their bullying really upset you that much?"

"They're not tears of sadness. It's because you two came to my rescue, even after all those horrible things I said yesterday. I'm so happy. That's why I'm crying."

"You already apologized for yesterday, though. Look, let's just high-five and move past it."

"That's how you popular kids deal with things. I don't know that stuff."

After we left Starbucks, we decided to walk Yuuko home. We were heading through the same rice fields I'd walked along yesterday.

Kenta just kept on blubbering and sniffing.

"Kentacchi, that's enough. So gross! Come on, wipe those tears."

Yuuko offered Kenta a handkerchief. "Thank you," he burbled, wiping his eyes and blowing his nose noisily.

Yuuko's outfit was much more revealing than the one she'd worn when we had gone shopping with Kenta. Her shoulders were fully revealed and at least half of her back. You could even see a line of cleavage. The dress was a pink knit one, and it clung to the contours of her body. Her thighs looked full and delicious.

Her outfit had certainly worked to stun Ren and co into submission. That dress was clearly Yuuko's secret weapon, her own personal Excalibur. Sexcalibur. Heh.

Yuuko watched Kenta snorting into her handkerchief.

"Er, you can keep that."

"...I figured."

Kenta glugged down some of the mineral water we'd bought on the way out of the mall and seemed to finally calm down.

Then he mumbled something. It sounded like "This is for the best... Right?" Then he continued. "...I mean, I know that the responsibility for this was all on me, despite everything you two have done for me. But looking back on it...maybe we went just a bit too far?"

"Hmm, well, yeah. In light novels and anime, things tend to get heated during the big ending confrontation. Lots of harsh words, that kind of thing. But ultimately, the story always wraps up with the good guys forgiving the bad guys, right? Like, that's the standard, feel-good ending."

"Yeah... Wow, King, I was really shocked when you turned up and went crazy on Ren. I guess I was kinda useless, though, huh?"

"...Heh. Don't mention it." I put one hand on my hip and stuck my tongue out. "Hmm, still, I don't think we went too far. All I did was pay them back for being huge jerks to you today. I think it was the perfect amount of payback, if you ask me."

I actually meant it.

"Yeah, I really don't care if their precious feelings got hurt from the way I burned them. If helping a buddy doesn't mean settling the score with the ones who hurt him, then what is justice anyway?"

Yuuko reached out and poked my belly.

"Hee-hee, you lost your cool for once, Saku!"

"No, I didn't. That was just me acting. I'm always cool."

Honestly, I never expected Yuuko to show up then.

"To be honest, I kept waiting for my chance to jump in. But I had faith in you, Saku. So I decided to wait until you'd said your piece. Man, I was really mad! I wish everyone had been able to get along in the end... But they were being super mean to my friend. Of course I was gonna take Kentacchi's side. I feel like it's only fair to get mad for a good friend when he's being wronged!"

"Oh... You guys..."

"But if you still feel bad about how things ended up, I know a way to make you feel better. Just remember that guys like that hurt people indiscriminately and never feel bad about what they've done. And they never go after the strong ones. Only the people they think can't fight back. They forget that some people will throw their shit back at them; that's on them!"

I kicked a stone along the path in front of us.

"Isn't it better to remind people like that how it feels to be on the receiving end of harsh words and violence? I feel like it'll end up doing them a favor. Definitely wasn't planned, but when you think about it, we did them a service today."

"But…now you've got more people out there who are going to be hating on you, King. All because of me…"

I laughed, looking at Kenta walking along with his shoulders slumped.

"I haven't told you my philosophy yet, have I? It's what's behind my whole cool-guy aesthetic. *Death is better than an unbeautiful life.* That's the code by which I live, and it's what leads some people to call me a narcissist. But I won't change, no matter the pressure. Because the thing I'm most afraid of is looking in the mirror and not liking the guy I see looking back at me."

I felt something stir within my soul. It felt old—and sort of familiar.

"I want to be beautiful. Like the moon I saw that day. Like a glass marble, trapped in a bottle of Ramune soda. The one from that book I read once."

Kenta was mulling over my words carefully.

I looked at him and gave him a meaningful smile.

"And by 'beautiful,' I mean cool and attractive and have tons of girls fussing over me. You get me?"

"King… I was actually starting to feel really inspired, but now you've ruined it…"

✳

We had reached Yuuko's house now.

It didn't quite feel like spring anymore, but real summer was still a while off. It was the end of April. The strange in-between nature of the seasons mirrored the unsettled feeling among the three of us.

Now we had gotten past the first month of the second year of high school, with all its new encounters. What would happen next?

I remembered what Kura said.

*"Getting sidetracked and taking the long route is where the real spice of life is to be found."*

He was right. It would be a shame to let this detour come to an end without realizing what I'd gained from it.

Had I managed to become a compass, one that Kenta could navigate by? Would I be a light to him if he got lost in the dark again, to show him the right path?

"I guess we're done with the detour now."

I turned to Kenta.

"…Huh?"

"These past three weeks. You filled the hole in your boat, right? You're no longer sinking alone in the ocean. Now we've come to the end of our agreement."

"I…I understand. I always knew it was coming, and after what I said to you yesterday, I thought I was prepared… But these past three weeks have been so amazing. It's hard to believe it's really over. Sorry."

"Still, we had an agreement."

Yuuko looked at me, and I could see she wanted to say something. I shook my head.

There's a limit to how much of a burden we can all carry. If I shouldered the responsibility of looking after everyone I met in life, I'd end up having to drop something else I cared about, before too long.

It had gotten dark all of a sudden, without any of us realizing it.

When I looked up, I could see the moon shining brightly above us.

Things always change before you know it's happening. People. Cities. Seasons.

So we had to move forward. If we stopped for too long, time would overtake us all.

"The detour ends here," I said, repeating the idea to myself once more.

"…I understand. I guess…we decided that from the start, didn't we?"

Kenta looked up at the sky, as if remembering something.

"You know, that day you broke my window and busted into my room…was like you broke a glass cage that I was trapped in… It was like you brought me something precious, something I'd given up looking for long ago—something I couldn't remember what it was supposed to look like…"

Kenta placed a hand over his chest, smiling ruefully.

"Gosh, what am I even saying?" He laughed. "But beginning tomorrow, I know I have to start writing my own story. You've brought me here, King, Yuuko, all of you have. But I can't rely on you any longer. I have one final request, though. When we see each other in school…could you please ignore me? If we stayed at any level of friendliness, I have the feeling it would only get my hopes up…"

Kenta swallowed hard. "But…," he trailed off again, before taking a deep breath and continuing. "I need to get over my weaknesses and find my own strength. Until the day comes when I can stand on the same level as people like you. When that day comes…would it be all right if I asked you again? To be my friends, I mean…"

His eyes filled with more tears. Tsk, after all that time he spent scrubbing his face.

"These past three weeks… I won't ever forget them. I won't forget the things you taught me, King, the way you scolded my mistakes. The advice you gave me, Yuuko, and all your smiles… I won't forget any of them, not until the day I die!"

Kenta gasped for breath.

"Thank you both… Thank you both so, so much!!!"

Then he bowed low before us.

In the moment, he seemed to have ceased being a boy and become a man.

A man who stood tall and proud.

I stared at Kenta, taking in the image of him. Then I turned to Yuuko beside me and spoke in a soft voice.

"My dear, has this man hit his head? He's saying some incredibly strange things."

"Oh my. It's your fault, my dear, for being so cryptic! The poor fellow has gotten the wrong idea!"

"It's that light novel mentality he's got. Everything always has to be so dramatic and sentimental."

"Now, now, dearest…"

Kenta lifted his head and looked at us in confusion, wiping away his tears with the back of his hand.

"Listen, Kentacchi. When Saku said it's over, he meant this teacher-student, master-disciple, king-subject, demon lord–minion, weird as heck kind of relationship, you know!"

"…Wh-what?"

"Starting tomorrow, let's be friends for real. That's what he means! After all we've been through together, we can't very well go back to being strangers now, can we?"

"…Huh?"

"Honestly, I'm shocked you thought what we have together could be so easily discarded! And after I put on this itchy outfit I hate just to help you out, too! Hmph!"

*Oh please. You know you love your Sexcalibur dress, Yuuko.*

"B-but…are you sure?!"

"Of course! We're friends, aren't we? Still, it's not like I'm offering you an official initiation into Yuuko Hiiragi's Angels or anything…"

"It's Team Chitose."

"…Like I said, I'm not telling you to join Yuuko Hiiragi's Angels, but definitely let's chat it up in the classroom, Kentacchi! We'll want to know all about your new life! And let's eat lunch together sometimes! Oh, and once you've tidied up your bedroom, invite me over! We can play video games together. Oh, no funny business, though, all right? ♪"

Yuuko winked at him in her racy dress. *No funny business, sure, Yuuko.*

"After all, we've done a lot for you, so now it's time for you to pay us back! With friendship, okay? You can't just abandon us now!"

Finally, I figured I should speak up, too. "You know, Kenta, you never asked us to be your friends for real in the first place. You just decided to act like the poor, downtrodden martyr character. Right? Sidey McSide Character?"

"King…you deliberately misled me, didn't you? You knew I would get the wrong idea! So you acted all solemn and serious…"

"Come on, man. I can't let my rom-com end without a little practical joking."

"This is the first time since we've met that I honestly feel like punching you!"

"Listen, Kenta. Don't throw a punch without being prepared to get punched back. You gotta know what you're getting into."

"Shut up, King! That's enough! I get the picture!"

*

After seeing Yuuko home and saying good-bye to Kenta, I headed home along the usual riverbed path.

I walked along wearily, listening to the slight burbling of the river, smelling the fresh greenery, bathed in moonlight.

Soft light emanated from the houses lining the riverbank. I could smell something good cooking. I could also hear water splashing from an upstairs window. Someone was taking a hot bath. But was it a cute high school girl, a MILF housewife, or an old man with a potbelly?

Sometimes, I would hope a little. Sometimes, I would get a little disappointed. Sometimes, I would just walk by without thinking anything at all.

But for whatever reason, she was always here when I really wanted to see her.

"…Hey, Asuka."

"Oh, hey. I wasn't expecting to run into you today."

"That's weird. I was certain I'd run into you. And could you come up with a better nickname than *hey*? I hate having to share a name with someone else. If you're up for it."

"Hmm? What a weird thing to worry about."

*

I told Asuka about everything that had happened this April, as succinctly as I could. Asuka nodded, listened carefully, and made satisfying expressions of surprise and amusement as I spoke.

"I think that's a great story. It's got innocence; it's got character development; it's uplifting. Like watching a group of boys release sky lanterns on a summer's night."

I felt my cheeks growing warm as I gazed up at the night sky.

"What would you have done, if you were me?"

"Hmm. But I'm not you. I'm me. Probably, I would have tried to talk things out with Kenta and then gone with him to talk to Miki, the three of us. The incident with Miki was the start of everything. So if we just sorted that out, everything would have been fixed."

"That's the difference between you and me, Asuka. I thought that if I focused on changing the outcome of what happened, then we'd get to the root of it as a natural consequence."

Asuka gave me a knowing smile.

"Hmm, I think that my way would have worked, but it would have left Kenta with some ties to that incident, and I don't know what would come of that. What you did, though—that set Kenta free."

"…You're overthinking it. I just did things my way 'cause that's all I know. I can't approach these things directly."

Why was it that I always felt like I'd become a little boy again whenever I was with this girl?

"But you kinda like that aspect of yourself, right?"

"…Hmm. I guess."

Suddenly, Asuka reached out and pushed my bangs aside, gazing into my eyes. I froze, even though the touch of her slim, warm fingers tickled me.

"You've changed a little. Your mental park is filled with kids playing with sparklers now."

Asuka's eyes were filled with a deep, rich color.

"Me? No way. I'm the same as ever. Just a guy playing at being a hero, I guess."

"Hmph, always trying to act so cool. But fine. Play the hero. I promise I won't crash your stage and be the villain."

She gave me a teasing grin. But at the same time, I felt like she could see right through me. She leaned in, bringing her lips to my ear.

"You're such a complicated guy. You act like nothing ever

affects you, like you're so cool, but in reality, you're very kind. Always helping others. You're only unkind toward yourself."

I looked away, wanting to escape. Then I manufactured a breezy smile, trying to chase away my own uncomfortable thoughts.

"Nope, true kindness is jumping into a muddy river to save a young kid from being bullied by his peers."

Asuka tipped her head to one side.

"Now, see, you've put me up on a pedestal. Like Yuuko and Kenta have done to you. But I'm just me. Asuka Nishino."

I could hear a fish jumping in the river. It made a tiny plopping sound.

"I can't shoulder the burden of other people like you do. I'm not as good as you are. I only help out the people I really wanna help and do what I can, nothing more. Speaking of which, after this, I'm gonna go home, eat the omurice my mom made, and read some of *The Door into Summer* by Heinlein before passing out."

"Wow, what a carefree, easy existence."

She reminded me of Kura, a little.

It was like Kura said… Nobody has a truly moral compass. You have to decide for yourself what's right and what's not right. That's all there is to it.

But some people didn't even check their compass. Almost as if checking it would rob them of the joy in the world around them.

I gazed into Asuka's eyes. What was it like in her world?

"By the way, how do you like your omurice? Do you like it when the omelet is placed on top and then splits open so the runny egg comes out? Do you like it with cheese? What kind of sauce do you like on it? Ketchup? Demi-glace sauce? White sauce? I like a really flat, thin omelet tucked nice and tight around the rice, slathered in tons of ketchup. Like the way we ate it when we were kids, you know?"

Right now, it seemed her world was entirely focused on dinner. Red ketchup, yellow yolk, green parsley on the side. Like a traffic light. Here I was thinking we were having a philosophical discussion; meanwhile, she was only thinking with her stomach.

"Do you have any plans for Golden Week?"

"Um, nope. Not a one. I don't like making plans in advance. I find it's more fun to wing it and decide what I want to do when I wake up every day. I'd hate to lock myself in to something and have to miss out on something even more fun that came along later. So you got any dates planned? You can tell me; I'm your big sis."

Asuka tucked her windswept hair behind her ear and grinned at me, her eyes wide and fixed on mine.

"I was thinking about asking this older girl on a date. But she just squashed my plans. I'm going to come stand outside your window tomorrow morning and wake you up, Asuka. I'll be out there doing warmup exercises."

"Ooh, sounds fun. Then, when it gets hot, we can jump into the river. Get all muddy and wet. Then I can change into your stinky gym clothes and walk home."

"They don't stink. You wanna go in the river right now?"

She grinned, as if remembering that day. "It would be nice, though, wouldn't it?"

Before I could ask what she meant by that, she shook her head. "Forget it."

"...But it's better this way. It's better for us to run into each other here, randomly, at the riverbank. That way, I can always be the cool older girl, and you can be the adorable boy I like to joke with."

"You think getting any closer would ruin the relationship?"

"Could be."

It felt like I was always chasing some spirit version of her.

Afraid that she would fade away into darkness before me, I said good night.

\*

Back home, I went out onto my balcony, like I did that night a month ago.

There was another full moon above, a perfect circle, as if drawn with a compass. The moon had done a full orbit around the Earth, since that day Kura came to me with his request.

The cherry blossoms were long gone, and the trees were now lush and green. The new students had more of a light spring in their step when they walked to school. Kenta had come out of his room. And now I had switched to short sleeves whenever I was lounging around at home.

The night was indistinct and hazy around me.

Somewhere far-off, a young man was jumping into the sky. Somewhere else, a young girl was getting into her horse carriage.

Chewing on the remnants of an interrupted bad dream, the plump *baku* spirit, consumer of nightmares, smiled.

I would be having good dreams tonight.

I took my phone out of my pocket and, on a whim, opened up the underground school gossip website. There was a new entry that mentioned me.

A smile spread across my face.

Saku Chitose from Class Five is the king!!!

Idiot. I told him to stay off social media.

It was the Monday after Golden Week. I woke up earlier than usual and headed slowly along the riverbank in the direction of school. Once I entered the classroom, I was immediately met with the sight of a face I'd gotten entirely too familiar with over those three weeks.

"Hey, Kenta. You're early."

"...Ah, King. Good morning!" Kenta turned to me, looking somehow refreshed.

"How long are you gonna keep calling me that? You can just call me Saku, like normal."

"Ah, I guess I just got used to King. It feels weird to call you Saku now."

"Eh, suit yourself."

I slung my bag on my desk, pulled the chair out from in front of Kenta, and sat down on it.

"So what have you been up to?"

"Oh, right! Listen to this, King! Kura is a complete demon! Look at all the homework he gave me. And he wants it done by the weekend!"

Kenta opened up a cloth tote bag he'd brought along with his Arc'teryx backpack. It was bursting with printouts and workbooks.

"Yikes, that's a lot. Still, you deserve it. And Kura never assigns more work than he knows a person can handle. Remember how he gave you some breathing room once you came back to school? Well, now he's letting you know you need to work your butt off if you wanna make it up."

"Yeah, but… There's a *ton* of homework here. I wasn't in class, so there're so many things I don't really understand just from reading the textbooks… Heyyy, King…"

"Don't give me that look. What happened to all your big talk about taking charge of your own life by yourself from now on?"

"That's totally unrelated! Come on, King, help me out! Help me study!"

Still, asking me straight out like this instead of hinting and whining…? That was proof Kenta had really grown.

"Aw, man, seriously? Just when I thought I'd gotten you off my back at last."

"Oh, I know! I'll treat you to a coffee! You'll do it for a coffee, right?"

"Don't insult me. Cute girls get my help for coffee. For guys, the going price is much higher."

"Oh, then I'll treat you to a bowl of Hachiban's. Hachiban's would do it, right?"

Kenta was nothing if not persistent.

"…Tch. All right. But you'd better throw in two marinated eggs and a side of fried rice. And fried chicken, too."

"Anything for you, King! Hail to the King! Huzzah!!!"

"Exploiting the generosity of the king for your own aims. Tch."

Still, for a bowl of ramen, I could help Kenta study. The ramen would keep things transactional. Just so he didn't get any funny ideas about us.

I looked down at Kenta, who was scowling at his stack of printouts. "You know…," I began. "…You know, you really have become one of those plain guys who has hot-guy aura. And those glasses really suit you."

Kenta blinked at me warily. "Wh-what? Don't get all weird on me, King."

"Don't get the wrong idea. I'm the type to praise beauty when I see it, whether it's on a girl or guy. It feels better to pay someone a compliment than to put them down."

"You're right. But when you say something like that to girls, they'll get the wrong idea. You should be careful, you know, King."

"Yeah, but what if you've got a girl next to you who thinks she's worthless? Don't you want to boost her spirits?"

"I know what you're like, King, so I understand you don't mean anything by it. But it's you doing things like that that makes you gain more haters. Maybe I don't have any right to say this, but you should be more discriminating, instead of being nice to everyone you see."

"Hmm. I do try to draw the line... But hey, I'm not sure I want to get advice from the likes of you."

While we were chatting, the rest of our group trickled into the classroom. Kaito's forehead was beaded with sweat. Probably had morning practice.

"'Sup, Kenta? We heard from Saku. Your revenge plan went pretty well, huh? So now that you're done with that Miki chick, you and I should go out and try to pick up girls together!"

"Uh, I don't think I'd have any success if I went with you, Kaito..."

Kazuki should have had morning practice, too, but he didn't have a hair out of place.

"Kenta, you should come to me for advice on girls. Not Saku. You take his advice, and you'll end up going down entirely the wrong path."

"Yeah, I figured."

*Oh, shut up, dumbass.*

Nanase and Haru walked into the classroom together.

Nanase patted Kenta on the shoulder.

"Hey, Yamazaki. You did good, huh?"

Haru slapped Kenta on the back. "Great job! I'm seeing you in a whole new light!"

"Ah yeah. Thank you both… Thank you for everything…"

Yua smiled her usual soft, sweet smile at Kenta.

"I guess today marks a new start for you, huh? If you need help with anything, please come to me!"

"Uchida… Thank you."

Yuuko bounded into the classroom, squealing: "Good mooorning!!! …Kentacchi! They just opened this new crepe shop in front of the station! Do you wanna go after school?"

Kenta smiled charmingly. "King can come, too, right?"

"You betcha!"

Atomu was watching this and had had enough. "Keep it down," he snarled. "It's too early in the morning for all this noise." Nazuna, Inaba, and Inomata were also giving us death stares.

Then Kenta turned to me, looking like he'd just remembered something.

"Now you can go back to focusing on being the awesome OP star of your own harem rom-com story, King. But you know, I hate getting bad endings, so just make sure you don't get yourself stabbed in the back."

He gave me a cheeky grin.

"You've really gotten ballsy, haven't you? Next time we play soccer, get ready for me to pass the ball to you every chance I get."

I grinned back at Kenta, before getting to my feet and going to open the classroom window.

A warm May breeze came in, rustling the curtains. The scent of new greenery surrounded us, filling the glass terrarium in which we all lived.

The sky was blue. The sun was warm, heralding the coming of the next season. It made the dust motes floating in the classroom air sparkle.

Someone was always catching feelings for me. And someone was always out to get me.

But every now and then, someone went from hating my guts to becoming one of my best friends.

Yep, everything in my world was just as it should be…

# AFTERWORD

Hello. I'm Hiromu, recipient of the thirteenth Shogakukan Light Novel Merit Award.

I'd like to introduce myself, but as this is my debut work, and I have so many people to thank, I think I'd better start there so I don't run out of space.

Guest Judge Labo Asai. It was a privilege just to have you read my novel entry. I can't express how thankful I am for the six pages of A4 paper you gave me, containing your thoughtful feedback. I based my revisions on your advice. I especially loved the part where you wrote: "*I don't even know what genre to categorize this as.*" I also want to thank everyone involved in evaluating and assessing my work from cover to cover. Thank you very much.

Thank you to H and Y for reading my novel and giving me your opinions both before and after entry into the competition. And thank you to N for making me such a cool signature and business cards! In particular, H, with their background in mainstream literature and publishing, managed to pull me out of the otaku swamp I was festering in and made me an actual light novel author. Even though you were very critical of the content of my work, you were the one who kept telling me that it would be a hit, and when you read the novel before entry into the competition, you kept telling me: "You've got a winner here; mark my words." I can't tell you how much that encouraged me. Now, just like you said you would, you can go ahead and tell everyone: "See that kid? I discovered him!" ...Lol.

Now then, now then, on to the person in charge of the illustrations, raemz! I regret that I didn't have many opportunities to tell you what I thought, but I have to say that getting into contact with you was one of the best things that could have happened to my novel! Every day, I was anxiously awaiting, thinking to myself *Will they upload the pics today...?* like a lovestruck teen. Then, when I saw the illustrations you sent, I could only squeal: "*Kawaii! Kawaii! KA! WA! EEExyczzzz!!!*" like some gross old fart. I could look at your illustrations for hours and never get bored. They get cuter and cuter the more I look at them. I call it: *the raemz effect.* Let's both keep working hard together in the future, too!

Now, to Iwaasa, my editor, who has done more for me than anyone else. At first, we pushed each other's buttons and even ended up in a sort of cold-war type of situation, but you are a wonderful editor who really respects and cares about the vision of your authors. When you read the second draft, you said only: "I see, I see" (quoted verbatim), and I thought, *Editors really don't have any appreciation for a person's feelings!* (lol). But now I've gotten used to you! Now when you send me messages with emoji, I tell myself: *Today, Iwaasa is feeling especially personable!* I call this: *Looking for Iwaasa's humanity.* But thanks to you, this novel has become several magnitudes better than it was before the competition entry. So thank you very much.

And finally, to everyone who picked up a copy of this title...I thank you most of all.

See, I told you I had a lot of people to thank. So in the remaining space, allow me to introduce myself... (To be continued in Volume 2, if that's cool?)

Hiromu